'Fantastic. Di_____ ___?'

'He went to kiss ___ goodbye on both cheeks and we sort of collided noses,' I confided.

Julie rolled her eyes. 'Jeeze, that's pathetic, Lara. But not to worry. It can easily be improved upon. When are you seeing him again?'

'Well, we didn't actually arrange anything,' I admitted sadly.

'So, call him and arrange something now, you idiot. Don't let this one slip through your fingers, Lara, for heaven's sake. I think I can remember his number if you didn't have the sense to take it down yourself.'

'Julie, I can't just call him if he hasn't called me,' I protested. 'That would look so sad. I'd have to kill myself straight afterwards.'

'Not if you had an excuse, you wouldn't.' She pointed towards a crumpled cricket jumper which was lying haphazardly across the back of a chair. 'Look, he left that jumper behind. Deliberately, if you ask me. It was freezing by the time he left here on Sunday night so he would definitely have noticed its absence.'

Also by Chris Manby

Running Away from Richard
Lizzie Jordan's Secret Life
Deep Heat
Flatmates

About the author

Chris Manby grew up in Gloucester and published her first short story in *Just Seventeen* at the age of fourteen. Now in her late twenties, she lives in London and writes full-time.

Second Prize

Chris Manby

CORONET BOOKS
Hodder & Stoughton

First published in Great Britain in 1997
by Hodder and Stoughton
First published in Coronet paperback in 1998
by Hodder and Stoughton
A division of Hodder Headline

This Coronet paperback edition 2001

10

A CIP catalogue record for this title
is available from the British Library.

ISBN 0 340 68962 5

Printed and bound in Great Britain by
Clays Ltd, St Ives plc

Hodder and Stoughton
A division of Hodder Headline
338 Euston Road
London NW1 3BH

ACKNOWLEDGEMENTS

Three cheers for Hodder and Stoughton – especially my editor Kate Lyall Grant and the brave girls from publicity, Katie Gunning, Camilla Sweeney and Katie Collins, who looked so great on the fantastic cover of my last book, *Flatmates*, which was designed by Alison Groom and a wonderful art department.

Equally gushing thanks to all my family. To Peter Hamilton, Helen Pisano and David Garnett for bearing the brunt of my writer's angst. To my real flatmates Jane Glover and Chris Skelton for occasionally doing their share of the housework and to Guy Hazel for never letting me forget the danger of writer's bottom.

I'm particularly grateful to Vi and Don Stevenson, for always having great books about the house. Since they weren't allowed to read the last one, this book is dedicated to them.

CHAPTER ONE

'Cheer up, Lara. It might never happen.'

As far as I was concerned, it already had. But I tried to put on a happy face. I was, after all, handing round the nibbles at my very best friend's engagement party. I was not, repeat not, going to think about everything that the 'e' word meant to me right at that moment. Such as the fact that when Julie moved in with her new fiancé Andrew I would not be able to afford the rent on our lovely little flat in Battersea on my own. And therefore I would probably have to move into a dreadful bedsit in somewhere unspeakable like Balham, where it would be simply impossible to entertain visitors and thus increase even further my chances of being left on the shelf at the grand old age of twenty-five.

While I played the hired help at her intimate soirée for fifty, Julie, the generous hostess, was describing the design of her wedding dress to Andrew's elder sister, Clare. When I walked by with a red-hot plate loaded with recently reheated M & S dim sum, Julie grabbed me and pulled me to her so fast that I only narrowly escaped scorching her chest with the plate and dropping all the wontons on to the floor. Not that she didn't deserve it.

'And this,' she announced drunkenly as I tried to rescue the nibbles and dusted the crumbs off my jumper, 'is my chief bridesmaid, Lara. Lara, Clare's just been saying that we can use the bridesmaids' dresses she had made for her wedding. That way we can save a bit of money and fit in with the "something borrowed" bit at the same time.'

'That's nice.' I tried to sound jovial. 'What colour are they?'

'Peach,' replied Clare.

I knew she was going to say peach because peach is the one colour I most definitely cannot wear. It makes me look not so much sallow as recently exhumed from the grave. But instead of telling her this unfortunate fact, I said, 'Clare, that's really lovely of you. But weren't your bridesmaids very skinny? I might have to lose some weight.' As I said that, I stuffed two crispy wontons into my mouth at once and followed them with a slug of Julie's highly calorific Malibu and pineapple. Come hell or high water, that peach dress was not going to fit me by the wedding day.

I returned to the kitchen and opened a couple more cardboard boxes as the sausage rolls in the oven (Quorn, not real meat, of course in view of the current fashion) turned from stiff frozen white to pale gold. I laid the delicate little vol-au-vents out in a circle on an oven tray and was so distracted by my own misery at the impending bridesmaid torture that I absent-mindedly picked up one of the ice-cold things and popped it straight into my mouth. Ugh! Frozen puff pastry and cold mushroom sauce. I spat it out on to the tray in front of me and then quickly picked the resulting debris off the other little puffs, hoping that no one would notice but not really caring that much if they did. I wasn't exactly full of goodwill to all men that night.

'Remind me not to have one of those,' came a voice from the doorway. I had been caught in the act. I turned around sheepishly to see a giant of a man blocking my view of the hall. 'Hugh Armstrong-Hamilton,' the big guy announced grandly as he held out his hand. Neither Julie nor I knew anyone double-barrelled or anywhere near that formal so I guessed at once that he must belong to Andrew.

'Friend of Andrew's?' I asked perceptively.

He nodded in confirmation. 'We work together at Partridge Skelton.'

'The merchant bank? Lovely. I'm Julie's friend Lara Fenton, chief bridesmaid and deserted-flatmate-to-be,' I replied bitterly. I must have been pretty pissed by now. I noticed that the bottle of cooking wine I had opened at the beginning of the party – to flavour the cook and not the edibles – was down to just half a glass's worth in the bottom. I swigged that straight from the bottle for courage.

'Got any ice?' Hugh was asking.

'No,' I replied. But he wasn't the only one who needed some now. Up close and when I could get him in focus, I realised that the man who had just invaded my kitchen retreat was completely gorgeous. He had that flawless skin which is wasted on men and would have saved me a fortune in foundation. As he squatted down to examine the contents of our freezer, which was long due a defrosting, I couldn't help staring at his broad back and at the way his thick dark hair curled over his collar like a little wave breaking on the sand. He was divine. Sod the vol-au-vents. I could have eaten him.

'I could just scrape some of this stuff off and have a margarita I suppose,' he was saying, tapping at the ice that was crusted to the freezer walls and sending little white crystals fluttering like snowflakes to the floor. I laughed, nervously and far too loud.

'But there isn't any tequila,' I told him. He closed the freezer and stood back up again. He seemed to take longer to stand up than normal people do, which was probably because he was a good foot taller than anyone else I knew. Suddenly I wished that I had decided to wear my sexy little black dress and not just slipped on my tatty jeans in a lonely-spinster-to-be protest. I found myself blushing when he looked at me and tucked my hair back behind my ear in a way which was supposed to be endearing, leaving a streak of flour across my cheek as I did so, which I wouldn't notice until much later on.

'Do you want a hand with those?' Hugh asked. I was holding the tray of vol-au-vents somewhat crookedly and he had just watched two of them roll off the tray and on to the filthy floor. I looked at them forlornly. He must have been thinking that I was completely incompetent by now.

'You can put these in the oven if you like. They'll be done in twenty minutes.' I said as I handed him the tray, trying hard to brush his fingers subtly as I did so. I had read something about doing that to create an intimate moment. Just at that intimate moment, however, Julie poked her head around the door and screeched, 'Lara, put that poor man down and come out here at once.'

Put that poor man down? I had only tried to stroke his fingers. But I blushed to the roots of my hair straight away and began to stutter. 'But we . . . I mean, I'm not . . . I'm not doing anything to him.'

'Yeah, right,' slurred Julie. 'Come out here. I'm sure that the lovely Hugh can spare you for a moment or two.'

Hugh shrugged and smiled. 'She sounds like she really needs you out there,' he said. So I made for the door sharpish before Julie had time to open her mouth again.

'What do you want?' I asked her urgently.

'I've got someone for you to meet. Someone lovely.' She let the word roll off her tongue.

'I was with someone lovely in the kitchen,' I hissed.

'Did you know you've got flour all over your face?' she replied.

'Have I?'

'Yes. I'll rub it off. Now you must come over here and

CHRIS MANBY

meet Simon Mellons. He works with Andrew at Partridge Skelton and he's very, very single. Just your type.'

'You mean to say he's desperate too?'

She shot me a weary look and began to weave her way through the crowd, dragging me along behind her. As we neared Andrew, I noticed the average-looking chap he was standing next to guffaw with laughter about something and spit chewed-up vol-au-vent out all over the mantelpiece as he did so. Apparently, this was Simon Mellons. Up until that moment, I might have given his lime-green chenille jumper the benefit of the doubt. In fact, I might have given him the benefit of the doubt right up until the moment when he picked up a bit of the recently expelled vol-au-vent and put it back into his mouth again.

'Not my type.' I muttered. But Julie didn't let go of my arm.

'What do you mean? He's perfect for you. Give him a chance. You haven't even spoken to him.'

'No, honestly. I don't need to. His surname's Mellons, for goodness' sake. Besides I should check the oven.' I pulled away from her again and this time I managed to escape but as I stepped backwards, I trod heavily on to someone's foot. I turned round to face Hugh Armstrong-Hamilton. He had spilled a glass of something down his front with the shock of my weight on his instep. Two glasses of something in fact. An elegant blonde who I wouldn't have allowed into the house relieved him of one of the empty glasses and said, 'Lucky I've already had enough to drink, Hughie-dear.'

'Sorry,' I muttered, then I fled without waiting around to see if my apology had been accepted.

I had decided that the party was over for me. I had got drunk, been obnoxious to my flatmate's future sister-in-law, narrowly escaped being set up with a grade one dweeb and acted like an imbecile in front of the only man worth batting my eyelashes at. I went to my bedroom, thinking that I would lock myself away from the crowd and then knock myself out with a couple of Nytol. But someone else had already had that idea. Well, they had locked themselves away in my room but from the sound of my bedsprings, I guessed rather angrily that they weren't doing any sleeping. There was nothing for it. I couldn't hang around amongst all these gorgeous attached people feeling as rough and single as I did. So, I left my own home in the middle of Julie's engagement party and walked the long miles from Battersea to Putney, where I knew my mother would be waiting for me with lots of tea and sympathy. At least, she would be once I'd woken her up and got her to let me in.

Despite the fact that it was four in the morning by the time I arrived, Mum seemed pleased to see me. Dad didn't even wake up. I stayed at their house until early afternoon the next day, letting Mum make a fuss of me and be generally motherly, while Dad made the most of the diversion and smoked an illicit cigar in the lounge. Just after lunch though, Mum started asking the dreaded b-word questions and when I said that there was still no future son-in-law on the horizon, she told me that she'd heard that lesbians could adopt these days or do it with a test-tube if they wanted to so that no poor woman need grow old without grandchildren, just in case I had something to admit.

As you can imagine, I had to go back to the flat pretty quickly after that. I was feeling a bit of a heel for skipping the post-party tidying up, but had convinced myself by the time I got to our road that Julie didn't actually deserve my help anyway since she hadn't called Mum and was obviously therefore not exactly worried about what had become of me. As it turned out, I needn't have felt bad at all. When I pushed open the door to our lovely little home at roughly four o'clock, I found that one reveller was still lying right behind it, fast asleep by the shoe-rack, face-down in a pair of trainers I had been meaning to throw away for quite some time. So much for missing the tidying up, I scowled. The house was still a tip and my vol-au-vents were still in the oven. Sadly, they were completely burned and stuck like limpets to the tray.

I tried the door to my bedroom again. This time, thank goodness, it wasn't locked. My latest plan was to hang about in there, flicking through the pretty-coloured bits of the Sunday papers, until someone else woke up. No way was I tackling that mess on my own. But it was not to be. My bed was full. I counted three heads on the pillows and four sets of feet at the other end, so someone under that duvet was either very short or up to something I didn't want to think about right then.

Slinking into the kitchen to put the kettle on, I found a solitary tea bag in the caddie but no milk. In fact the fridge was completely empty. Someone had even licked the margarine pot clean! Desperate for a cuppa and unable to drink black Darjeeling, I thought very, very dark thoughts towards my ex-best friend Julie indeed.

'Oh, hello. What happened to you? I'm afraid I burned your vol-au-vents.'

It was Hugh Armstrong-Gorgeous, standing at the door to the kitchen again but this time with his huge arms full of groceries. He set the straining bags down on the kitchen table and I eyed a carton of semi-skimmed covetously. 'I forgot how long you said they needed to be cooked for,' he continued. 'But when I tried to find you, you seemed to have disappeared.'

'I went out to get a bit of fresh air,' I told him.

'Must have been a big bit. You were gone all night. Still, if this was my flat, I don't think I'd have bothered coming back until Monday or Tuesday. It's a right tip, isn't it?'

'Yes,' I agreed. I noticed with disgust that someone had stubbed out a cigarette in the tub of my delicate Peace Lily and heaven only knows how much alcohol the poor plant had had to endure before that final indignity. It was now drooping almost as much as I was. I picked the fag butt out of the soil and flicked it on to the filthy floor which was awash with several further butts in a solution of cheap red wine. No amount of Baby

Bio and sweet-talking was going to bring that poor lily back to life.

'Bet you don't know where to start?' Hugh continued almost gleefully. 'Luckily no one threw up in the bathroom.'

'That's a blessing then,' I muttered.

'But I'm afraid that someone did throw up in the corner of the sitting room. Behind the sofa. Just so you don't get a shock when you look behind there.'

'Thanks. It's very kind of you to let me know,' I said sarcastically. Sick in the sitting room? I wondered who had invited that particular pig and, more importantly, who had let them get away without mopping up their own mess? I could see Julie now. 'Been sick? That's OK. Just push the sofa over it for the moment and Lara will clean the mess up in the morning.' Fume. Fume. Fume. Fifteen years of solid friendship were rapidly being eroded away by the results of one foolish night.

I put the kettle on again. But I had used the last tea bag so I had to reheat the black Darjeeling I had made earlier in the microwave instead. I didn't expect it to taste right and it didn't disappoint me. Hugh, meanwhile, rinsed a wineglass out beneath the cold tap, then thought better of it and decided that for hygiene reasons he had better drink straight from the juice carton instead.

I watched him slyly as he downed a pint of orange juice with his head tipped back and his Adam's apple bobbing like a buoy. He still looked pretty delicious, even after a night of drunken debauchery, and I started to wish

SECOND PRIZE

I had taken the opportunity to smarten myself up at mum's before coming back to the flat. Where had he slept, I wondered, and more importantly, who with, since multiple bed occupancy seemed to be the order of the day? I hoped it wasn't the ice-brittle blonde whose drink I had spilled all over Hugh's jumper. Just while I was thinking about this, Hugh put the empty juice carton back down on the table, since the bin was already full to overflowing, and asked me, 'So where did you stay last night?' with a rather conspiratorial air. 'Julie didn't tell me that you had a boyfriend.'

Bloody Julie. Robbing me of my mystique. I bet she'd also told him that I hadn't had a snog in two years. 'Well,' I replied, barely concealing my annoyance, 'Julie doesn't know everything about me after all, does she?'

'Oh, that's pity,' said Hugh. 'Because I was going to ask you if you'd like to join me for a late lunch but I imagine that you've probably got other plans.'

Damn, damn, damn. 'No. I stayed at my parents' house, actually,' I blurted out quickly. 'They live in Putney.'

Hugh smiled slyly. 'Julie said that was where she thought you would be. So where should we go for lunch?'

Mum had given me so much food that morning that I felt like Mr Blobby after a fortnight-long binge but how could I resist Hugh's charms? 'There's a pub round the corner that does Thai food,' I suggested. 'They might still be open. But I'd really like to get changed first, if you can bear to wait? My shirt smells terribly smoky.' (And my armpits were probably much much worse!)

'Actually, I think that someone might be sleeping in your room,' Hugh said tactfully.

'I had noticed.'

'And anyway, I think you look fine as you are. Come like that.'

I looked down at my jeans. I supposed that they weren't too filthy considering what they had been through and, in any case, he had already seen me looking my worst. Putting on my gladrags now wouldn't repair the damage already done, would it? But I could really have used a quick tooth-brush. I knew that if I didn't it would be sod's law that Hugh, the most gorgeous bloke I had met in at least two years, would try to get a snog.

Just then, Julie stumbled past the kitchen door in the red DKNY petticoat thing that had cost her a fortune but still looked as though she had bought it from BHS, obviously not having bothered to get undressed before she went to bed. She waved vaguely. Her face had the pallor of someone who had been at sea for fifteen years and never quite found his sea-legs.

'I'll just put some lipstick on,' I said, mindful of my own complexion. If Julie looked like shit, then I usually looked like shit that was two days' old and natural light wasn't going to be half as flattering as our dark kitchen.

'Honestly, Lara, don't bother,' Hugh grabbed my arm

and pulled me to my feet. 'Let's go now before every-one else wakes up and we get sucked into doing the hoovering.'

'I had almost forgotten about that. You know what, Hugh? I think I really ought to stay behind and help out . . .' I protested, suddenly getting an attack of butterflies about the impending late lunch. 'Since I do live here.'

'I'm not taking that for an answer,' he retorted. 'You were in charge of the vol-au-vents last night. Come on. You've done enough.'

Hugh was right. I had been a one-woman catering team, hadn't I? Perhaps I had done my share of the work. Perhaps Hugh did like me in my tatty jeans. Perhaps I wouldn't really have run out of things to say to him by the time we got to the bottom of the stairs.

'Come on,' he insisted. 'Before I fade away with hunger.'

'OK.'

I decided, unusually for me, to take a big risk. I gave up on my disgusting Darjeeling without further persuasion and followed Hugh out into the early autumn sunshine. After all, how big a cock-up could I make over lunch if I made sure that I kept to Diet Coke? And I knew that the mess in the flat would still be there for me to sort out no matter how late I got home.

CHAPTER TWO

In fact, the mess was still there on Tuesday night. Julie and I were having a war of attrition about the clearing-up ever since I had found a used condom under my bed and was probably reacting in much the same way as my mother would have done – all frosty silence and meaningful glares over the breakfast table. By Tuesday night, however, I was sick of living in squalor and I decided that when I got back from work I would have to give up my protest and get stuck in at the sink straight away. Fortunately for her, Julie had the same thought and was back just before I was. If I hadn't walked in to find her up to her elbows in Fairy Liquid, she might well have got monogrammed tea towels as a wedding present.

'Thought I'd better do something about the state of this place,' she muttered.

'Yes,' I replied. 'Good idea.'

'Those burnt vol-au-vents have totally ruined this old baking tray,' she continued. 'I just can't seem to get them to shift . . .'

'Really? You should try using more elbow grease,' I said, not without a hint of sarcasm.

'Look, Lara. I'm really sorry things got a bit out of hand on Saturday night. I promise you that I didn't tell those people that they could use your bedroom as a sex nest. In fact I think they took a bit of a liberty as well, if it's any consolation.'

'That's OK,' I replied. 'At least my duvet's having a love life.' I had shoved all my bed linen straight into the washing machine on Sunday night, without daring to check it for dubious stains, and then put it through a boil-wash twice, just in case.

Julie turned to face me, dripping soapy bubbles all over the floor as she paused in scrubbing at the ruined baking tray. 'And what's that supposed to mean?' she asked as a sly smile spread across her lips. '"At least my duvet's having a love life"? From what I gather, you're not doing too badly yourself any more.'

'What?'

'You sly old cow. You never tell me anything. You went out for lunch with Hugh Armstrong-Hamilton and Andrew called me this morning to say that the foolish man just can't stop talking about you now. The Stock Exchange is going to be on the verge of collapse pretty soon if he doesn't stop mooning about Lara Fenton and get on with his work.'

'Really?'

'Yes, really. Well, maybe "mooning" was a wee bit of an exaggeration but Lara, he was charmed by you, you lucky mare. I chased after him for months and months and months. I had to give up when he blatantly started to set me up with his friends in an attempt to get rid of me. That's how I met Andrew.'

'You didn't tell me.'

'Well, it is a little bit embarrassing isn't it? And I still don't think Andrew really knows that he was only my second prize.'

I could almost feel myself puffing up with pride like a little mushroom vol-au-vent. Had I really caught the eye of a man that Julie Whitgift couldn't attract? Maybe at last the tables were turning and I was going to be the one who was out every night with a different man, while she stayed in with her knitting. Though obviously it was a pretty hollow victory now that Julie had settled down of her own accord and was most definitely going to beat me to the altar. 'So, he's a bit of a catch, is he?' I asked in a nonchalant kind of way.

'Just a bit, La. He's the whole bloody shoal.' She ticked off the reasons on her fingers. 'He's handsome. He's funny. He's reasonably clever. And apparently he's got more money than you could shake a stick at.'

'You must be joking?' I said. 'We went halves on that lunch.'

'So? He could have been testing you out, La. Just making sure that you weren't after him for his fifteen thousand acres in the Shires.'

'Fifteen thousand acres? Wow. Is that a lot?' I couldn't help asking before I added quickly. 'But you know I don't think like that about men, Julie. I don't care how much money and land they've got to their names as long as they've got a nice personality and a reasonable face.'

'Yes, Lara. But you were always a wee bit strange in that regard,' Julie replied. 'So, what happened?'

'We talked.'

'About what?'

'Usual things. His work. My work. Whether Thai food is better than Indian?'

'Any long silences?'

'Not really.'

'That's good. Did he say whether he's still single?'

'No, but he didn't say that he wasn't. And the blonde girl he was talking to at the party is definitely just a friend. She goes out with one of his workmates in fact.'

'Fantastic. Did you kiss him?'

'He went to kiss me goodbye on both cheeks and we sort of collided noses,' I confided.

Julie rolled her eyes. 'Jeez, that's pathetic, Lara. But not to worry. It can easily be improved upon. When are you seeing him again?'

'Well, we didn't actually arrange anything,' I admitted sadly.

'So, call him and arrange something now, you idiot. Don't let this one slip through your fingers, Lara, for heaven's sake. I think I can remember his number if you didn't have the sense to take it down yourself.'

'Julie, I can't just call him if he hasn't called me,' I

protested. 'That would look so sad. I'd have to kill myself straight afterwards.'

'Not if you had an excuse, you wouldn't.' She pointed towards a crumpled cricket jumper which was lying haphazardly across the back of a chair. 'Look, he left that jumper behind. Deliberately, if you ask me. It was freezing by the time he left here on Sunday night so he would definitely have noticed its absence.'

'I can't do it,' I whined. 'If he was interested in getting together again he would have called me by now.'

'Not necessarily. He might not have wanted to seem too pushy at first. Call him now,' Julie commanded. 'At the very least he deserves to know what's happened to his jumper, doesn't he?'

'Since you put it like that . . . I suppose it wouldn't hurt so much if I gave him just a little call . . .' I picked up the jumper and carried it with me as I skipped over to the telephone. Had he really left it behind deliberately so that I would simply have to get in touch? The mere thought of that scenario was making my heart beat faster. Funny thing was, I could have sworn he was wearing a navy-blue sweatshirt complete with red wine stain and not a cricket jumper when we walked to the pub. Oh well. Julie called out Hugh's number as she stood elbow-deep at the sink. She obviously knew it by heart, which was sad.

'Is it ringing?'

'Yes, it is.'

There was no time to back out. Hugh picked up the phone after just two rings. It entered my mind briefly that

19

he might even have been waiting by the phone for me to call and I instantly lost all semblance of composure.

'Er, hi, H-Hugh,' I began. 'It's L-Lara. Lara Fenton. The girl at the party in Battersea. We went for lunch on Sunday. Remember?'

'Of course I remember. Hi, Lara. How are you? Finished that tidying up yet?'

'I'm fine, thanks. And we're just starting the tidying up now as a matter of fact. I'm only calling because you seem to have left your jumper behind,' I added hurriedly.

'My jumper?'

'Yes. It's a woolly cricket jumper with maroon and gold stripes around the neck.'

'Maroon and gold stripes?' He was obviously playing the innocent. 'Nope,' he announced after a second's thought. 'I don't think so. That's really not my kind of thing, I'm afraid. Must belong to someone else.'

'Are you sure?' I asked.

'Yes. I'm sure I'd know if I'd lost my own jumper. And I swear I've never owned a cricket sweater in my life.'

'Oh. I suppose you'd know.'

A moment of awkward silence yawned open like an abyss before me and I wanted to fall straight into it.

'Well, I'm sorry to have bothered you then,' I muttered. 'I'll see you around.'

'When?'

'What?'

'When will I see you around?'

'Whenever?'

SECOND PRIZE

'How about this Thursday?' he asked. 'I'll come over to your place about eight o'clock. That be OK with you?'

'OK?' I squeaked. 'OK? That'd be lovely. Thursday it is, then.' He said goodbye and put down the phone. I almost tripped over the Hoover as I raced back to Julie, trying to calm down the growing heat of excitement in my cheeks with the mystery jumper. 'It isn't his jumper,' I informed her innocently.

'I know it isn't,' she said flatly. 'It belongs to Andrew. But I also knew that you'd never phone Hugh Armstrong-Hamilton in a million years if you didn't have an excuse to do it.'

'What!! How could you do that to me?' I put the jumper down on the table and picked up a damp tea towel which I used to flick Julie with hard across the back of her head. 'You bitch,' I shrieked. 'You set me up!!'

'I got you a date though, didn't I?'

CHAPTER THREE

J ulie's claim that she had 'got me a date' was perhaps a little premature. I booked Thursday afternoon off work and panicked my way up and down the length of Kensington High Street trying to find a suitable outfit for dinner with an earthly god. Three hours of hard foot-slogging later I got back on to the Tube completely empty-handed and prayed all the way home to Battersea that my long black jersey dress with its flattering stomach-flattening front panel would be clean enough to wear.

It wasn't of course. Julie had borrowed it for a drinks-spilling party in Fulham and not bothered to wash it out afterwards. So I spent another hellish hour laying out the cleanish contents of my wardrobe upon the bed and trying to narrow down a short-list of possibles from a jumble sale's worth of panic buys.

There was the added complication that I didn't know where Hugh was planning to take me. We had already been out for lunch together. Did that mean that he was 'serious' enough about me to want to take me out to dinner or were we going to spend the evening in some smoky little pub? And if we went to a restaurant was it going to be Pizzaland or Daphne's? Julie had spent the past two days periodically sighing, 'He's so rich, you lucky bitch', so we might well be going Michelin. On the other hand, I had heard that the seriously stinking rich were notoriously tight with their cash so we might just as well be doing McDonalds.

Anyway, I got my options down to a blue silk shift dress that I had bought in a Browns sale and a pair of voluminous navy palazzo pants which would go quite well with a white top I'd inherited from Jools when she lost half a stone and subsequently an inch off her boobs. Both the trousers and the dress had been bought at extreme times in my life. The shift dress when I had just split up from my university boyfriend and lost eight pounds in a single week without even trying to stay off the chocolate, and the trousers at the very peak of my 'life's so good I've got fat' stage. Now that I was in between those extremes neither the pants nor the dress fitted properly but with the help of an elasticated belt and underwear with a high Lycra content respectively, they would just about do. They would have to.

At the very height of my sartorial dilemma, Julie returned from work. She was much much earlier than usual – her job in advertising generally required a three-hour lunch that had to be made up for at night – but she was obviously as eager as I was for my big date to arrive. Walking into my room to see how the transformation was getting on, she took one look at the clothes laid out upon my bed, shook her head violently and said, 'No, no, no. You can't wear those. What about your long black dress?'

'It is hanging, unwashed, from the back of your bedroom door,' I replied in a remarkably civil tone for someone so deep in panic that I needed a police diving team to get me out.

'Whoops. Then I suppose I'll have to lend you something of mine.'

She disappeared into her room and returned moments later with armfuls of stuff that I just knew I would never get into. But Julie wasn't about to let the fact that I was at least a size bigger than she was become some sort of problem. She had me squeeze myself into a rust-brown coloured jersey creation with buttons all the way down the front. On Julie, this long dress had looked stylishly monastic. On me, with all the buttons straining fit to burst across my bust, it looked like the splitting skin of an overripe conker.

'I can't wear this,' I wailed. 'You can see my bra through the gaps.'

'It's sexy,' she assured me as she stood back and admired her handiwork. 'Just a little flash of lace here and there. Drives the boys wild.'

'More like a flash of grey cotton and safety pins,' I told her. 'I remain unconvinced.'

'Stay there.' Julie rummaged in my jewellery box and fished out a brooch. She used it to pin together the worst area of seepage.

'There you go,' she said triumphantly. 'No one will notice your underwear now.'

'But this looks even more ridiculous,' I moaned. 'No one ever wears a brooch at that height. Besides which, it's a disgusting brooch.' It was a silver and diamanté hedgehog that had been given to me by my grandmother on my twelfth birthday. I had loved it at the time but now it was just a little bit too twee even for someone who owned more than one pair of teddy-bear print pyjamas. I couldn't bear to throw it away since my grandmother had recently passed on to the other side but equally, I had never actually intended to wear it again.

'It looks OK, Lara. Honestly it does. Just relax a bit, will you?'

'It draws too much attention to my tits.'

Julie sat down on the edge of the bed and considered my opinion. After giving my 36Cs a critical once-over, she nodded and said, 'Yes. Perhaps you're right. It makes you look massive. Haven't you got one of those minimiser bra things?'

'A minimiser bra? My chest is my one and only asset!!' I protested. I unpicked the hedgehog brooch and put it back into the jewellery box but not before giving it a little kiss to make amends for the fact that I had pronounced it disgusting.

'Well, do you want to make a feature of your bust or not?' Julie continued. 'Make your mind up, will you? You've only got half an hour.'

'Oh, I don't know. I might just have to cancel this date

altogether,' I said forlornly as I collapsed on to the bed. 'I'll have to ask him if we can go out tomorrow instead and make sure that I get my black dress clean tonight.'

'No way,' Julie insisted. 'It's way too late to cancel tonight's date politely and if you ask him to go out tomorrow instead you'll look like a proper saddo.'

'Why will I look like a saddo if I ask to see him tomorrow night?' I was confused.

'Because how many hip and groovy people do you know who don't have their Friday nights booked up for weeks in advance? He'll think you've got no friends, Lara.'

'But I'm not actually doing anything tomorrow night, am I?'

'You'll just have to pretend that you are. Honestly, Lara, you've got to make him think that you're a valuable commodity to be desired and respected, not just some desperate old slapper grasping for any date that'll have you.'

'I'd rather be a desperate old slapper with something to do on a Friday night than a lonely wannabe commodity,' I protested. 'Can't I pretend that tomorrow evening is the one Friday night this year I have free? I could pretend that I've been keeping it clear to deep-condition my hair but that I'll sacrifice my beauty routine especially for him?'

'He won't believe for an instant that you use a conditioner,' Julie sneered as she examined my split ends. 'But I suppose it isn't really an issue since it's not as though Hugh won't have already arranged to go out with his friends tomorrow night anyway.'

Just then, the telephone rang. Julie leapt to her feet. 'I'll answer it. I'll answer it. You've got to get those buttons shut somehow. Breathe in a bit more, can't you?' She skipped off into the kitchen and left me to wrestle with the jersey dress. Perhaps if I put on a plain black vest beneath and undid all the buttons as far down as the waist? That might look quite chic. I considered my vest collection. Perhaps not.

'Lara!!! It's for you,' Julie shrieked.

I looked at my watch. Just quarter of an hour to go before Hugh was due to arrive. I prayed that it wasn't my mother, calling to find out whether I had remembered to handwash my navy-blue cardigan or if I had enough vitamin-enriched vegetables in my fridge. Julie was holding her hand over the mouthpiece. As I walked towards her she was whispering instructions frantically. 'It's Hugh,' she said. 'He may just be calling to say that he's going to be late but if he wants to rearrange, remember that you're far, far too busy to see him until next Tuesday.'

'But I'm not too busy,' I reminded her in a hiss. 'I haven't got anything to do all weekend or on Monday night.'

'I don't care. Listen to your Auntie Julie, Lara. If you want to succeed with this one, you have simply got to play hard to get for a while. Be strong for me.'

She handed the telephone to me and gave a thumbs-up sign but did not retreat to another room. It was clear that she was going to stay right beside me to police every little thing I said.

'Er, hello, Hugh,' I muttered. 'Have you had a nice day?'

Julie winced at the pleasantry.

'Nice as a day at the office can be, thank you, Lara,' he replied. 'Listen, I'm terribly sorry to do this to you at such short notice but I'm afraid I'm going to have to blow you out this evening.'

'Blow me out? Why?'

No, no, no, Julie shook her head. I was obviously meant to be disinterested in his reasons.

'Something's just come up,' he said simply. 'An old friend is in London for one night only and I really must see her because she lives such a long way away from town. I feel such a heel, Lara. I do hope you can forgive me for messing you around like this.'

'Oh, it's OK,' I squeaked as my heart sank to my shoes. 'I should probably put in a couple of hours on a project I've been doing for work anyway.' Julie looked as though she was going to die. 'Could we, could we perhaps rearrange for a later date?' I asked tentatively.

'Of course,' said Hugh. And very enthusiastically too, I thought. My confidence in his interest was instantly restored. 'How about tomorrow night? We could go to this great little Italian restaurant I know for dinner, eat a bit of pasta and then perhaps go on to a club.'

I bit my lip.

'Tomorrow night?' I asked.

Julie shook her head so violently that I thought her eyes might pop out.

I swallowed hard. 'Tomorrow night? Oh, Hugh. That

sounds just wonderful but I'm afraid that I'm already booked up for the whole weekend.'

'Really?'

''Fraid so. I'm playing squash. Yes, I'm in a squash tournament,' I elaborated. 'Would next Tuesday evening do instead?'

It would. We made the necessary arrangements and I bid Hugh goodbye.

Julie was sitting on the kitchen table, still shaking her head. 'Squash tournament?' she said incredulously. 'Squash tournament? No one ever plays squash on a Friday night, Lara. Now he'll think you're really weird. Or worse, what if he asks you to have a game of squash with him one day? You haven't got a clue how to play!!'

'All right, all right! Stop going on at me,' I begged her. 'At least I managed to turn him down for tomorrow night. That was what you wanted, wasn't it? It's me who's got to sit in all on my own now when I could have been having dinner at an Italian restaurant and then going on to a club to dance the night away in his big strong arms.'

'Is that what he suggested?'

I nodded.

'Oh, I bet he means La Traviata. I went there once with him, Andrew and a girl they both knew called Caroline. She was a right bitch, I can tell you. Acted like her shit doesn't smell. But it was the best Italian meal I've ever eaten. And really expensive too. Andrew paid something like twelve pounds for a piece of bread with tomatoes on it. Bruschetta, I think it was called.'

SECOND PRIZE

'Thanks a lot, Julie,' I hissed. 'I could have been eating out there tomorrow night but instead I'll be having tomatoes on toast *chez nous*.' I did a mental inventory of the contents of the cupboards. In fact, I probably wouldn't even be having that unless I went round M & S with my Chargecard. There were still two weeks until pay-day and I was already banging my head against the limit on my overdraft.

'Cheer up, Lara.' Julie put her arm around my shoulder. 'I'm sure he'll take you to La Traviata another day. And just think, when he does, that bruschetta will taste all the better for your having waited for it. If you approach this whole thing properly, La Traviata might even be the restaurant where he asks you to marry him, like Andrew did me in Le Manoir.'

'Aren't you jumping the gun just a little bit?' I asked. 'We haven't even had our first date yet, for heaven's sake.'

'So? Andrew knew that he wanted to marry me just two days after we met.' She put the kettle on and continued to muse about the legendary proposal. He had gone down on one knee of course. 'In front of all those people eating their dinner. I was terribly embarrassed at the time but when I look back on that moment now, I can see that it was just so romantic of him. I really couldn't have asked for a more wonderful, sensitive man to share my life with.'

I had only heard this story about a million times so I left her to her dreaming and went to take off the borrowed dress before I lost the ability to breathe within its confines.

I rescued my own black dress from the back of Julie's door and stuffed it into the washing machine with the Fairy washing liquid ball. But I was so pissed off about not being able to see Hugh for another five days because of Julie's stupid seduction system that I must have put it in on the wrong cycle, because when I came to get the dress out again an hour or two later, it had shrunk.

So, I spent Friday night trying to stretch my black dress back to its former proportions and when that tactic failed miserably, I spent the rest of the weekend shopping for something similar to replace it. Once again, I was having no luck on the shopping front. The fashion for flattering clothes had obviously passed and the shops were full of Day-Glo dresses that all stopped at just the wrong spot on my thighs or my calves. From the knees down, I had decided, my legs were passable, but show even a half-inch above that, and my cover was blown. Likewise, an unflattering line across the calf might draw too much attention to my slightly unladylike ankles.

Julie came with me into town. She was hunting for 'going-away' outfits for her honeymoon and two hours into the shopping trip, she had enough carrier bags full of stuff to set up her own stall in Covent Garden. I had purchased nothing. Absolutely nada. Over coffee in a little French place with real Parisian waiters (or maybe just Islingtonians with good accents), Julie tried to persuade me that a pair of silver-fishscale flared hipsters I had tried on in Miss Selfridge did in fact make me look good and not like a half-descaled cod.

'You should get them for your date on Tuesday,' she said as she stuffed down an almond croissant. 'Hugh likes a wacky girl. Believe me.'

'I am not getting those stupid hipsters,' I replied as I slavered at the mere thought of being able to stuff down an almond croissant with such impunity. 'You just want me to buy something quickly so that you can stop helping me to find that perfect dress and suggest that we go home.'

'That's not fair. I've been really helpful to you today.'

'No, you haven't. You just keep shoving lime-green hotpants suits and bright yellow kaftans in my direction. You don't care whether I look good on Tuesday night or not. In fact, you'd probably prefer it if I looked a right state, wouldn't you?'

'I would not, Lara. That's so untrue.' She looked almost genuinely surprised and hurt. 'I want this date with Hugh to be a success almost as much as you do. But it's very difficult to go shopping creatively with someone who's so set in her ways about clothes, you know. You should give some of my suggestions a chance. You're always looking for something in boring black or navy blue when silver and pale green could be just the colours you want. You won't know unless you try them,' she added wisely.

'I do believe that it was you who suggested I wear black and navy blue in the first place,' I reminded her tartly. 'You said, if I remember rightly, that they might help to "de-emphasise" the width of my bum.'

'I didn't, did I?' Julie blushed. 'But that was in the old

days. You've really shaped up since I said that. Let's go back to Miss Selfridge and try those trousers on again.'

'Have I really shaped up?' I asked, fishing for compliments.

'Yes. You really have lost quite a bit of weight since you got that exercise bike.'

I'd ridden the damn thing twice.

'I've always been jealous of your curves, La. You've got a real bust and a tiny waist. I'm just straight up and down,' she added wistfully, as she folded the last of the croissant into her mouth. Like the crow with the cheese, faced by the wily fox, I was flattered back into stupidity.

So, when Julie had finished her coffee, we trooped back to Miss Selfridge and walked straight up to the disco-diva-type section where the silvery hipsters were hanging by the thousand, reduced from £45 to just £6.99 a pair, popular though Julie insisted they were. Julie picked out a pair in size twelve and a pair in size fourteen. I carried them through to the changing room obediently, feeling the crinkly plastic coating on the fabric and wondering just how much fun they would be to wear after you'd had a bit of a dance in them and were covered in sweat. Depended on what your kind of thing was, I supposed.

The changing room, this not being my day at all, was one of those dreadful communal changing rooms that remind you that shopping for clothes, like being hit by a bus, is one of those occasions that requires matching underwear. I wasn't wearing matching kit, of course, so I tried the trousers on in the quietest corner I could find, pulling them up beneath my skirt and not taking my skirt off until I was sure that the zipper on the hipsters was going to fasten all the way.

As far as I could see in the mirror, which was being hogged by two fifteen-year-old size sixes who kept asking each other if they looked fat, the hipsters were no real improvement on my memory of the same. I turned round and round like a dog with worms chasing its tail in an attempt to get a good back view in the impossibly placed glass. I was getting pretty dizzy before I realised that it wasn't going to happen and decided that I would just have to trust in the judgement of my best friend. Unwise though that was considering her track record.

Julie was waiting outside the changing room, fingering a skinny black sweater with a fake rabbit-fur collar that I just knew she would have to have by the time we left the shop.

'Your opinion?' I asked. I tried to ignore the other shoppers while Julie put her fingers to her chin and pulled a face of barely veiled concern. 'My legs do look like a fish's tail in these, don't they?' I insisted. I looked down at the flappy hems which covered my feet and wondered if I even had any shoes high enough to stop them from dragging through the dirt when I walked.

'Yes,' Julie agreed with the fishtail comment. 'But remember that mermaids are considered to be beautiful worldwide. I think those trousers are fantastic and you should definitely get them for Tuesday night. I'll just check the rear view. Turn round.'

It was probably a good job I couldn't see her face because less than a week later, when I finally got to see my own back view in those terrible trousers, the truth really did hurt. At that moment in the shop, Julie started making cooing noises which I took to be signs of encouragement but which were probably just sounds of suppressed hilarity. She ushered me back into the changing room to put on my sensible clothes again and had my credit card out of my bag and ready for use when I re-emerged with an uncertain look upon my face.

'You sure you don't fancy this bustier thingy too?' She dangled a matching bra-top in front of me.

'I'm Lara Fenton,' I reminded her. 'Not Elton John.'

'You're probably right,' she agreed but she still held the thing up against me, drawing amused smiles from a *Vogue* cover-girl-type standing behind us in the queue. The bustier might have suited Ms Vogue, but of course she was about to buy something with considerably more style.

'You would tell me if I looked really stupid, wouldn't you?' I asked Julie one more time as the shop-girl swished my card through the till and rang up the amount, which looked like a bargain if you didn't know what I was buying.

'Of course I would tell you if you looked stupid,' Julie replied sincerely. 'Come on, La. Am I your very best friend or what?'

I suspected that the correct answer that afternoon might very well be 'what'.

CHAPTER FOUR

T uesday night came far too quickly. I could barely concentrate at all at work and the project I had spent all of an hour typing out with two fingers came back from the boss to my desk blood-red with corrections. But I fled through the door at five thirty on the dot mindless of my responsibilities. Incredibly, both the Tubes and the buses were with me. By the time I got home, I was foolishly thinking that it just might be my lucky night.

The silver trousers lay shimmering on the bed awaiting their first foray into the outside world. Despite trying to make me buy the matching bustier while we were in the shop, Julie had suggested that tonight I team the trousers with a plain black skinny polo neck to make sure that I didn't go over the top with the glitter look. Since I didn't have a plain black polo neck of my own, she had lent me one of hers. Except that it wasn't exactly plain. It was the skinny top with the fake rabbit-fur collar that I had known she wouldn't be able to resist that Saturday afternoon. It looked great on the hanger, really cool, but when I put it on, that jumper itched like it was made from hungry fleas.

I had to trust in the gods that I didn't look like a total prat as I finished dressing and waited for Hugh to arrive. The biggest mirror in the whole house was on the doors of the bathroom cabinet. I did try standing in the bath in an attempt to get a full-length view but almost ended up flat on my back when my stockinged feet slipped on the enamel. I wisely gave up after that. Knocking myself out just before my first date with Hugh Armstrong-Hamilton wouldn't have been *très* cool.

At least I knew that my hair and make-up were OK and, from where I was sitting on the sofa chewing my nails down to stumps, my feet looked fine too in a pair of black lace-up platform boots from winter 1993 that I had thought I would never wear again. In fact I can't believe I didn't throw them away after the day when I dislocated my ankle on a stationary escalator at Charing Cross.

Julie had done me the honour of being out of the house while I endured the painful minutes from half past seven to eight o'clock. I had told her that I didn't want her to be around while I waited for Hugh to arrive, winding me up and making me nervous as she was wont to do. She claimed to be working late anyway, though I had a sneaking suspicion that Hugh and I might pass her 'just coming in' on our way out.

When the doorbell finally rang, the shock of the noise breaking the silence of the empty flat almost killed me. I hadn't dared even turn the television on while I waited, in case the bell decided not to work and I missed a quiet knock. Now I leapt to my feet and quickly brushed myself down. I took a final slug from my courage-giving gin and tonic and three deep breaths for luck. With my hand on the door handle I offered up a small, silent prayer: 'This is my first date for almost two years, God,' I muttered. 'And I think we both know that I really, really deserve it. Please don't let it be a disaster like the last one was.' Seconds later, I wished I hadn't invoked that last terrible date because when I finally opened the door to Hugh and he handed me a huge bunch of bright pink flowers, I found myself saying 'Hello, Guy.' (The name of the last chap, who had broken my heart by coming out of the closet a week after we first went to bed.)

I wasn't sure whether Hugh had heard me fluff his name but he must surely have seen the accompanying blush. I buried my face in the flowers in a feeble attempt to hide my cheeks and promptly broke out with a violent sneeze that sent petals all over the floor. I've been a martyr to my hayfever for years.

'Come in, come in. Can I get you a drink of something?' I asked, indelicately wiping my nose on my sleeve and tripping over my own feet in those stupid boots as I headed back inside.

Hugh hovered on the doorstep, probably taking in my outfit, while I searched for a vase for the flowers. There was not a vase in the house that didn't contain a floral tribute to Julie from Andrew, so I emptied out the blue plastic bin from the bathroom, filled it with water and put my flowers in there instead, hoping Hugh would think me rather avant-garde.

'Gin and tonic? Vodka and tonic? Lager and lime?' I recited the contents of our fridge as I tried to 'arrange' the carnations without the benefit of natural artistic talent.

'Actually, Lara, I was wondering if we might go straight out when you've sorted out those flowers. It's just that I said we'd meet up with some friends in the restaurant at half past.'

'Oh.' I was crestfallen. 'Some friends?' Our first date and we were meeting up with some of his friends? Obviously, this was not what I had hoped for but I tried to put on my happy-go-lucky face anyway and slipped Julie's black jacket over my shoulders. 'OK. I'm ready,' I told him at last with a carefree shrug. 'Where are we going?'

'La Traviata.'

I took that bit in with a smile.

Considering Julie's rapturous review of the place, La Traviata didn't look all that posh to me. In fact, I had passed it by a dozen times on my way to the library without giving the place a second thought. Hugh and I walked there. I must admit that I was expecting to be driven but he told me as we walked that he didn't have a car. Too expensive to run and having nowhere to park in Chelsea was his reasoning. I was rather disappointed, since while I agreed with what he was saying and was actually far too green to run a gas-guzzler myself, I was still a sucker for a man in a sports car.

SECOND PRIZE

Anyway, back to La Traviata. From the outside it looked like a pretty bog-standard Italian restaurant with a burgundy-red canopy and a little courtyard fenced off from the street with old wine barrels. Unfortunately it was too cold to sit outside and enjoy our food with added petrol fumes so we were ushered straight inside to join a table that was already occupied by two well-groomed-looking girls.

Hugh introduced me.

'Lara Fenton, these two lovely ladies are Antonia Fisher and Cecilia Devine.' They took me in beamingly but next to their magazine-cover glossiness I suddenly found myself growing rather self-conscious about my artfully frizzy hair. Hugh continued to explain the connection. 'Antonia and I grew up together in Gloucestershire. Cecilia is Antonia's significant half.'

'Really?' I don't know why I said that so incredulously. Even after Madonna's erotic experiments I suppose I still expected lesbians to have crew cuts and ride bikes. By contrast, Antonia and Cecilia looked typically Cheltenham Ladies, all long, straight hair and ski-tans, with Antonia still wearing the obligatory single string of pearls beneath her tight red T-shirt by DKNY.

'Lara lives with Andrew's fiancée, Julie,' Hugh explained. 'You might remember Julie. She came to dinner once at Caroline's house.' Antonia and Cecilia shared a look and a giggle. They put my back into hackles instantly with what was definitely a show of hostility to my best friend's memory but I was never to find out just what

41

had been so funny because right at that moment, the door to the restaurant swung open again and in walked two more people. A much more conventional-looking couple this time. He was almost as tall as Hugh but blond-haired and slightly stocky. She was as slim and graceful as a young willow tree, with chestnut-brown hair that tumbled across her shoulders like molten silk where mine hung like frayed string. She was wearing a deep red version of the black dress that I had just shrunk down to Barbie-size in the wash. In fact, she was Barbie-sized.

'Hughie, darling. How good to see you.' The girl leant across my shoulder to plant a kiss on his cheek and when she drew away again, he was beaming inanely and I was suddenly unspeakably jealous, not to mention choked by her heady perfume. 'It's been so long.' I don't know why, but it sounded as though she was saying that for effect as well.

Hugh regained his composure and straightened himself up just enough to introduce me. The gilded couple were Tim Winterson and Caroline Lauder. More friends from Hugh's childhood in glorious Gloucestershire. Remembering what Julie had said, I wondered if this was also Caroline of the scentless poo.

Anyway, it seemed that the newcomers knew Antonia and Cecilia pretty well too and they soon launched into meaningless gossip about friends they had in common and probably also my common friends. I stuck my nose into the menu and tried not to feel left out as they laughed at their private jokes. Thankfully, there was quite a lot to read and not all of it was in Italian.

The waiter hovered. I ordered. The rest of the party were still far too concerned with the mysterious parentage of a recently-born child. The waiter tutted. Hugh ordered the special for everyone. Fusilli Napoli. I was already having spaghetti. I felt even more left out than before. But then the conversation between the girls took a turn which was obviously intended to drag me into proceedings, while the boys moved closer together at the other end of the table and talked shop about the City. I got lost at the first PEP.

'I have some friends who are thinking about getting married just before Christmas,' Antonia informed me. 'Isn't that when your flatmate's marrying dear old Andy Pandy? We were wondering what colour the bridesmaids are going to wear, since a winter wedding rather seems to limit you to red velvet and holly green, don't you think?'

'Julie's chosen peach actually,' I announced as I fiddled with a breadstick, worried about the sudden harshness of my London accent against Antonia's plummy tones after sitting in silence for so long.

'Peach?' repeated Antonia. 'That's funny. Didn't Andrew's sister go for peach as well?'

'She did indeed, if I remember rightly,' chipped in Caroline. 'But she got married in April. It's an awfully odd choice for a wedding in the middle of winter, don't you think?'

43

'Not really,' I defended, but I prayed that someone would change the subject before they worked out that the bridesmaids' dresses were in fact going to be handed down. They didn't look like the kind of people who had ever had to understand economy with their understated casual chic courtesy of Ralph Lauren and Calvin Klein.

'Peach? Well, that's certainly given me something to think about,' said Caroline, almost sarcastically, as she flicked a rogue breadstick crumb from her spotless burgundy bodice. Was she the bride-to-be, I wondered? I couldn't see an engagement ring, but then Tim asked Caroline something about her TESSA and the conversation about weddings was over as suddenly as it had begun.

I was already feeling twitchy about the appropriateness of my silver trousers when I slipped out to the loo, to escape a conversation about share prices to which I couldn't possibly contribute, and caught my back view for the first time. It was devastating. Not only did my backside resemble a Christmas bauble, in shape if not in size, but I still had the price tag hanging from the belt hook of my trousers. I tugged it off. Oh, calamity. It wouldn't have been quite so bad if it had said £45 but the original price was obscured by £6.99, written large in bright red ink. I imagined that Antonia's knickers alone had probably cost twice that. Everyone must have seen the label, I thought as I clutched my hands to my head with shame. If the loo window had been big enough I would have crawled out through it right there and then. In fact, I more than considered it, but it had been thoughtlessly bricked in.

Thwarted, I slunk back to my chair feeling very embarrassed, thinking that my best bet was to pretend to be invisible until dinner was over. But as I was crossing the restaurant to our table I managed to get the heel of one of my ridiculous shoes caught up in a treacherous trouser flap and before I knew it, I was face down in my spaghetti, which had arrived during my absence. To give them their due, everyone pretended not to have noticed as I slowly brought my head up from the plate but I could feel myself going as red as the bolognese all the same. I pressed napkins to my cheeks as though they could soak up the blush along with the tomato sauce while everyone else continued to scoop up their Fusilli with merry abandon. When I finally felt calm enough to eat, I tried to twist the long strands of pasta tightly around my fork but they never made it like that to my mouth and inevitably, at the end of each mouthful, I would have to suck in a single strand like a blackbird digesting a worm. Even more inevitably, Hugh always seem to choose that moment to ask me a complicated question, causing me to gesticulate my answers wildly while I forced the spaghetti down and tried not to choke.

By this time the front of Julie's skinny black top was splattered with red spaghetti sauce dots, though I couldn't see the strand of pasta that dangled from the fluffy collar. I caught Cecilia smiling at me indulgently on more than one occasion and wondered if I should complete the picture of sophistication I had presented by asking for the HP sauce. Caroline wiped the corners of her mouth delicately with her napkin. I tried to follow suit but picked up a napkin on the wrong side of my plate only to find that it was full of chewed olive stones which fell out all over the table with a clatter as I brought it to my mouth.

'Coffee?' the waiter asked, when I had finished making a mess of the tablecloth with my chocolate mousse.

No way. Boiling water? I didn't think I should risk it.

When the bill finally came round, Antonia fetched her calculator out of her handbag and split the total into six. I gave Hugh thirty seconds to say he'd pick up my tab but he didn't. So I laid out my forty quid along with the others (Julie had been right about one thing: it was *expensive* with a capital E) and resigned myself to tomatoes on toast for the rest of the week, if not for the rest of the month. But by this point I didn't really care. I just wanted everyone to settle up quickly so that I could escape, get out of that Mafia money-laundering restaurant and get Hugh to myself because my cheeks were never going to go down until under cover of darkness or, preferably, under the covers.

But as we filed out of the restaurant into the clear night air, Cecilia suggested that we all went on to a nightclub. I was desperately wondering how to get out of it, knowing that I now had less than £5 in my purse, when Hugh saved my life by saying, 'Well, you four may not have to get up in the morning but Lara and I have jobs to go to, so I think we'll give clubbing a miss tonight.'

I agreed, thankfully, and heaved a silent sigh of relief. But there was just one more social agony to endure before Hugh and I parted from the others and he walked me back to my flat.

The kissing started. Mouths descended on me from all directions. Cecilia did one cheek, Caroline did both. Antonia and I crashed noses and Tim ended up kissing my forehead while I stood rooted to the spot by nerves, like a confused toddler surrounded by canvassing politicians. There is no social ritual more peculiar than kissing. No embarrassment worse than going for a second cheek when only one is going to be offered. Besides, I was brought up in the kind of family where I rarely saw my father kiss my mother let alone someone they had only just met. All those germs. How revolting! I couldn't wait to get home and give Hugh some more of mine.

I wondered if Hugh had been as eager as I was to be alone with him but he was strangely quiet as we walked back to Battersea, nowhere near as chatty as he had been that Sunday afternoon when we ate bad Thai food at the back of the pub. Perhaps he was nervous, I thought. I certainly was. He had his hands stuffed firmly in his pockets and his face was as blank as my bank balance. I tried to slip my arm through his as we walked along but we came too close to a lamppost and had to part to get past.

'I felt horribly embarrassed when I came back from the toilet and fell over my trousers,' I said in an attempt to refire the conversation which was getting dangerously near death.

'Lavatory, Lara.'

'Pardon?'

'It's lavatory, not toilet. And not pardon, but what.'

'Eh? What do you mean?'

'Oh, don't worry about it. It's a public school thing.'

'Oh.' I wondered if I was meant to find it funny. My mother had spent years and years telling me 'don't say what, say pardon'. I told Hugh I went to a state grammar.

'Really.' He was pretty disinterested.

We had reached the bottom of the stairs which led up to my flat. Hugh stopped. I had skipped up three steps before I noticed that he was no longer with me. 'Want to come in for a coffee?' I asked, trying to sound tremendously inviting but at the same time not too eager. No lights were on in the flat and I had high hopes that Julie was not at home so that we could commandeer the sitting room since I only had a single bed.

But Hugh just shuffled his feet on the pavement and said, 'Some other time perhaps. I really have got to be up early in the morning.'

Disconsolately, I walked slowly back down the steps and kissed him goodbye. No messing about with cheeks this time, just a little peck on the mouth. He didn't try to clutch me to him and force his tongue down my throat as I had hoped he might. The plan had been that as soon as he felt my molars he would be overcome with passion and change his mind about not coming inside. As it was, he could barely have felt the brush of my lips against his before he turned his head away.

'I'll give you a ring,' he called as he headed off quickly in the direction of Clapham Junction.

'Oh. OK,' I said sadly. I waved until he was out of sight and was still hoping against hope that he might reappear at the door, having decided that he did want a night of passion after all, when I was cleaning my teeth and putting on my nightie.

As I had suspected, Julie wasn't in. At least that meant that she wasn't there to gloat over my failure to entice Hugh inside, but it also meant that I had no one to do a post-mortem with. He had said that he would call. Now as I lay in bed picking at a rather persistent spot, I needed someone to convince me of that because, after my spectacularly gauche performance in front of his terribly cultured mates, I somehow doubted that he would.

CHAPTER FIVE

'He said he would call, so he'll call,' said Julie impatiently. She was trying hard to be sympathetic to my plight but with just two months to go before the wedding of the century, an invitation wording crisis was keeping her rather preoccupied.

She was sitting on her bedroom floor, leafing through a huge ring binder stuffed to bursting with all sorts of wedding stationery. Most of it was vile. Some of it criminally so. I steered her away from a particularly nasty set printed with cutesy pink hedgehogs dressed up like the bride and groom.

'But they're my favourite animals,' she protested.

I wondered whether she'd like to borrow my brooch for the Big Day.

Finally, and not without a little guidance, she settled upon effortlessly-tasteful plain white card with the words embossed upon it in silver. 'But it's so boring,' she said sadly as she filled out the order form. 'I wanted to be more individual than this.' I pointed out that she could choose from a variety of swirly typefaces that would add just the right touch of originality but she was determined to be unconsoled.

'Don't ever get married, Lara,' she advised me woefully. 'Organising a wedding is nothing but a nightmare from accepting his proposal to the Big Day itself. I mean, I'm putting all this effort in so that cousins I haven't seen in fifteen years can come and laugh at my dress while they're stuffing their faces with prawn vol-au-vents and champagne at my father's expense. You can't begin to know how stressed out I am.'

She couldn't have begun to know how stressed out her father was, I thought, but instead I said sadly, 'I can only hope I get the opportunity to find out myself one day.'

'Oh, Lara.' Julie cocked her head to one side and gave me a half-sympathetic smile. 'One day your prince will come. Really he will. Besides, I'm sure that your date with Hugh wasn't such a big disaster as you're making it out to be. He wouldn't have walked you home otherwise.'

'I think that was just his polite upbringing showing through. Julie, it's been four days since I saw him last. Do you think perhaps I should give him a call? To say thankyou for taking me to dinner or something?'

'No,' she snapped. 'Absolutely no way.' She looked at me as though I had suggested roasting a kitten in the microwave. 'You can't call him. Especially not if you went Dutch.'

'But you got me to phone him the first time.'

SECOND PRIZE

'Yes, but that was different. When you called that time you were phoning as a casual acquaintance to enquire about the ownership of a stray cricket jumper. If you phone him now, you'll just be a desperate old slapper wanting to know why he hasn't called you.'

'Oh, God,' I moaned. 'This is all too hard. Why do we have to play these stupid games all the time?'

'Just follow my rules,' Julie said wisely. 'And he'll be eating out of your hand within a month. Believe me, La. You must practise the subtle arts of patience and indifference when it comes to relationships. It is the only way to catch a man. It's how I caught Andrew.'

That's funny, I thought. I seemed to remember her patience and indifference while courting Andrew consisting of waiting until he had turned the corner at the bottom of the road before calling his answerphone 'just to hear his voice'. I felt like a surly young monk at the foot of the Buddha. The only way to catch a man? I wasn't so sure. But Julie assured me that she had 'results' from her Draconian dating system and, since I hadn't had any results for quite some time, I let the phone sit silently in its cradle and tried not to stare at it too much.

As I sat at my desk the next Monday morning, inputting the corrections to my latest big project, I couldn't help thinking back to how I'd been feeling just a week before. Then, with my first date with Hugh still to look forward to, I had been as happy as I ever was during office hours. I had even made everyone in my section a cup of coffee

53

without being asked. Now, I was finding it hard even to raise a smile at Malcolm the office junior's jokes which normally made me roll about on the floor in uncontrollable hysterics. Well, nearly.

'How do you make five grannies shout "Bollocks"?' he asked when Maureen, the office dragon, was safely out of sight and earshot in the ladies'.

'I don't know,' I said out of habit. 'How do you make five grannies shout "Bollocks"?'

'Get another granny to shout "Bingo"!' came the reply.

I couldn't bring myself to laugh. Perhaps it wasn't actually funny, but I knew that it was more likely to be that I was in a foul mood because Hugh hadn't phoned. I was Lara Fenton, one-date disaster. I had missed out on a double-barrelled surname and fifteen thousand acres and I just knew it was because of those stupid silver trousers and my inability to eat spaghetti with aplomb.

I turned back to my project before the screen-saver could kick in and betray the fact that I had been staring blankly at the screen for at least fifteen minutes. I had been working as a junior consultant for Hartley and Hartley Ltd. for almost eighteen months. The company dealt in Human Resources and the section I worked in had particular responsibility for comparing wages and staff benefits across various different industries. Other companies could then buy our results to check that they weren't overpaying their poor worker ants. Hartley and Hartley certainly couldn't have been accused of that. Of all the companies I had canvassed for my project, I had yet to find one which paid less than my very own firm so, as you can imagine, I often felt disgruntled and rarely bothered working late.

The Wages and Benefits Research Department had five staff in all. Me, Malcolm, Maureen, Linzi the temporary secretary who was saving up to go home to Australia for Christmas, and Joe. Joe was a graduate trainee like myself but he had started a year before me and thus seemed to see himself as very much my superior. He was a gangly chap and though he had recently turned twenty-six, he possessed the spotty skin and bum-fluff of a fifteen-year-old boy. And the way he looked matched his personality. Apparently his favourite way to spend a weekend was fishing in the ponds on Clapham Common. I had never heard him talk about a girlfriend. Malcolm thought he might be gay. But I knew better on that score. Joe rarely missed an opportunity to squeeze past me en route to the filing cabinets.

'Cheer up, it might never happen.'

'If one more person says that to me today,' I told Joe angrily. 'It bloody well will happen to them.'

'What's the matter with you?'

'Premenstrual tension.'

Joe recoiled to fiddle with a filing cabinet. He obviously didn't have sisters. But sadly the effect of his embarrassment wasn't all that long-lasting. Moments later he was back again, this time actually perching a shiny-trousered buttock on the edge of my desk. He tapped his pencil

rhythmically against the top of my monitor in an attempt
to attract my attention.

'Lara . . .' he began.

'What?' I snapped. 'What do you want now?' It was a
great impression of a girl with period pain.

'Er . . . nothing.' Joe stood up again and fiddled with
his Mickey Mouse tie. He took two steps towards his
own desk, then two steps back towards mine as if he
was engaged in some bizarre dance. 'No, hang on,' he said
eventually. 'It's not nothing actually, Lara. Listen, I was
wondering what you were planning on doing tonight?'

'Me? What I'm doing tonight?' I repeated incredulously.

'Yes. Are you doing anything? Anything special?'

Poor Joe suddenly looked as though he was frantically
searching for a stone to crawl back under after accidentally
blurting out a string of what might as well have been
four-letter words. 'I'm going to quiz night at the County
Arms and I thought you might like to come along,' he
continued. His voice was getting higher and higher.

I softened suddenly. I may have been in a foul mood
because of Hugh but I had never been the type of girl
who kicks a puppy and asking me out had obviously
taken every little drop of courage Joe possessed in his
rangy body. 'Would you . . . would you like to come
with me?' he tried one more time.

It certainly wasn't as though I had anything else to do
that night.

'It starts at eight o'clock.' Joe was almost begging now

and Maureen, who had returned from the ladies', was watching avidly and not all that secretly from behind the cover of her monitor, waiting to hear my reply. If only Hugh had been so desperate for my company, I thought. If only Hugh had been going red in front of my desk, begging me to spend an evening with him at the County Arms.

Suddenly, I took leave of my senses and the decision-making part of my brain began to mutiny. I decided that it would be good for me to be out of the house for an evening. At least then I wouldn't be able to stare at the telephone while it didn't ring. And I didn't actually have to tell anyone that I was going to a pub quiz with Joe the Schmoe from work, did I?

'OK, Joe,' I said, without too much enthusiasm.

'OK? You mean yes?' he repeated incredulously.

I nodded. 'Yes, I suppose I do mean yes.'

Joe gave a huge sigh of relief that seemed to deflate his whole body. 'Shall I meet you there?' he asked.

'Yes.'

'You know where it is?'

I did.

'Great. I'll see you later. I can't believe it . . .'

Joe practically skipped off to his desk and when he got there, he picked up his telephone straight away. He was probably ringing his friends to crow about his success. As he crossed the room, I was sure that even Maureen had given him the thumbs-up sign. Minutes later, she sidled over to my desk with an unasked-for cup of tea that had just the right amount of sugar. Tea made by Maureen was as rare as a useful junior member of the royal family.

'So you're going out with Joe then?'

'You were listening to every word of the conversation so you must know as well as I do what I am going to be doing tonight,' I replied, not really caring too much if I offended her.

'That's what I like to hear,' she continued regardless. 'Two young people going out and enjoying themselves together. You kids of today are always too busy thinking about your careers to go looking for love. It'll only lead to disappointment if you put love off for too long. And Joe's a lovely lad. Perfect son-in-law.'

'Thanks for that, Maureen. I'll bear it in mind.' She'd been talking to my mum.

Too busy thinking about my career, I mused. Huh! If only Maureen knew how much effort I had put into the search for love for the whole of my adult life and most of my adolescence. If I'd put the same effort into my career I would have been heading-up British Aerospace and not just pushing paper at Hartley and Hartley.

For the rest of that afternoon I had to endure knowing winks from Malcolm every time he brought me my photocopying and I also had to diligently avoid catching Joe's eye and so giving him any more encouragement. For a short while, I considered backing out. But there would be no pulling a sickie because Joe would know that I had been perfectly well all afternoon.

At the end of the day, Joe stopped by my desk on his

way out of the door. 'I'll see you at eight then. Don't work too late,' he told me. I was still working ultra-slowly on the corrections to my project, thinking that perhaps I could still call Joe on his mobile and tell him that I'd got caught up. That night I almost prayed for my boss to emerge from his office and give me a task that would last until midnight. But he didn't. The selfish git.

'Who are you going out with?' Julie asked me for the twelfth time as I got ready for my big date later that evening. 'Why won't you let me know his name?'

'Because if I tell you his name it won't mean anything to you anyway.'

'Not even his first name?'

'Julie, no. I swear you don't know him.'

'Well, he can't be much of a catch if you're going out looking like that.' Julie looked at my tatty jeans and scruffy sweatshirt disdainfully. 'Are you going down the dogs or something?'

'We're going to a pub quiz actually.'

'Jeez, what kind of a date is that, Lara? A pub quiz? I think I'd rather stay in and watch the washing machine.'

'Or the phone,' I added, since that was what I had been watching for the past seven nights. 'Look, I've got to go now. I'm going to be late. If Hugh Armstrong-Hamilton should deign to call while I'm out painting the town red, you can tell him that he's missed his chance.' I tried to sound blasé about it, but I still couldn't help thinking it was more the case that I'd missed mine.

Joe was waiting for me outside the pub. Probably just in case I tried to pretend I hadn't seen him in the murky darkness inside and buggered off before he could catch me. He was wearing a nice clean T-shirt and new jeans with a neat crease down the front of each leg. As I walked up to him, he went to kiss me on the cheek. I had hoped he wouldn't try to be that continental. I turned my head away simultaneously and he got me wetly on the ear.

'You turned up,' he said.

'Yes, I know. Unbelievable isn't it?' I replied.

I had assumed, and even hoped, that Joe and I would be meeting up with some other friends of his but once we got inside the County Arms it quickly became obvious that a night at a pub quiz was Joe's idea of a romantic tête-à-tête. Joe went to the bar to get the drinks in – a pint of lager for him and a Diet Coke for me since I was determined to stay sober – while my job was to find a good table. I was torn between getting a table right in the corner or one right next to the bar. The one in the corner would have minimised the chances of being spotted by anyone who knew me but at the same time, I figured that Joe might think I wanted privacy for another reason altogether if I chose a corner seat. That risk was far too great so I chose a table right next to the bar and resolved to keep my head down. If I was caught, I could always say that I was seeing Joe for a bet.

Joe returned with the drinks, a pencil and a piece of paper. We started to talk, falteringly, about the people at work, and I longed for the quiz to start so that I wouldn't have to hear about Maureen's dodgy waterworks again. To my horror, as he was talking I noticed that Joe had a crop of thick black hair protruding from one of his ears and I couldn't tear my eyes away from it, so Joe ended up looking over his shoulder every five minutes thinking that someone I knew must be coming in.

'Seen someone you know?' he asked.

'No,' I said. Thank goodness that was true.

'You keep looking over to the door.'

'Do I?' I blustered. I was hardly going to tell him about the outcrop. 'I've got a lazy eye,' I explained. 'Sometimes it just drifts off all over the place.'

'Oh, really,' Joe replied. 'I've never noticed that before.'

'Most days I can keep it under control. But when I get excited,' I shrugged playfully. 'Hey, the thing's just got a mind of its own . . .'

At last the quiz started. We didn't have to talk any more and as Joe moved to sit beside rather than opposite me so that he could see the quiz-master, I didn't have to look at his ear any more either. Joe was in charge of the pencil. He had already divided the piece of paper into neat little squares headed up with all the categories. He had obviously done this quiz a few times before.

'Who won the World Cup in 1966?' the quiz-master began.

That was easy enough. I thought we might be on our way to winning a tenner.

'Who was Prime Minister before Margaret Thatcher?'

I racked my brains but just about got it.

By the time the quiz-master asked, 'Name five elements in the periodic table beginning with "M",' I was almost getting into it. Joe was a mine of useless information and he really came into his own over the chemistry questions. I was even beginning to think that this quiz was more fun than watching the telephone and that if we won this round, then the sky was the limit. There would be an inter-pub competition to go on to with £500 for the eventual winning team. I could use that money to buy a decent pair of trousers.

'Mercury, Molybdenum?' I suggested.

'Did you make that one up?'

'Mesopotamia?'

'No. That was a country, stupid, not an element.'

'Are you sure?'

'Yes, of course I'm sure. Didn't you do chemistry?'

'No. It clashed with domestic science.'

The quiz-master collected up our entries just before Joe and I broke into a fight and we had another nervous drink while we waited for our score to be returned. To my amazement we discovered that we had won. We had got just two questions wrong. (The elements, of course.) The quiz-master ceremoniously presented us with a brown envelope, stuffed with two crisp fivers. I felt strangely elated, which might have been because I had switched to lager with vodka chasers during the geography section to aid my concentration, but whatever the reason, I kissed my team mate on the cheek. Joe blushed rather prettily.

SECOND PRIZE

It was my round. I took my share of the winnings and went to splash out on two pints of Carlsberg and some dry-roasted peanuts. The juke box had been turned back up and I was grinding along to James Brown's 'Sex Machine' when it suddenly struck me that I hadn't thought about my disastrous love life for at least an hour. Pub quizzes were obviously the cure for a broken heart.

It was then that I saw him.

Standing like the angel of death at the opposite end of the bar.

Hugh Armstrong-Hamilton. Very slightly larger than life in his stuffy pin-striped suit. For a long moment I was frozen like a rabbit in the headlights of a fast approaching car.

'What do you want, love?' the barman asked.

'Yes. Love,' I murmured.

'Eh?'

My senses returned to me like a sledgehammer to the brain. Hugh still didn't appear to have spotted me so I slipped back into the anonymity of the crowd around the bar without getting the drinks and sidled over to Joe.

'Joe,' I said urgently. 'I've come over a bit funny all of a sudden. I've just got to go outside and get some air.' He put a hand to my forehead. 'No, I'm not feeling hot, Joe. I'm feeling sick. I've got to go. Look, I'm sorry about this. I'll see you tomorrow, OK?' With that I snatched up my jacket and fled for the door, praying that Joe wouldn't follow. Of course he did, so I had to spend a quarter of an hour on the pub steps with my head between my knees, pretending to feel queasy and hoping that he'd give up on me and suggest that I went home.

Joe didn't.

But Hugh did.

'You OK down there?' he asked, seeing me in a recovery position on the pub steps. 'Oh, good God. If it isn't Lara Fenton. Been getting a bit tanked up again, have we?' Joe glared at him furiously.

'No,' I squeaked. 'I just came over a little bit queasy. It's rather hot in there.'

'Maybe you ought to get her a taxi home.' Hugh was addressing Joe.

'No,' I protested, wanting nothing less than to share a taxi with Joe. There were far too many speed bumps on my road that could throw us dangerously together on the back seat of a black cab. 'I'll be fine. Honest I will. He lives in the opposite direction from me anyway.'

'But I don't. Why don't you come in a taxi with me instead? I'll be passing right by your house. Makes sense.'

'Do you want to go in a taxi with him?' Joe asked me in a hurt voice. He looked as though he knew he was about to lose me to the City-boy upstart.

I clutched my head and pretended to get another wave of nausea. A huge part of me wanted to get in a taxi with Hugh but the remaining part of me was struggling to hang on to some sort of self-respect. After all he hadn't phoned me that week. Why should he want to be with me now? But Hugh had already hailed a car.

SECOND PRIZE

'Come on, Lara,' he said. 'I think it's time to go home.' Taking the decision out of my court, he hooked his hands under my armpits and lifted me to my feet.

'Lara, are you sure you're going to be all right with him? Will you give me a call to let me know you're safely home?' Joe was squeaking. Hugh towered above him and tried to look more friendly giant than threatening. 'I'll take good care of her. We're old friends.'

Joe nodded. Unconvinced.

'I'll see you tomorrow morning, Joe,' I told him. 'Thanks for a lovely evening.' Helplessly, I followed Hugh into the taxi and left Joe behind on the pub steps, looking like a puppy without a bone. It was going to be very hard facing him in the morning.

But not half as hard as facing Hugh right at that very moment. What had I done?

Now what, I asked myself as we spun away from the pub. The words 'we're old friends' rang in my ears. I was in a taxi with a man who had said that he would phone me but hadn't. What were we going to talk about? Was he going to tell me what I did wrong on our first date to make him so put off? Or was he going to tell me that he'd lost my number? No, he wasn't. Instead Hugh began to chat away as happily as he had done that afternoon in the Thai pub. It was as if we were simply friends and it didn't matter that he had forgotten to call. Perhaps that was all he thought we were.

'Never seen you in the County Arms before,' he said.

'It was my first time. I promised Joe I'd help him in the pub quiz. We won it, in fact.'

'Well done. I've never tried the quiz though I go there quite often. It's on the way back from work and they've got plenty of pool tables. Do you play pool? No, I forgot. Squash is your sport, isn't it? We must have a game one day. You know what? Andrew's only gone and asked me to be his best man,' Hugh added seamlessly. 'So we'll probably be seeing quite a lot of each other over the coming months since I hear that you're the chief bridesmaid.'

'You're going to be the best man?' I said incredulously.

'Yes. Bit of a surprise that.'

He was telling me. Julie had kept that particular bombshell to herself, I seethed. It was all I needed. To see more of Hugh. A constant reminder of my unattractiveness to the opposite sex.

'Are you OK, you still look a bit peaky?'

'Oh, I'm fine, really.' I laid my forehead against the cool glass of the window. 'Perhaps I had a bit too much to drink. It's just that . . . It's just that I feel I shouldn't have imposed upon you like this.'

'It's no imposition, Lara. Honestly.'

'Well, after last Tuesday night, I didn't think I'd ever see you again.'

'I'm sorry. Was it really that awful for you? I know it can be a bit awkward when you join a group where everyone else knows each other so well.'

'No. It wasn't that. But when you didn't call me afterwards, I assumed that it must have been awful for you.' There. I'd said it. And now the taxi-driver was pulling up outside my flat and there was no time to repair the damage I'd done. Maybe we'd be able to laugh about my stupidity in thinking that he had once fancied me by the time Andrew and Julie's wedding day came round. I handed Hugh a crumpled fiver to cover my part of the fare and went to open the cab door before he saw how red in the face I had got.

'Thanks for seeing me home, Hugh.' I slammed the door behind me.

'Wait a minute, Lara. Don't rush off like that.' He had quickly opened the taxi window. 'Can't I come in for that coffee you offered me on Tuesday night now?'

I was dumbstruck. Coffee? He wanted coffee now?

'You going on or getting out here, mate?' asked the taxi-driver, while I hovered.

I just looked at Hugh and sort of nodded. 'I'm getting out here,' he told the driver before jumping out of the car with what seemed like incredible haste. This time when I walked up the stairs, Hugh was right behind me.

'Did I really say I'd phone?' he asked again as I fiddled with my key in the lock. 'I've had such a busy week, Lara, I must have forgotten what I said. I wouldn't have left you waiting for me to ring, I promise. Perhaps I thought I was waiting for you to call me instead.'

I walked up the stairs in a dream. This was totally bizarre. He suddenly seemed as keen on me as Julie had

once claimed he was. I opened the door to the flat and
ushered him inside, hoping against hope that my flatmate
wasn't in. There was a note on the kitchen table saying
'See you tomorrow. Hope your big date with the mystery
man went well!!!!' I screwed it up quickly before Hugh
could read it too and settled him down at the table while
I made tea.

'Yeah. Work's been a nightmare lately. Andrew's mind
just doesn't seem to be on the job at all since he's
decided to get married so I'm having to take up the
slack. Anyone would think that he was going to jack
in his job and become a housewife as soon as Julie puts
a ring on his finger.' I laughed at the thought. That was
Julie's plan.

'Everyone at dinner the other night really liked you,'
Hugh continued.

'Really?' I knew that he was lying to make me feel
better about the whole restaurant débâcle.

'Yes. They all thought you were great fun.'

Must have been the wacky outfit.

'Especially in that wacky outfit,' he confirmed. 'In fact,
Caroline liked you so much that she's asked me to invite
you along to join us at a party she's throwing at her new
house next weekend.'

'What? Oh!' I was so surprised by this revelation that
I dropped the biscuit barrel, spilling chocolate diges-
tives and garibaldis all over the floor. I thought that
Caroline had been the one who hated me most. I hadn't
noticed any of my jokes making her face crack into

even the weakest of smiles. While I was scrabbling to salvage the unbroken biscuits, Hugh elaborated on the deal.

'It's out in South Wales, I'm afraid. Caroline inherited a farmhouse there when her great aunt died last year. She's been doing it up. Parts are still a little bit ramshackle but the downstairs section of the main house is almost habitable now. She says it's a house-warming party but I suspect that we'll all end up wielding paintbrushes, knowing how she feels about DIY. It's quite a long way so we'd have to stay for the whole weekend of course. What do you say?'

What did I say? One minute I'm thinking that Hugh ArmstrongHamilton hates my guts because I say 'toilet', the next he's inviting me to accompany him to a weekend house-party.

'Antonia and Cecilia will be there,' he added as a further incentive, obviously unaware of how little encouragement the chance to see those two posh witches again would be to me.

'Are you sure that your friends really want me to be there? I mean, you've all known each other for years and years. Won't I be a bit of a spare part?'

I was sitting down now, and suddenly Hugh reached across the table to take my hand. 'Of course you won't be a spare part, Lara.' He raised my fingers to his lips and kissed them one by one, then he dragged me halfway across the table so that our lips met above the tomato ketchup bottle. I almost fainted with surprise but just about kept myself together by trying to work out when I had last cleaned my teeth.

'Please say that you'll come with me. It'd be such a good laugh.'

'I'll have to let you know . . .' I murmured, pulling away ever so slightly, mindful as ever of Julie's instructions for keeping him keen with indifference as his fingers stroked my burning cheeks.

'Don't take too long deciding or I might have to try extra persuasion.'

Extra persuasion? Yes, please!!!

Hugh got up from his seat and walked around the table to kneel on the floor beside my chair. Before I knew it he was kissing me again and pretty soon he had his hand up the back of my shirt. At last, my heart squealed, a proper snog!!! It would probably have been the most wonderful moment of my life so far if it had not been for the fact that I was wearing my oldest chewing-gum-grey bra. The one which had not two but three rusty safety pins holding it together. (I had put this vile device on earlier that evening to ensure that no matter how drunk I got, I was never tempted to take my top off in front of Joe Madden. How was I to know that I'd end the unpromising evening in the arms of someone I would gladly have stripped off a layer of skin for?)

'Oh, Hugh,' I sighed, longing to melt into his caress and make it a moment to cherish forever. But I knew I wouldn't be able to relax until I had put that bra out of my mind.

CHAPTER SIX

I didn't go back into work for the rest of the week. Luckily, my fabulous bit of acting outside the County Arms tallied well with my story that I had been struck down by a mysterious bout of sickness and diarrhoea. Thankfully, my boss was a little bit queasy about that kind of thing so he didn't press for details.

I spent the rest of the week planning for the exciting weekend ahead. It would entail a major shopping spree of course because I had decided that I was not going to let myself feel uncomfortable about my appearance in front of those snooty posh girls again. I needed new underwear, new casual wear and a strong pair of walking boots. I needed a new little black dress and a pair of amazing evening shoes as well, just in case. The spree took my credit card right up to its limit, but by Friday afternoon I was the proud owner of a suitcase full of gear that even Princess Diana would have been proud to go away with. Not to mention an amazing Louis Vuitton suitcase that cost about as much as I would spend on a house. But, as

Julie frequently pointed out, I was investing in my future. To catch a big fish like Hugh Armstrong-Hamilton you had to expect a little bit of initial outlay.

Julie was, however, just a little bit concerned about my progress so far. After the kiss in the kitchen, things had happened pretty quickly that night and when Julie came back to the house in the early morning to tong her hair before leaving for work, she was disgusted to discover that we were three for breakfast.

She said he'd think I was a fast piece.

I was just relieved to discover that he wasn't gay. (That had happened to me once before. Or maybe that guy was just being kind.)

On the strength of my first-night *faux pas*, Julie had prophesied grimly that the longed-for weekend would never happen. But it seemed that it was going ahead. Hugh called round the very next night with a bunch of flowers to replace the carnations that I had allowed to shrivel and die while he didn't call. We went for a drink in a fancy wine bar down the road and talked and talked and talked about our lives until the barman started sighing loudly and put the chairs up on the tables around us.

For people from such different backgrounds, it seemed that we had so much in common. We had both owned Donovan's Greatest Hits compilations and neither of us could stand to eat baked beans unless they were Heinz and piping hot. It sounds cheesy, but it really was as if I had known Hugh forever by the time he left my bed for the office on Thursday morning. He even had a nickname for me, Dumbo, because I thought Rioja was a type of cheese . . .

He called me twice that Thursday afternoon to check that I hadn't forgotten where and when we were going the next day. I was in charge of hiring the car that would drive us down to the back of beyond. I was surprised to discover that I was also going to be in charge of driving it.

'Perhaps he can't drive,' said Julie. 'But that's really weird. Everybody learns these days. Perhaps he's been banned for some terrible reason.'

'Perhaps he just doesn't like driving.' I wouldn't have a word said against my new man.

As I waited for the hands of the clock to creep towards five o'clock that Friday afternoon, I finally sensed myself becoming nervous. I remembered how intimidating Caroline, Antonia and Cecilia had seemed in the restaurant on that dreadful first date. Tim was but a vague memory since he had hardly said a thing all night. I took another look at myself in the mirror, hardly recognisable as good old Lara Fenton in my neat pink Ralph Lauren polo shirt and brand-new Versace jeans. But I looked like one of them now. Perhaps things would be easier this time.

Five o'clock struck and my alarm clock rang out from the bedroom. I had set it for five just in case, though there was little chance of me falling asleep in my current wired-up state of mind. Now I had to drive into the City and pick Hugh up from outside his office. I grabbed my bag and threw it into the back of the Clio I had hired, hoping he wouldn't think me a cheapskate for having asked for the smallest car the rental place had. In reality, it was the only car I thought I might be able to park without crashing.

As it was, I had badly mis-timed the drive into town, hitting the rush hour right at its peak and going dreadfully wrong in a number of one-way systems. When I finally saw Hugh, standing on the corner outside the illustrious marble-clad buildings of Partridge Skelton, he was frantically looking at his watch. I knew then that he wouldn't have cared if I turned up in a Sherman tank as long as I got to him within the next thirty seconds. When I did reach him, it was just as Julie's fiancé Andrew walked out of the lobby with the vol-au-vent dweeb from the party in tow.

'All right, Hugh, my man.' Andrew punched his workmate on the arm. 'Off on your dirty weekend, eh? I wouldn't have asked Lara to drive if I were you.'

I smiled tightly as I opened the passenger door. I wasn't going to let Andrew wind me up. So what if I'd once reversed into a bollard?

'Don't forget that we drive on the left in this country, eh Lara?' Andrew laughed at his own joke and the dweeb joined in.

Hugh jumped into the car beside me and kissed me perfunctorily on the cheek. 'You're late. You're heading in the wrong direction. We want the M40.'

'I know, I know,' I snapped, trying to suppress my road rage and get back into the traffic without stalling the car in front of Andrew and the dweeb. 'But this was the only way I could get anywhere near your office,' I explained.

There was no way I could do a U-turn in the terrible traffic so I had to drive for another mile in the wrong direction until I came to a roundabout with Hugh shouting, 'You could have turned in there,' every time we passed a side road with a no entry sign.

I felt like an elastic band that had been stretched just a little too far and the feeling didn't begin to subside until the sprawling outskirts of London had given way to the fields of Oxfordshire. Finally, Hugh began to chat rather than chastise. He loosened his tie and brought a half-eaten packet of wine gums out of his pocket. I was starving. I hadn't eaten since Thursday in order to squeeze into my new jeans more comfortably but when he finally offered me a wine gum I had to refuse since it was a green one and I thought it might be common to ask for another colour.

CHAPTER SEVEN

'I'm really glad you decided to come along,' he said. 'It should be a bit of fun. Relaxing.'

I certainly hoped so. I had spent all that month's salary on getting together the right wardrobe and hiring the car to get us there. And now I had a crick in my neck from getting tense in the rush-hour traffic which I doubted I could get rid of before I had to drive back into London again. Some serious relaxation was exactly what I needed.

'There are horses to ride in the nearby village, if you fancy going out for a trot?'

'Horses?' I shrugged my shoulders. I hadn't ridden since I got bucked off a donkey on Brighton beach aged seven years old. But I could just imagine Caroline and the lipstick lesbians, squeezing their tight thighs into curve-hugging jodhpurs and being manfully in control of their mounts. 'I was rather hoping to get some reading done,' I told Hugh by way of an excuse. 'So maybe I'll do that while you guys go for a ride by yourselves.'

'Nonsense. You've got to come for a hack. I know just the horse for you.'

Go for a hack? I'd rather have chopped wood. I could see that I was going to have to feign a broken leg. Still, the idyllic countryside and the bracing walks sounded good.

It had been pitch dark before we even got out of London, so now, as we left the motorway somewhere in Gloucestershire, it was pretty well impossible to see anything other than the Cat's-eyes twinkling in the middle of the road. Hugh was navigating, but surprisingly, he wasn't very good at it. He would shout 'Turn down that little road there' just as we'd sailed on past, then sigh impatiently as I tried to turn the car around again and double back. After one particularly narrowly missed turning I insisted that we stop the car and take a proper look at the map before things got any worse and we ended up in Scotland.

I pulled the car into the side of the pitch-black country road and flicked on the map-reading light. I didn't have a clue where we were. Hugh pointed vaguely at a squiggly B-road studded with ridiculous place names but that was as much help as he was going to be. He stopped looking at the map then and started looking at me instead.

'What's wrong with you?' I asked irritably.

'This light really suits you,' he told me. 'It's like the candlelight in La Traviata.'

'I wish it was. Though I would just as happily be in a

SECOND PRIZE

Little Chef right now. I'm fed up of being in this bloody car,' I told him. 'And I'm getting really hungry.'

'For what?'

I felt Hugh's hand creep on to my knee beneath the atlas. He squeezed my thigh affectionately and leaned across two pages of Gloucestershire to kiss me. Pretty quickly, I couldn't have cared less where we were or when I had last eaten. My heart hammered against the walls of my chest as Hugh's hot tongue probed the inside of my mouth and his hand sneaked beneath the bottom of my shirt.

'Fancy a quick one?' he asked.

'What? A quick one? Not here?'

'Yes, here.'

'Well, OK then.' But I insisted on finding a better parking space first since the last thing we wanted was to be shunted from behind while we were up to something that could land us in jail in these backward parts of the country.

So, as a result of Hugh's navigation, my lack of driving confidence and our brief diversion, it took us almost seven hours to reach Caroline's 'little' place in Wales. And as I turned the car into the driveway, I knew instantly that something was wrong. The road felt softer somehow, as if it wasn't there. Of course, when I opened the car door and stepped out on to what I had hoped would be the driveway, I sank in a mudbath that came right up to the top of my socks.

'Oh shit,' said Hugh.

'Exactly,' said I.

Caroline and Tim emerged from the house far more sensibly dressed in great big green wellies. They were carrying a torch to seek us out and I was sure that Caroline shone it for an unnecessarily long time in my eyes before she kissed Hugh hello and he dissolved into his usual pathetic grin.

'We thought you'd never get here,' Caroline exclaimed.

'Lara kept getting us lost,' Hugh told her by way of an excuse, which was strange because I could have sworn that he had insisted on navigating.

'Well, never mind. You've made it at last. Everyone else has been here for hours and hours.'

Tim, who had yet to say a word, picked both our bags out of the car boot and carried them effortlessly inside. I wondered what his relationship with Caroline actually was. He seemed to dote upon her while she generally acted as though he wasn't really there. At best, she afforded him the same respect and affection as a butler.

The others were sitting around the kitchen table, nursing half-finished glasses of brandy. That is just what I could do with, I thought, as Hugh air-kissed the giggling girls. I stood in the corner of the bright, warm room, waiting to be shown to somewhere I could freshen up a little. In the light, I examined the damage to my new shoes. Tim suggested that I took them off and stuffed them full of newspaper to help them keep their shape while they dried out in front of the Aga, but I had a horrible feeling that they were already well beyond repair. Red suede loafers, just two days' old, and I hadn't had time to Scotchguard them in readiness for this trip. Tim insisted on attempting to rescue them anyway and eventually I joined the others at the kitchen table in my woolly socks.

The talk revolved mainly around people's plans for the weekend. Of course, they all wanted to go riding and I found myself being dragged in. I bravely admitted that I hadn't ridden 'for a while' but stopped short at saying 'for about eighteen years and never on a horse'. Caroline also had great plans for hiking up the mountain which apparently towered behind the house. I certainly hadn't seen that in the dark and hoped that the next morning would reveal it to be little more than a hill. The new jeans had just about cut off all my circulation below the waist.

As they talked, I let my gaze wander around the kitchen, taking in the feel of the place. If this house was what Caroline considered to be little she would have needed a microscope to find the front door to my flat. The vast floor of the kitchen had obviously been quite recently replaced with reddish Italian tiles. A British racing-green Aga dominated the left side of the room and high above the scrubbed pine table hung one of those things they used to dry laundry on in the old days but, instead of dripping with vests and knickers, it was wreathed with dried flowers. Absolutely decorative and quite stylish. But I couldn't help thinking that it had probably been bought just like that in some elegant Knightsbridge shop.

'So, what is this little gathering in occasion of, sweetheart?' It was Antonia speaking, filling a lull which had occurred in the conversation. I switched my attention from the laundry thingy back to the table. Antonia looked at Caroline at the other end of the table and raised her glass as if she were getting ready to propose a toast. 'Just house-warming, is it?'

'Well, not exactly.' Caroline stared down into her own glass and then glanced across the table to Tim. 'Some of you know already.' Antonia and Cecilia smiled as though they might have guessed. She took a deep breath. 'This weekend is actually in honour of the fact that Tim and I have decided to get engaged.'

'At last!! Congratulations,' Antonia beamed widely and raised his glass. 'You sly old mare. Your mum and dad will be delighted.'

'We wanted to present it to you all as a fait accompli.' Caroline raised her left hand from her lap and laid it down again gracefully upon the table so that we could all admire the glittering diamond and sapphire engagement ring. 'We're going to do it just before Christmas. Just something small and intimate. We thought there would be no point waiting much longer.' Tim nodded. I remembered the conversation about bridesmaids' dresses at La Traviata.

We all cooed politely over the news. Only Hugh sat back from the table, sipping his brandy and saying nothing. I turned to look at him, expecting him to be smiling serenely or something like that but he wasn't. Instead he seemed to be almost glaring at Caroline, as if he didn't quite approve. I saw her catch his eye and swiftly look away again to rest her loving gaze on Tim.

After the excitement of the engagement announcement, the evening began to tail off pretty rapidly. Antonia and Cecilia went to bed first. Hugh was yawning theatrically. I was desperate to get him between the sheets after the agony of having to keep my hands off him for almost three hours.

'Oh, I forgot. You don't know where you're going to be sleeping yet,' said Caroline, finally taking the hint of our barely concealed yawns.

'I thought you'd never say that.' I rose unsteadily to my feet, grateful for the thought of an impending bed, and winked at Hugh.

'Well, Hugh's in the blue room in the west wing. And I thought that Lara might like to have Great Aunt Felicity's old room since it's one of the few rooms in this place to have a fireplace that's clean enough to have a fire.'

'A fire? Oh, how lovely,' I replied gratefully but inside I was devastated that Hugh and I were to be accommodated in separate beds. I wondered how far apart the rooms were and consoled myself with the thought that it might be rather romantic to have to creep through the house in the darkness to find him.

'Tim, would you be a sweetie and show Lara where she's going to sleep?'

Tim relieved me of my case manfully. Hugh picked up his own bag and moved towards Caroline who led him out of the kitchen through the door which the girls had used on their way to bed. To my surprise, Tim and I left the kitchen through another door entirely.

'The east wing,' he explained.

This door led to a dark narrow staircase which ascended creakingly for what seemed like thousands of feet. At the top of the stairs was a rickety landing from which led two more doors. Tim shone the torch with which he had been lighting our way on to the floor boards and I noticed to my horror that you could see right through into the room below our feet.

'Shit,' I gasped automatically. 'Is that safe to walk on?'

'If you keep right behind me and step exactly where I step, you'll be OK.' Tim took my hand and led me across the few floorboards that were still intact to the bedroom on the right. 'This was Great Aunt Felicity's room. Don't think there's a ghost but let me know if you discover otherwise.' He put my bag down on the narrow bed and busied himself with the lighting of two oil lamps. 'I'll be in the room right next door if you need me,' he said. 'But bang on the wall if you do. Don't, whatever you do, try to cross the landing on your own or you might end up in the kitchen rather more quickly than you hoped.'

No fear of that, I thought. But I longed to ask Tim why he wasn't sharing with Caroline.

'I'm really sorry it's got to be like this,' he continued. 'Caroline is so slow at DIY. She told me that she was going to replace those floorboards months ago; instead she spends all her time and money putting unnecessary frills and furbelows in the kitchen and forgets to bother with the vital repairs. Still, I'll fetch you in the morning, when I wake up, and guide you safely downstairs again.'

'Thank you.'

'My pleasure. Then I'll say goodnight.' Tim left me to myself.

'Goodnight.'

I could barely believe it. No sneaking to see Hugh that night. I was trapped.

I sat down on the bed next to my case and surveyed my new surroundings, not daring to investigate too far in case the floor of this room was in the same state as the landing. A fire did indeed blaze, or rather flicker, in the grate but a blackened chimney breast told me that the chimney wasn't exactly efficient. I undressed quickly by the light of the oil lamps and slipped under the chilly sheets. Thank goodness I had used the bathroom before coming upstairs because I sensed that I wasn't even going to be able to risk creeping out of my room to use the loo, let alone to visit Hugh on the other side of the house, though I was comforted to find that there was a crackle-glazed chamberpot beneath the bed.

As I lay there wondering whether the sheets were just cold or actually damp, I looked at the shabby wallpaper which was printed with vast yellow cabbage roses and then at the photographs of austere-looking Victorians that lined the mantelpiece like a guard. And this mausoleum was apparently the best room in the house? If that was the case, I laughed to myself, the others must have been sleeping in rooms that even a Conservative council might have declared substandard.

I turned on to my side and tried to go to sleep. The oil lamps flickered a shadow show upon the walls. The house creaked and groaned around me and although I knew what I was hearing was just the sound of the timber beams contracting as the house cooled down, I couldn't help thinking that knowing my luck, I would be the first person sleeping in that room to meet the Lauder family ghost.

CHAPTER EIGHT

That first night in Wales I had terrible dreams. I dreamt that it was already morning and that I had walked across the dangerous floorboards of the east wing landing alone and then down into the kitchen wearing not a stitch. The others were sitting around the kitchen table eating breakfast and when I walked in, stark naked as the day I was born, they stopped what they were doing immediately and stared at me open-mouthed.

Caroline was the first to speak. She stood up on her chair and pointed down at me where I cowered like a leper on the red Tuscan tiles. She was saying, 'What is Hugh doing with someone who looks like that when he could be with me?' I was trying to cover myself up with a tea towel but Cecilia whipped it out of my hand and Caroline continued to point at my shivering body. 'Look,' she said. 'She's even got cellulite.' The others laughed heartily at that. It was every girl's worst nightmare.

I awoke sweating, though the fire had long since burned down to a pile of warm grey ash. Outside my window a branch went tap tap tap against the pane like the fingers of a ghost. The wind whistled across the hills. I pulled the covers tightly up to my chin and tried to go back to sleep but to no avail. Instead I lay wide awake until my watch said that it was seven o'clock and I thought that I could at last politely ask Tim to take me back downstairs.

I tapped on the wall between our rooms for about half an hour but there were no signs that Tim had heard me. I was getting desperate, I really needed to use the bathroom. So, I slipped my big new jumper over the top of my silky pyjamas and decided that I could probably risk the landing on my own.

I opened the door. In the grey morning light, the landing looked even more precarious than it had done by the light of Tim's torch. I couldn't get across it without knowing which boards were rotten but I figured that I could just about get to Tim's room if I stayed close enough to the wall. I sidled up to his doorway, clinging on to the wall like a rock climber. Tim was still sleeping like a baby when I creaked open the door. He was obviously used to the noises of this old house and they hadn't bothered him one bit. I walked towards the bed and cleared my throat quietly. 'Ahem, Tim. Good morning. I wonder if you might help me get downstairs.'

He woke with a start but I was very glad to see his face soften into a smile when he saw that it was me. 'Did you sleep OK?' he asked.

I lied with a nod. 'I slept wonderfully well but then I've always been a bit of an early riser.'

'What time is it?' he asked.

'About seven.' A time I hadn't seen deliberately since the day I left school.

'Wow. That's late, for me. OK. Let's cross no-man's land and get ourselves some breakfast, shall we?' He jumped out of bed wearing nothing but his pig-patterned boxer shorts. I turned away out of politeness as he dressed but he kept talking to me and from time to time I couldn't help turning towards him. It seemed rude to have my back to him as I answered his questions. He had a fabulously hairy chest.

'So you're officially Hugh's new bit?' he asked.

'Well.' I took great umbrage at being referred to as a 'bit', no matter who I was supposed to belong to. Suddenly the pigs on Tim's shorts seemed very appropriate.

'Have you been seeing him long?' he persisted.

'I'm not exactly seeing him. I've only known him for about three weeks. That night in La Traviata was our first proper date.'

'Aah,' Tim said wisely. 'I thought it was a bit unlikely that he'd actually managed to make something last for more than a month.'

'Oh.'

'Sorry, Lara. I shouldn't have said that, should I? What with you being in the first flush of love. Perhaps he's been cured.'

Tim led the way to the dangerous landing, leaving me full of infuriating questions.

'You've got me all curious now, Tim,' I said as I took

his hand and stepped across an extra large gap. 'Cured of what?'

'Don't worry your pretty little head about it.' I pursed my lips. The last time I had heard that line from a man I had been about five years old.

'I've worried about bigger things than a man in my time,' I assured him as I took the last three steps on my own. 'You know, I even know how to drive.'

Tim smiled. At least he knew he had sounded a jerk.

We were the first up. Tim was remarkably wide awake considering the time. I was still feeling slightly groggy having only had two or three hours' proper sleep in that dreadful old room. Tim whirled around the kitchen, breaking eggs and grinding coffee. Pretty soon the air was filled with the enticing scents of breakfast. I was ravenous. I hadn't even had a wine gum since Thursday night.

'That's what I like to see, a girl who appreciates good food,' said Tim as I stuffed down the greasy eggs he had ladled on top of my thick brown toast. I washed them down with coffee so strong it made my head throb immediately. Tim was frying tomatoes and bacon, singing as he worked.

As he was putting on a bit of a show, I didn't feel so bad about trying to get a closer look at him. I must admit that I had noticed that he was pretty fit while he was hopping around the bedroom in his boxer shorts. He was very tanned. The contrast of his biscuit-brown skin made the whites of his eyes and his teeth almost sparkle. He flipped another fried egg over so that it would be cooked on both sides. As he did so, he bit his lip in concentration. It was the expression of a small child. Had Julie not been engaged, I think he would have been her type.

Unfortunately, my private Tim show was soon broken up. The smell of breakfast had obviously wafted into the west wing of the house and one by one the others descended the stairs to join us. Antonia looked almost unthreateningly plain without her lipstick and mascara though Cecilia would have been beautiful wearing a sack. She took over from Tim at the cooking and got the eggs done much more efficiently but without the same aplomb. Caroline and Hugh were the last to arrive at the breakfast table. Caroline was looking slightly hassled. Hugh kissed me 'good morning' on the top of my head and pinched a piece of cold toast from my plate.

'And how was your night in the famous east wing?' Cecilia asked me. 'Did you see the ghost?'

'What ghost? Tim said there wasn't a ghost.'

'Oh, good old Tim. He does like to protect us feeble ladies, doesn't he? I'm sure I saw it when I had to stay in there. I've refused to go near that room ever since.'

'What was it you saw?' Antonia asked wickedly.

'Just an old lady. Probably Great Aunt Felicity, but heaven only knows what she'd done with her head . . .'

'I don't think Lara needs to hear about that,' Tim cut in swiftly. 'Is everyone ready to go for a ride this morning?'

'I'll have to get changed first,' I said, looking at my teddy-bear pyjamas. Cecilia roared as though I had made a great joke.

'I think I'll stay behind,' Hugh said quietly. 'I've got myself a terrible headache after all that brandy last night and I'd like to catch up with some reading.' I looked at him accusingly but he avoided my eyes.

'I'll stay with you,' I tried. 'I'd like to do some reading too.'

'No way, Lara,' Caroline chipped in. 'Don't let him spoil your fun just because he can't take his brandy. You've got to come out with us. You really must see the countryside around this place and get some fresh air into those London lungs of yours. Besides, Hugh can be a real monster when he's got a headache. I wouldn't want to be within a mile of him when he's like that.' She smiled at him fondly.

'Do you want me to see if I've got some painkillers in my bag?' I asked him, resting my hand on his knee beneath the table.

'No, thank you,' Hugh removed my hand rather abruptly and got to his feet. 'Don't bother with that. I'm just going to go back to bed for a while. I'll see you all later on.'

I watched him disappear again in a mood verging on desperation. I couldn't believe it. He was going to let me tackle a hack all on my own. I wished I'd had the courage to tell him that I was only good at indoor sports. When I had the chance to practise.

The remaining breakfasters split up and we went to our various rooms to get ready for the morning's ride. Tim helped me across the landing though I was sure I could almost tackle it myself by now. When I got into Great Aunt Felicity's room again, the stale smell of night was overpowering. I decided that I would open some windows and get some fresh air inside. I drew back the curtains and gasped.

Behind me, the hills of Wales rose up like the backs of a dozen sleeping dinosaurs. For as far as I could see, there was nothing but grey-green hills dotted with the white smudges of tenacious sheep and even the occasional patch of snow on the very high ground. Growing up in Putney, I hadn't imagined that views as magnificent as this existed on the island in which I lived. Mountains. Real Mountains. I expected to see Julie Andrews streaming down the slopes singing 'The Hills are Alive' at any minute.

But in this beautiful view there was no sign of human life. No other houses but the one I was standing in. Not even the skeleton of a pylon taking electricity to the valleys beyond. No wonder Hugh had said that this place was isolated. How different it was from my little flat in London, where I spent night after night able to hear the snoring of the man next door through my bedroom wall though I didn't even know his name. Oh, splendid isolation, I thought. A long-dead creative urge stirred deep in my heart. If I lived out here, I could paint the best pictures in the world. I wished that I had brought my water-colours with me. Perhaps Caroline had some. Perhaps I could say that I simply had to capture the view on canvas while the light was good and thus get out of the dreaded ride.

'Water-colours?' Caroline looked puzzled when I asked.

'I'm afraid I don't. Only paint round this place is emulsion. Come on, Lara. Stop trying to stall for Hugh's sake. We'll be late at the stables.'

Feeling thoroughly ticked off, I clambered into the back of Caroline's green Range Rover to sit sandwiched between Antonia and Cecilia. We drove out past my hired Clio which was listing badly in the deep mud. Tim commented that we ought to drag it out of the mire that evening, adding smugly that I had probably buggered the clutch. I was so envious of Hugh, reading beside the cosy fire in the sitting room while I had to endure the lecturing and braying of his friends in the back of the car. I wished I had insisted on staying with him. We could have snuggled up together in front of the fire. I comforted myself with the thought that the answer according to Julie's rules would probably have been to give him space anyway.

When we reached the stables, I decided straight away that I didn't like the look of the horse that was assigned to me, though everyone assured me that he was the sweetest little thing in the county. Everyone had learned to ride on this disgustingly pungent nag apparently. He was brilliant with kids and beginners, though I'm sure they had no idea quite how much of a beginner I was. The horse was snuffing the air noisily, breathing out great clouds of vapour from his violently flared nostrils. When I approached his stall he eyed me disdainfully and was obviously planning to have me off his back before we even left the yard.

SECOND PRIZE

Thankfully, I didn't have to tack the beast up. That was left to someone who knew what he was doing. The stable boy Martin looked a friendly enough lad so I confided in him that I hadn't ridden for some time and wasn't sure that I'd even be able to get on the monster's back. Martin promised me that he would give me a leg up, but when he did, it became quite clear that it was just an excuse to feel my bum. Tim saw him hassling me and came across to take over. He helped me on and gave me a brief tour of the controls: one set of reins. To stop, pull hard.

The beautiful Caroline seemed strangely twitchy while we were tacking up. Just as she was about to get on to her horse, Martin rapped on the window of his office and told her that she had a call.

When she came out of the office again, she took Tim aside and whispered a few things in his ear. Then, she abandoned her pony, got back into the Range Rover and sped off in the direction of the farmhouse as though her tyres were on fire. Antonia asked what was up, thankfully, because, while I was desperate to know, I would have felt too rude to ask myself.

Tim sighed. 'It was Hugh. He says that the log man has turned up at the house with the week's firewood and he's got no money to pay him. Caroline's gone back to sort it out but she says she'll catch us up.'

Cecilia raised an eyebrow. 'Hugh's got no cash? How much can a pile of logs possibly cost?'

'Hugh's like the queen, he doesn't carry money,' I said, for a bit of a laugh. I didn't get one.

So it was Cecilia who led the way out of the yard on a beautiful dark brown horse. I knew that there was probably a more poetic word for the magnificent creature's colouring but I couldn't remember what it was. Cecilia sat very upright in the saddle as she rode. It was as though someone had stuck a broom handle down the back of her bra. I struggled to look half so elegant as I brought up the rear on my old dappled nag.

Pretty soon, my horse, whose name was Horatio because he had a gammy eye, was lagging far behind. I saw Tim's mount pass through an arch of bare-branched hazel trees and watched forlornly as they began to gallop into the distance, entreating me to follow. If only I could. I dug Horatio in the side with my heels but he wasn't having any of it. Eventually, Horatio gave up walking altogether and dropped his head to the short winter grass.

'Oh, come on you b-word,' I shouted, slapping my heels against him again and again. Horatio continued to munch grass silently. The others were just spots in the distance now, cantering up the hill without bothering to look back. I gave a sigh, abandoned any thought of catching them up and slid from my saddle on to the frosty ground. I held Horatio's reins helplessly and watched him chew. I knew as soon as I did so that getting off had been a big mistake because I would never be able to get back on.

When I figured that Horatio must have had all the grass he could eat, I tugged on his reins and tried to make him turn back towards the stable. I could easily walk there, get a nice cup of tea and wait for the others to return. A much better idea than trying to catch them up, I thought. I pulled the reins. Horatio dug his hooves in. He didn't want to go inside.

'Come on, you git. I don't want to stand out here in the cold all day. I'm frozen.' But Horatio didn't care. 'It's all right for you,' I told him. 'You're covered in fur. I've just got this stupid bomber jacket to keep me warm. And right now it's not.' My fashionable padded jerkin wasn't really made for the cold. 'Come on.' I gave the reins an almighty pull, momentarily jerking his head away from a juicy blade of grass. Horatio eyed me angrily. He whinnied loudly. Then he promptly pulled the reins free of my hands and cantered off home. Without me.

'Oh buggeration,' I shouted. 'Horatio. Horatio!!! Come back here, you stupid horse.' I could see it now. Horatio running loose through the village. Straight into the path of an articulated lorry. A nag's worth of dog meat. I was going to be in big, big trouble. Not to mention horribly embarrassed when it came out that I couldn't even control the horse they kept for the children. I tucked my stupid hard hat under my arm and started to follow in Horatio's footsteps, trying to comfort myself with the thought that he wasn't adventurous enough to run amock in the village. By the time I got back he'd be in his stall, stuffing down yet more bloody grass. I looked behind me to the distant hills. The other riders were not even dots on the horizon any more.

It was while I was looking for a sign of the others that

I tripped over a displaced clod and landed knees down in a pile of Horatio's poo.

'Shit, shit, shit!!!' I said literally. I looked at the knees of my smart new jeans. Not just shitty but ripped by a stone that had gone through the denim and imbedded itself in my knee. Sitting down on the ground with a thud, I held my head in my hands while I waited for the skies to open and add insult to injury with a nice spot of freezing rain.

However, suddenly, I heard a familiar whinnying behind me. Horatio! He'd come back for me. At least now I wouldn't have to return to the stable *sans* horse. I scrambled to my feet, swearing and getting my stupid hat out of my eyes. But Horatio wasn't alone. His reins were held firmly in the left hand of Tim Winterson. Tim saw me standing all forlorn in the field and laughed out loud.

'I think you lost your horse!' he shouted.

'I had noticed,' I replied.

Tim handed me Horatio's reins. 'Jump on. We'll cut across that field there and catch the others up in a minute.' I held the reins as though I'd never seen such things in my life.

'Actually, Tim,' I said bravely, 'I was thinking that I might walk back to the stable now. I'm getting a little bit cold.'

'Riding will warm you up.'

'No, I don't think so. But a cup of tea might just do the job. I'll see you back there.'

'Lara, you are not going to walk back all the way to the

stables and wait there on your own.' Tim was dismounting now. 'Here, I'll help you get back on Horatio. Is that what you're worried about?'

'I . . . er . . . I have hurt my knee,' I added hopefully.

'Can't be that bad if you're still standing on it. Here, I'll help you up,' he insisted. I put my hands on the saddle dutifully and Tim tried to lift me up. 'Throw your right leg over when I push up.' I threw my leg over. But I must have been a bit too enthusiastic because before I knew it, the whole of my body was sailing over the horse after it. I landed without grace on the frost-hard ground. Thankfully I had put my helmet back on. But that didn't save my bum, which would be black and blue for weeks to come.

Tim raced around the backside of Horatio to see what had become of me. He lifted me to my feet and looked at me in a concerned way as I dusted myself down. 'I really would rather walk back to the stables,' I insisted once again. 'I'm not really much of a rider.' This time, Tim had to agree that I was right.

So we walked back to the stables. Tim led his own horse and Horatio since thanks to that fall I had grazed my hands too badly to even hold the reins. Tim was most apologetic for having forced me to take the horse out in the first place but I forgave him graciously. I suppose I could have refused to go more vehemently myself.

'Growing up here and in Gloucestershire, as Caroline and I did,' he told me as we strolled along, 'one sometimes forgets that not everybody learns how to ride.'

I smiled at him forgivingly. 'Quite. On the estate where I come from,' I told him, 'we all learn how to break into cars instead. Much faster than horses and easier to get going.'

The stable boy didn't seem at all surprised to see us back early and Horatio went back into his stall without giving me a second glance. I hissed in his furry ear that I hoped that next time I saw him, he'd be Pedigree Chum for my grandmother's Yorkshire Terrier. Tim unsaddled his horse which nuzzled him affectionately before it was led away.

'Martin,' Tim called when he emerged from the stable. 'Has Caroline showed up again yet?'

'Ha'n't seen 'er if she has,' Martin replied in his thick accent.

'Oh.' Tim's face creased into a frown as he joined me on the low wall by the car park. 'That's strange. She seemed really keen for a ride this morning. Perhaps she changed her mind when she saw the frost. Hope she hasn't forgotten that she's supposed to be picking us up.'

'Too right,' I nodded. 'It's freezing out here.' I was pretty disgruntled that Caroline hadn't turned up as well. How come it was all right for her to decide that she didn't want to go thundering across the country in sub-zero temperatures? I decided that if a ride was suggested again, I would volunteer to drive and get Martin to pretend there had been a call for me saying that the woodman needed help with his chopping.

SECOND PRIZE

'Oh well, Lara. Looks like we're going to be hanging around here for a while after all. Do you want a cup of tea?'

I wanted a large brandy but tea would just about do. Martin soon brought out a teapot and two badly stained mugs. I wondered whether they had ever been washed, but I tried to suppress the thought because I was so desperate for something around which to warm my stinging cold hands.

Antonia and Cecilia came back not long after us. Tim looked perturbed as he helped them unsaddle their horses. I could see him scanning the road to the yard for the Range Rover and not finding it, his moody expression grew worse. 'Where is Caroline?' he asked. 'I suppose I should call and tell her to hurry up.'

'We don't mind waiting here for a while,' said Antonia.

'Yes, but Lara and I do. We've been sitting here for almost an hour. She's forgotten us.'

'Of course she hasn't.' Antonia sent Martin to fetch more tea and we waited.

And waited.

Caroline kept us waiting for an hour and a half in the end. When she finally turned the Range Rover into the stable yard, she gave Tim an apologetic wave. Getting into the back of the car and sitting right behind her, I noticed that her hair seemed freshly washed.

'Thought you'd forgotten us,' said Tim as she kissed his cheek.

'Oh, I thought you were going to be ages. I didn't

want to hang around with that Martin boy. You know what a lech he is. Always staring at my chest.' I could vouch for that, but Tim seemed strangely unsatisfied with the answer. 'How's Hugh's headache?' he asked, almost sarcastically.

'Oh, he's fine too.' She turned momentarily to address me. 'I think those headache pills you gave him really worked.'

I hadn't given him any pills.

When we got back to the farmhouse, Hugh was in the kitchen dicing onions. He greeted everybody with a smile but pulled me towards him for a special hug and a kiss that almost made me forget about the pain in my knee. 'How was the ride?' he asked interestedly. 'Hope you didn't end up on Horatio.'

'I did,' I told him. But suddenly I didn't mind any more. Hugh hugged the misery of riding that malicious bag of bones right out of me. Then he asked me to stand beside him at the sink and scrape clean some carrots, popping little pieces of red pepper into my mouth while I worked, as though I was a baby bird. 'I wish you'd come with us,' I told him.

'I wish I had too. I'm sorry if I was a bit grumpy this morning, Lara. I barely slept at all last night. I promise I won't neglect you any more.'

Over lunch, the black mood that had sprung up over the riding incident seemed to have totally dissipated. The others talked about their childhood. Holiday games. Secret dens they had made in the woods. Even though I couldn't find a way to chip in with a tale of my own, it was quite interesting to listen to them, until Tim mentioned a birthday party held for someone called Fiona and Caroline suddenly changed the subject to horses again.

Then, that afternoon, Hugh said that he felt well enough to go for a walk in the fields beyond the farm-house. I went with him of course and as soon as we were clear of the yard he took hold of my hand. Despite the grazes I had gained while riding I didn't care that he squeezed my hand so hard that it felt as though the bones were going to break. I was simply overjoyed to have him to myself once more.

After an hour or so, we stopped by a stone wall and looked back over the frosty fields we had crossed. Then Hugh turned to me and kissed me on the lips. Softly at first, but pretty soon he was getting rough and tickling my tonsils with his tongue.

I sighed with delight as he took my head in his heads and tipped it backwards so that he could kiss my throat. I thought that I had never been so happy. Out there in the beautiful countryside being kissed by the most amazing man I had ever met. Hugh's eyes met mine and I noticed that they were crinkled up in a genuine smile.

'Your pretty face really livens this old place up,' he told me. 'I'm so glad you decided to come.' I smiled like an idiot. I was glad too.

We turned then and began the walk back to the house. Hugh held my hand tightly all the way back across the fields, sometimes making it difficult for me to avoid tripping over the sheep's droppings as I followed him without letting go. But when we got back to the yard, he dropped my hand again as though it had suddenly become too hot to hold. I noticed the change in his attitude, but I didn't say anything. Julie had told me that they didn't like public displays of affection, not a certain type of public school man.

The house was quiet. The kitchen deserted but clean. Everything had been tidied away. Hugh told me that he was going to take a bath before dinner. I dropped hints that I wanted to join him, but he made it pretty clear that I wasn't going to be allowed since the old bath was far too small for two. So while Hugh soaked away his aches and pains, I decided to take mine into the sitting room to warm them by the fire. I hoped that no one would be in there but it wasn't to be so.

As I walked into the sitting room, Cecilia and Antonia leapt apart. It was clear that Cecilia had been crying. Her beautiful brown eyes were red with tears and her porcelain cheeks were puffy and streaked. Antonia looked hassled too but when I turned up, she tucked herself into an easy chair and nonchalantly picked up a book as though she had been reading all along. I made to leave again, but Cecilia beckoned me back into the room. So I sat awkwardly in a corner of the sofa, flicking through an ancient copy of the *TV Times*. There was no other reading matter in the room but Antonia's book.

The most disappointing thing was that the stars in the magazine said that I was due for a love surprise but they were completely out of date and thus totally irrelevant. I tried to concentrate on an article about Delia Smith's fantastic home-making skills but it was hard to focus my attention with Cecilia sniffling from the other end of the sofa. She was dabbing at her cheeks with a balled up piece of tissue, her eyes fixed on Antonia, who was managing to ignore her rather well.

Finally, Antonia snapped shut her book, muttered, 'For God's sake, Cecilia,' and took herself out for a walk. Cecilia didn't attempt to follow her; instead, almost as if I wasn't there, she let her mouth drop open and gave out a tremendous wail.

I didn't know what to do. Was I supposed to comfort her or was I supposed to make myself scarce pretty sharpish? I considered what I would have wanted in the same circumstances. I would have wanted someone to comfort me undoubtedly, but something inside me was keeping me from reaching out for Cecilia and giving her a great big hug. I hoped it was the fact that she had been so sneery of me up until that moment and not the fact that she was interested in girls. But eventually, her unhappiness became too much to bear and my shyness was overridden. I put my arm carefully around her shoulder and she crumpled her face against my neck. She was still crying with her mouth open, just like a child. I had never seen such a beautiful face transfigured into a Halloween mask by unhappiness.

'What's wrong?' I asked hopelessly. 'Is there anything I can do to help?'

She continued to sob, stopping only to take noisy breathes. 'Have you and Antonia had an argument?'

'We're always having arguments,' Cecilia blurted finally. 'And it's always because of her.'

'Her?'

'Caroline.'

'Oh.'

I wondered what on earth Caroline could have done to cause these two to have an argument. At the restaurant in London and around the kitchen table in Wales they had seemed like the original three witches. They were as tight as Julie and I had been before Andrew came along and stole her away from me on Saturday nights.

'What's wrong with Caroline?' I probably could have phrased the question more subtly but Cecilia answered anyway.

'She's a bitch, that's what's wrong with her. She always has to have everything her own way. I wanted Antonia to come with me to my father's birthday party in Monmouth tonight. But she won't. She says that Caroline's dinner this evening is much more important. Even though we've been celebrating her engagement for the last bloody fortnight. I told Antonia that we could come straight back here first thing in the morning but she flatly refused. It's as if that girl has her in some kind of a thrall. You must have noticed it yourself.'

I had noticed Caroline being enthralling but not as far as Antonia was concerned. Perhaps I was as naïve as Julie often said I was.

'Caroline simply has to know that everybody loves her all the time. Everybody has to pay their respects, every bloody day. It's like being at the court of bloody queen Caroline. I'd never have got together with Antonia had I known there was a third party involved.'

'She's not . . .' My mind boggled. Caroline certainly hadn't given the impression of a girl who was inclined to swing both ways.

'No, she's not sleeping with Antonia, if that's what you're asking. She just likes to give the impression that she might be about to if I step out of line. She keeps everyone hanging on for a scrap of her affection like that. Antonia, Tim, Hugh. She can't bear for any of them to love anybody else.'

'Hugh?'

'Yes, Hugh. Don't tell me you haven't seen the way he looks at her? He's exactly the same as Antonia. And Caroline can't stand the fact that he's brought you here, believe me. That's why you're in Great Aunt Felicity's room. It was where she put me the first time I came down to Wales. To keep me separate from Antonia. She obviously thinks that you're the bigger threat to her supremacy this time.'

Cecilia's handkerchief had dissolved into soggy little snowflakes. 'If I were you, Lara, I'd try to forget about Hugh while you still can. It'll save you a lot of heartache in the long run. I wish I'd seen it all sooner. They're a closed shop, Lara, and you and I will never be allowed to do more than stick our noses against the window.'

'Really?' I remembered the way Hugh had kissed me in the field. It had felt as though he was letting me into his life then. And surely Cecilia was being over the top about the whole Caroline situation. Caroline didn't want Hugh or Antonia. She was about to get married to Tim.

'Huh! That engagement's a farce. She couldn't survive on Tim's attention alone. I don't know why Hugh, Tim, Antonia and Caroline don't just all live here together like one big happy family. Why do they continue to kid themselves that they can lead normal lives away from her? It's the cult of Caroline Lauder and she's the high priestess.'

The door creaked open behind us. Cecilia leapt backwards from my side like a cat with a match to its tail and tried to look innocent. She needn't have worried too much. It was Tim, not our hostess. But Cecilia still made her excuses and left. Tim took her place beside me and picked up the ancient *TV Times*.

'Ah, Delia Smith,' he noted with glee. 'This might be useful, since I'm going to be cooking tonight. We're going to have a little formal dinner in honour of the engagement. Give me a shout when you need to get across the landing to dress up.'

'I think I'll have a bath first,' I said, leaving Tim to glean some useful hints from the high priestess of cookery. 'Call me if you want some carrots diced.'

'Carrots? Huh. My princess Caroline won't be having anything so mundane as carrots.'

*　　*　　*

SECOND PRIZE

There was just one decent bathroom in the house and that was in the west wing, near Caroline's bedroom. But as I neared it, I could hear definite sounds of splashing which were punctuated by peals of laughter that told me the girls had made it up. So much for the bath being too small for two.

I didn't want to interrupt Tim again, so I decided that I would find Hugh and tell him about my extraordinary conversation with Cecilia. He would be amused, I thought, to hear about the 'Cult of Caroline'.

'Hugh! Hugh, are you in there?' I called through his keyhole. I heard a shuffling from inside, someone getting up from the bed and walking towards the door. Hugh opened it to let me inside. He wasn't alone. Caroline was sitting in the chair by the fireplace, nonchalantly picking at her nails. She smiled tightly but I guessed that she was almost as disappointed to see me as I was to see her there. I couldn't exactly tell her the Cult of Caroline tale.

'I'm waiting to get into the bathroom,' I explained.

'Oh yes,' said Caroline. 'The girls are in there. They'll be ages picking their spots. If I were you I'd go down to the sitting room and wait in the warm.'

'I got a bit bored waiting downstairs on my own. Besides, it's not too cold up here. I've got my thermal vest on.'

Caroline shot me a look of what I can only describe as exasperation. I was taken aback. Hugh, sitting on the end of the bed, made no effort to persuade me to stay. 'I'll be down in a little while, Lara,' he told me. 'In the meantime you could make yourself extremely useful and put the kettle on.'

'OK.' I retreated quickly. I hadn't felt like this since my parents sent me away from a room when I was young. I remembered that they had been having an argument and that I had interrupted it. I wondered if that was the case now. The wonderful Hugh who had taken a walk across the fields with me was gone again, replaced by the preoccupied Hugh of that morning who didn't seem to want to have me around. I slunk back down the stairs and asked Tim to point me in the direction of the phone.

'Hello?'

Julie was in. Tonging her hair. Getting ready to go out in the West End. When I heard the sound of my newest CD blaring out in the background I was suddenly really envious of her, back in jolly old civilisation. As far as I knew, there wasn't even a mono radio in this decrepit wreck of a house.

'Hi, Lara. What are you calling me for? You're supposed to be having a fabulous time in Wales.'

'Oh, I am,' I said, not half-lying. 'It's just that everyone's taking their pre-dinner siesta and I'm just a weeny bit bored.'

'How's Hugh?'

'Hot and cold.'

'A-ha. I knew something was up. You wouldn't have called otherwise. You'd have been far too busy taking your pre-dinner siesta with him.'

I looked over my shoulder to check that no one was listening in.

'Yeah. It's really weird, Julie. One minute he's all over me. The next, it's like I'm his sister or something. I can't work him out at all.'

'Hot and cold. And when does this happen?' Julie the love doctor tried to make a diagnosis. 'Hang on. Don't tell me anything for a second. I've just got to move these curling tongs to the other side of my hair.' There was much rustling as she manoeuvred the phone to hold it beneath her chin, then placed it against the other ear. I knew what she was doing because I'd seen her do it a hundred times. 'Right, I'm back,' she told me. 'Carry on.'

'Well, he was very affectionate when we went for a walk on our own earlier this afternoon, but when we came back, phut,' I made the sound of a dud firework not going off. 'It was as if he'd turned himself right off again.'

'So, what you're saying is that he's unaffectionate in front of other people?'

'Sort of. I think. But he gave me a big kiss in front of everybody when I came back from riding this morning.'

'You went riding?' she asked incredulously.

'More like walking. I only got as far as the stable-yard gates before my pony decided to give up on me and I had to get off.'

'I can't imagine you on a horse.'

'Neither could the horse. But I was OK with that

113

because I didn't really want to be shown up by my novice riding in front of the others. My horse would barely move out of the yard. And luckily, Caroline didn't even get to see my ridiculous attempt to get on the thing. She had to come back to the house to sort out some money for the man delivering the wood.'

'She went home while you were riding?'

'Yes.'

'And you said that Hugh kissed you when you came back from riding which means that he didn't go?'

'That's right.'

'Lara. Is Hugh affectionate towards you in front of Caroline?'

'No. No he's not.'

'Sheesh.' Julie was silent again while she concentrated on another part of her hair. 'I knew there was something going on between them the very first time I met that girl.'

'Between Hugh and Caroline? But Caroline's just got herself engaged to this bloke called Tim.'

'So, Prince Charles was married to Princess Diana, wasn't he, stupid? Wake up, Lara. Hugh is obviously soiled goods. Too much baggage. Anyone else worth getting excited about up there?'

'Well, no. Not really. There's Tim, who is Caroline's fiancé as I said, and those two lesbians I told you about.'

'What's Tim like?'

'Not really my type. Listen, Julie, do you really think that something is going on between Hugh and Caroline?

When he kissed me this afternoon it was like nothing I had ever felt before.'

'Why? Did he have two tongues?'

'No, stupid,' I groaned. 'But it was as if . . . It was as if he really, really liked me.'

'Then perhaps he really, really does. Listen, Lara, the doorbell's ringing. Andrew must have got here early and here I am still standing about in my underwear with half my hair still straight. Hang in there. But try to act a bit indifferent, will you? Remember the rules. And I'll see you tomorrow night.' She put down the telephone and I imagined her skipping across the flat to meet the man of her dreams. It was always so easy for Julie. She met straightforward men with straightforward emotions who wanted to kiss her in front of everyone they knew just to prove that they had her precious heart. I was beginning to wonder if I wasn't just a pawn in some complicated game. But hang on in there, Julie had said. And on the strength of that afternoon's amazing kiss I would. By tomorrow evening, I figured, Hugh and I would be back in London. We would be safely over the border, far away from Caroline and her machinations, if she even had any, and I could begin to work on consolidating my position in Hugh's heart.

While I was making my decision to keep trying for his affection Hugh walked into the kitchen and wrapping his arms around my waist, he kissed me lightly on the back of the neck. I was doing the right thing.

'That tea ready yet?' he asked.

I hadn't been anywhere near the kettle.

'Never mind,' he said. 'One kiss from your sweet lips is as good as any hot drink.' He swept me up until I was standing on tiptoes and used his tongue to probe the inside of my mouth.

'I wish they hadn't given us separate rooms,' I murmured. 'Perhaps I could creep over to see you tonight.'

'Don't you dare try and cross that landing in the dark,' was Hugh's reply. 'I don't want you falling through the floor and breaking your neck.'

'Well, why don't you have Great Aunt Felicity's room tonight and creep over the house to see me?'

'Because Great Aunt Felicity's room is the best in the house. You're the honoured guest, Lara. The blue room is absolutely freezing.' I remembered the blue room from my brief visit and it definitely hadn't been cold, but Hugh assured me that there was a terrible draught through the casement and it was clear that he wouldn't be budged. 'Besides,' he added. 'It would be very rude of us to creep about like a couple of sex-starved teenagers in Caroline's house. She's very old-fashioned.'

'Really?' Perhaps that explained why Tim was in the east wing too.

'Can't you wait until we get back to London?'

No, I couldn't wait, in more ways than one.

We made the tea and sat opposite each other at the kitchen table. I told Hugh Malcolm's joke about the grannies and the bingo and was delighted to be able to make him laugh. The way he had greeted me on coming into the kitchen had partially dispelled the worries I had been feeling and the sight of him smiling chased the last of my doubt into the distance. How heartless of Jools to suggest that I go after Tim instead. Compared to Hugh, Tim seemed so loud and unruly. So chauvinistic. So uncouth. I decided that I liked Hugh for his reserve in public situations. It wasn't just because he was afraid of upsetting Caroline, I told myself. It was because he was a gentleman.

About half an hour later, I got into the bathroom. The water was barely warm any more since everyone else had got in there before me, so I didn't linger long, but I washed my greasy hair quickly and tied it up in a French plait. I figured that I would sit by the fire until my hair dried and then, when I undid it, the plait would give me waves almost as good as a pair of Julie's tongs.

CHAPTER NINE

Something told me that Tim was more familiar with Delia Smith that he had let on. Despite having been the last in the bathroom, I was the first person to be ready for dinner and as such, I was honoured to be able to assist the masterchef as he turned salmon mousses out of their little moulds and frantically arranged a salad with the artistic talent of Leonardo da Vinci. When we had finished laying the table and placed a mousse in front of each chair, Tim stood back and wiped his brow.

'Looks good enough to eat,' I quipped.

'But not quite as good as you do,' he replied.

I blushed to the roots of my hair and smoothed the skirt of my new black dress down over my thighs nervously. It was a skinny sheath of clingy velvet, with a wide boat-neck and it had cost me a fortune. I hoped that·I wasn't going to be too dressed up. I was dreading seeing Caroline walk into the room looking artfully casual in something like a white shirt and faded jeans as soft as butter. But then Tim put my mind at rest. 'Keep an eye on those pans while I go and get changed,' he instructed, leaving me in charge of the asparagus.

'Are you dressing up?' I asked.

'Of course,' he said. 'It's a very special occasion.'

I sipped at a glass of cooking sherry to steady my nerves as I guarded the pans. Hugh had never seen me looking this smart and I hoped that he would be impressed into eternal submission when he saw how well I scrubbed up. I was gazing into the pale green water of the asparagus pan when he walked up behind me and squeezed me tightly around the waist.

'You look fabulous,' he breathed in appreciation and I prickled all over with pride. 'That dress is wonderful. Wonderful.'

'You can help me take it off later on, if you like,' I told him coquettishly. He didn't reply, but kissed me on the neck again with hot lips. I only knew that someone else had come into the room when he jumped apart from me as though he had suddenly received a 200-volt shock.

Cecilia and Antonia were wearing matching floppy trouser suits. Cecilia in blue and Antonia in palest peach. They were holding hands. The cross words of that afternoon had obviously been forgotten or smoothed over. They leaned against the sink together, sipping sherry and admiring Tim's handiwork. Antonia commented that Tim was a far better cook than his fiancée and Cecilia seemed visibly relieved by the revelation.

Tim reappeared soon afterwards to gather up the praise that was being heaped on his efforts. He passed on advice about how to make the smoothest mousse and how not to end up with half of it left in the mould when you came to tip it out. I couldn't have given a toss. I was remembering my vol-au-vent disaster and the very first time I had laid eyes on Hugh. I was watching him picking at a salad and just longing for dessert to be over so that I could show him that I'd even matched my underwear to the incredibly expensive dress I had bought in honour of him.

I suppose it was inevitable that Caroline would be the last person in the room, making a grand entrance as though the engagement was all but over and she was already the blushing bride. She took us all in with a sweep of her eyes across the room as she took her place at the head of the table, but her gaze seemed to linger slightly longer on me. It was then that I realised to my horror that we had bought our dresses from the same shop but that I had passed over the dress she was wearing because I couldn't justify the extra expense. I prickled uncomfortably as it dawned on me that she had shared this realisation too and was pleased to have the upper hand.

Now that the guest of honour had arrived, we were allowed to sit down. I was sandwiched between Hugh and Tim as we tucked into the salmon mousse. I wish I could say that it tasted as good as it looked but it didn't and pretty soon I found what must have been the only bone in Tim's carefully sieved mixture. Tim patted me on the back and I spat the bone out with such a trajectory that it landed just centimeters from Cecilia's plate. I'll never forget the look on her face as she picked it up with a napkin and disposed of it oh-so-carefully. Hugh continued to talk as though nothing had happened, without pausing to ask if I was about to die or not. I guess he might have been trying to spare my blushes as he had that first night in the restaurant.

Once again, the conversation revolved around people I didn't know but this time I was relieved that I couldn't be expected to join in. I had decided to concentrate on eating without making an utter fool of myself. My throat still tickled where the bone had made a scratch and at every mouthful I offered up a little prayer that I wouldn't gag. Tim cleared away the mousse plates and brought out the main course. The asparagus was pretty stringy. Hugh made a comment to such an effect and Tim retorted that I had been in charge of the veg.

The conversation continued to describe a world of which I knew nothing and found increasingly that I did not particularly care to understand. It was just like La Traviata, though this time I felt a little better because I knew I didn't look such a mess as I had done then. In fact, I was probably the most gorgeous girl at the table, since Caroline seemed barely able to raise a smile all night and she didn't look her best when she frowned.

During dessert, I felt Hugh's hand slip on to my knee. I looked down to check that I wasn't mistaken, then, seeing that his hand was indeed very much on my thigh, I twitched my leg muscle to let him know that I approved.

Had there been a tablecloth, I would have responded in kind but I just about clung on to decency though my heart was racing like a train. Cecilia was lingering over her chocolate mousse and I had to stop myself from asking her to hurry up so that I could drag Hugh off to a darkened room.

Finally, Tim had cleared away the last of the dishes and stacked them on the draining board. At that point, Caroline got to her feet and announced that she would be serving the coffee. Tim glowed with pride, as though she had said that she would now perform 'Swan Lake' *toute seule*. It seemed to me to be the very least she could do after all his valiant efforts.

Hugh's hand remained on my leg. I savoured the warmth of his palm through the sheer nylon of my stocking and allowed my mind to wander towards later on, when I planned there wouldn't even be ten denier between us, Caroline's puritan sensibilities or not. Hugh talked earnestly with Antonia about the best way to house-train her parents' new standard poodle while he kneaded my thigh. Caroline clattered coffee cups helplessly over by the sink until Tim went to her rescue.

They began the rounds. Tim passed out the cups and saucers and set a jug of cream in the centre of the table. Caroline followed him with the pot full of steaming black coffee. She poured out delicate amounts for Antonia and Cecilia while I longed for the pot to get lighter on her behalf. She seemed to be having trouble supporting its weight and I thought that she might drop it at any moment. Tim seemed to notice too.

'Do you want me to do that, darling?' he asked. 'It looks rather heavy.'

'No, sweetheart,' Caroline smiled acidly. 'I think I can just about manage to pour out a few cups of coffee on my own, don't you?'

She turned to the head of the table and poured out a cup for Tim. Next, she was alongside Hugh. I felt his hand slip guiltily from my lap as she approached. I saw Caroline's eyes widen and the next thing I knew, the coffee was cascading like a scalding waterfall straight on to my legs.

I leapt up from my seat, clawing at my thighs in pain. Hands seemed to come from everywhere, dabbing at my soaking legs. Someone poured a jar of icy water all over me, starting rather unnecessarily from the top of my head.

I ripped my stockings off. It seemed as though they were holding in the heat. My legs burned. My skin was redder than it had ever been in a hot bath or after a day in the sun. Tim ran to the sink and wet tea towels were passed along like buckets down a fireman's line to be pressed to my screaming thighs like cold compresses.

'Do you think we ought to call an ambulance?' someone asked.

'Pass me another tea towel.'

'Shouldn't we smother her in butter or something?'

'Haven't we got any ice?'

SECOND PRIZE

I must have fainted then because things got out of sequence for a while and the next thing I remember is Caroline saying, 'Well, if she hadn't been such a tart. Wearing that stupid short dress. She was asking for trouble.'

Someone silenced her. I was lying on the cold tiled floor. Tim was smoothing my hair back from my forehead. I felt as though my thighs had been pricked with a million needles, but they were still covered up with ice-packs so I couldn't see the damage.

'Lara, are you OK?'

I sat up unsteadily, clutching my hand to my forehead. 'I think so. Did I fall over? Must have been the combination of the shock and that water someone poured over my head.'

Caroline looked at the floor.

Tim and Hugh tucked their hands into my armpits and lifted me back on to a chair. It was time for the medicinal brandy.

'Looks like those lovely stockings saved you,' Cecilia observed.

It didn't feel like it. It felt like the coffee was still on my thighs, but I agreed with Cecilia anyway, because I didn't want to spoil the party. When I felt well enough to stand again, I went upstairs and reluctantly changed into my jeans. I told myself that I hadn't heard Caroline calling me a tart and when I re-emerged from Great Aunt Felicity's room, the others seemed satisfied that they'd done the concerned bit and the tone of the party was already starting to lighten again. We polished off a bottle of VSOP and moved on to the port. Three glasses of that helped to dull the pain.

Then some bright spark said, 'I know. Let's play a game.'

CHAPTER TEN

'A game? Like what?' asked Antonia. 'Not cards, I hope. I hate playing Hugh at cards. He wins all the time because he cheats like mad.'

'You know what they say,' said Tim. 'Lucky at cards. Unlucky in love.' He didn't look at Hugh who replied somewhat pointedly, 'Why don't we play Murder in the Dark instead?'

'No,' said Antonia, oblivious of the gibe. 'That takes up far too much imagination. All that trying to think up alibis and stuff. We could play hide-and-seek, though. This is a great house for that. Or Sardines. Yes, how about Sardines?'

'How about Sardines in the Dark?'

So it was decided. Sardines in the Dark. 'Sardines in the Dark?' I piped up. At the kind of parties I generally attended, we usually played Spin-the-Bottle, so I had to ask for the rules to be explained.

Tim was to be first Sardine. I felt somewhat at a

disadvantage in my invalid state and not knowing the house at all but Caroline ruled that we couldn't carry candles while we searched for Tim, in case someone set her Osborne and Little curtains on fire.

Tim left the kitchen. We counted to a hundred before we followed. I tried to stick with Hugh at the start of the hunt, but he told me that was cheating, and soon I was on my own. On my own, in a strange room, in the dark, feeling my way around the edges and trying hard not to encounter ornaments. In the distance, I could hear laughter and shouts from the others but whenever I tried to follow them, I found myself opening a door that led not into the hallway but into a cupboard filled with old tarpaulins and, I was sure of this, rats.

I decided that my best bet was to stay put. I decided that I would sit down on the first chair I came across and stay there until the game was over. That way I could make sure that I didn't send some hideous but valuable heirloom crashing to the floor even if I did get a reputation for being a bad sport.

I felt my way along the wall. My guess was that I was probably in the extra-posh sitting-room which had at least three armchairs somewhere. I couldn't believe how dark it was in there but the nearest street-lamp was probably on the east coast of Ireland.

Bingo! I found a chair. I was carefully edging my way on to it when something bit my bum.

'Ow!!! Help!!!' I shrieked.

'Shut up,' said the chair and I was manfully pulled down on to it.

'What?'

'It's Tim, you idiot. You've found me. Now keep quiet and we'll wait for the others. They walked straight past me a minute or so ago. I think that they're all upstairs right now.'

'You're not very well hidden,' I complained as I wriggled my shirt down over my bum a little more to make a better barrier between me and Tim's trousers.

'Ah, but you see,' Tim explained. 'This is the best way to hide when you're playing this game in the dark. Everyone goes straight for the cupboards or runs upstairs and looks under the beds. They don't think that I could actually just be sitting in a chair, covered by nothing but darkness.'

'Very clever. But it'll only take one more of us before we're spilling on to the floor and your cover will be blown.'

'Oh well. At least I got to have you on my knee.'

'Don't be so cheesy. You're an attached man.'

'Ssssh. Someone's coming back downstairs.'

'Well, this is a stupid game if you ask me,' said a familiar female voice. It was Caroline. 'We've looked absolutely everywhere in the house. He's probably slipped outside to hide in the stables.'

'Or in the pigsty,' said Hugh.

Caroline chuckled. 'Wherever. But if he is outside, he's cheating.'

Tim sniggered into the back of my neck.

'You know,' said Caroline suddenly. 'I thought for one awful moment that he didn't believe me when I told him that I had to come back here to pay the woodman this morning.'

'I'm sure he didn't even start to question it.'

'I don't know, Hugh. He seemed pretty disgruntled when I got back to the stables.'

'Don't know what he's got to be disgruntled about. He's engaged to the most beautiful woman in the world.'

I must have stiffened at that comment, because suddenly Tim clamped his hand across my mouth.

'Why did you drop that coffee over Lara, Caroline?' Hugh asked suddenly.

'I didn't do it deliberately.'

'Of course you did it deliberately, Caro. You saw me put my hand on her knee and you were jealous, weren't you?'

'Why would I be jealous of that mousy little tart?'

'The same reason that I'm jealous of Tim.'

'I was just fed up of seeing her show off in that hideous dress . . .'

What? Oh, come on Tim, I thought. I need to defend myself. I tried to claw his fingers away from my mouth but he just clamped harder. He needed to listen.

'What did you bring her here for in the first place?' Caroline continued.

'Why shouldn't I have some company of my own? You're getting married to Tim, aren't you? Why are you marrying him, Caroline? Of all the people you could have had.'

'Because he loves me. That's why.'

'He doesn't love you, Caroline. He's infatuated by you, sure. He looks up to you like he's your little dog. But he doesn't love you.'

'What else was I supposed to do when you left?' Caroline sobbed suddenly. 'You didn't want me any more.'

'But I did. I did.'

No, no, no. I didn't want Julie to be right. I bit down on Tim's fingers but still he wouldn't let me go. I couldn't even get up, because he had me clamped hard against him with his free arm and when I tried to kick out with my legs he trapped them between his own.

'You idiot, Hugh,' Caroline sounded as though she was sniffling. 'Why didn't you say something before?'

'How could I after Fiona?'

'Fiona, Fiona!! Is she always going to come between us?'

Who the hell was Fiona?

'No. But . . . Caroline, you know I couldn't come to you so soon after . . . I needed to wait.'

'But you waited too long and now it's too late for both of us.'

'It's never too late.' I heard him step towards her.

Oh, God. I really did want to become part of the furniture now. After all that thrashing about like a blind girl, my eyes were finally become acclimatised to the dark.

I was beginning to be able to make shapes out, just in time to see Hugh take Caroline in his arms.

'Caroline. My darling.'

'Hugh!'

The kissing noises were horrific, standing out against the silence like a bloodstained bullet hole in a white T-shirt. Tim suddenly let me go and stood up too quickly. I fell on to the floor, pulling down an occasional table on the way. Lights went on. People sprang apart. A punch was thrown. A punch was thrown back.

I watched with growing horror from my place amongst a pile of shattered porcelain. Looking away while Tim laid into my pretty-much ex-boyfriend, I caught sight of the severed head of a china dog I'd seen on the *Antiques Roadshow* and knew I was sitting on at least two thousand pounds' worth of shattered heirloom.

'Stop it!!! Stop it!!! Watch his face. What are you doing? Watch my porcelain!!!' Caroline was torn between saving Hugh's life or saving Great Aunt Felicity's vase.

I scrambled to my feet, using the Osborne and Little curtains to pull myself up. Tim was on top of Hugh, laying into him as though his fist were a pneumatic drill. Caroline was clutching a particularly vulnerable jar.

'Stop it!! Stop it!!' I joined in the screaming before the sight of blood could make me faint. Antonia and Cecilia had followed the sound of the kerfuffle downstairs. If Antonia hadn't been fifth dan tae kwon do, I'm sure Hugh would have lost an eye. Antonia laid Tim out with a single flying kick. Tim's backwards-flying head took out the precious vase.

'Aaaagh!! I don't believe it. You selfish pig.' Caroline ignored the casualties on all sides as she started to piece the porcelain together. I suppose it might have been shock that made her concentrate on the material side of the matter but if two guys had been fighting over me, I like to think that I would have kissed at least one of them better.

Cecilia fell to her knees and took Tim's head in her lap.

'You've split his lip,' she said accusingly to Antonia.

'Well, so what?' retorted Antonia. 'He's given Hugh two black eyes.'

'Oh my God. Not that as well,' Caroline pushed me roughly aside to get to the china spaniel.

'What happened?' Cecilia asked.

'Tim had a fit about something stupid and now clumsy Lara has managed to knock over a table full of Meissen,' said Caroline.

'Now, hang on,' I began. 'It wasn't like that at all.'

'You're lucky I've got insurance.'

She was lucky that I'm not a fifth dan.

'God, I don't believe it. It's not the money,' Caroline moaned as she held a dog's leg in each hand. 'It's just that some of these things can never be replaced.'

'Oh, my poor darling,' Antonia rushed to comfort her. 'We'll find another dog for you. I'm sure we will.'

'I can't understand what made them start fighting,' she whined.

CHRIS MANBY

I was too busy pulling a shard of china out of my thigh to put her straight. Cecilia looked up from her patient momentarily with an expression of disbelief.

'I want you all out of my house now,' Caroline shouted suddenly. 'All of you, before I call the police.'

'All of us?' asked Antonia desperately.

'No. Just everyone except you and Hugh, of course. You've got five minutes.' The chosen few stormed off to the west wing leaving me, Cecilia and Tim on the floor.

'What happened?' Cecilia asked again.

'We were hiding on this chair. Caroline and Hugh didn't know. They started kissing. Tim went a bit mad.'

'I'm not bloody well surprised. I knew there was something going on between those two. Ever since that Thursday night three weeks ago when Caroline stayed at my flat in London but wouldn't tell me who was taking her out. I guessed it was Hugh.'

'Oh.' That Thursday was the one on which Hugh and I had been meant to have our first date.

'Is Tim going to be OK?' I asked. He groaned painfully. 'Do you think he might have concussion? He hit his head on the way down.'

'Tim Winterson have concussion? Darling, his skull is thicker than the Great Wall of China. Here, you take my place and hold his head. I'm going to go and see that bitch Caroline. She can't just tell us to get out and leave him like this. He could be dying. They're supposed to be engaged.'

I let Tim's head rest on my painful thighs. What a

mess. Hugh hadn't even looked at me before trotting after Caroline to her room. Didn't I deserve an explanation and an apology almost as much as Tim did?

Tim opened a swollen eye and looked at me unseeingly. 'Caroline,' he moaned. 'Caroline, where are you?'

'She's just gone to get you an ice-pack,' I improvised. Tim was so groggy, I wasn't sure whether he could remember what had happened at all.

I smoothed his hair back from his forehead where a few strands were sticking to a nasty-looking cut. This wouldn't be the end of the engagement, of course. Or the end of me and Hugh, I tried to persuade myself. They were all just a little keyed up because we had drunk so much. I was still occasionally seeing two Tims myself.

But then Cecilia pushed open the door to the sitting room again. Her face carried the expression of a doctor coming to tell you that the transplant has gone wrong. She put her hands together in a gesture of prayer, then rubbed her chin nervously for what seemed like an age before she could summon the courage to speak.

'Caroline?' Tim moaned.

'No. It's Cecilia.' She knelt on the floor beside me and took his hand. 'Tim. It's bad news. Caroline gave me this.' She reached into her pocket and pulled out the ring. 'I'm afraid the wedding's off.'

'What wedding?'

'Your wedding to Caroline.'

Tim stared at her blankly.

'Perhaps we should tell him again later,' I suggested. 'Wait until the shock of that kick's worn off.'

'Hugh says he's finished with you too,' Cecilia said flatly.

'Oh.' I shrugged my shoulders. 'Oh. Er. Do you think we ought to get Tim into bed?'

'No. We're not staying here. Caroline's asked us to leave, remember?'

'Where are we going to go?'

'Back to London. You've got a car with you, haven't you?'

'Yes. But it's stuck in the mud. Besides, even if we get it out of the mud, I've been drinking way too much to drive home now.'

'This is the middle of nowhere, darling. There aren't any police until Cardiff.'

'Can't we wait until morning? I'm sure Caroline will understand that.'

'No. I've got to be away from Antonia now. We're splitting up too.'

'Why?'

'Why? This!!!' She pointed at Tim's split lip. 'This is why. She's a liability. Always storming in with fists and kicks. Never waiting until she knows what's happened before she dispenses her idea of justice. It's like going out with Judge Dredd. Come on.'

I didn't want to dash off like this. I still wanted to talk to Hugh. But Cecilia assured me that he had told her expressly that he didn't want to talk to me. So Cecilia and I compromised. We dragged Tim out to the car and pushed it out into the country road which led to the house. We pushed it as far as a lay-by, then we got in and waited until we decided that we felt sober enough to carry on.

Outside in the freezing cold, it didn't take very long for me to stop feeling pleasantly tiddly and for a very nasty hangover to set in to match my aching limbs. We got going just before dawn. I felt like we were escaping the Moonies but I wasn't quite sure that I wanted to.

CHAPTER ELEVEN

Tim was pretty much unconscious when we bundled him into the car, but he came round and started snivelling as we crossed the Severn Bridge. Cecilia tried to comfort him but she too was obviously feeling rather keenly the new hole in her life. I drove on in silence. I had only known Hugh for less than a month at that time but I was also feeling pretty blue. You don't fall off a horse, get burnt by a jugful of scalding coffee and get called a mousy little tart without feeling some sort of pain. And every budding relationship which got the worm and died before it had time to flower was another nail in my shelf as far as I was concerned.

'Have you still got the engagement ring?' Cecilia was asking.

Tim fished in his pocket and pulled the offending item out.

'You should throw it away,' Cecilia advised. 'It's probably cursed. Chuck it into the river.'

'No way,' I felt I had to chip in from the front. 'It looks

expensive, Tim. You should sell it and have a party with the proceeds.'

'I won't be throwing it away, or selling it,' Tim said sadly. 'It belonged to my grandmother. I was waiting to give it to the woman of my dreams and I guess I just didn't wait long enough.' He sniffed loudly. 'She was seeing that bastard all along. Every time she said she was visiting her godmother in London, she was visiting him.'

'Antonia just sided with her, of course,' Cecilia was ranting. 'She's known Tim for years longer than Hugh but she sided with Caroline. I couldn't believe it. When I told her that I thought Caroline was just a selfish slut who wants everything her own way, Antonia told me that Caroline was the selfish slut she loved, so I told her where she can stick our relationship. I won't be at all surprised if Antonia goes storming into Caroline's room tonight and announces that she's in love.'

'Disaster all round then,' I said banally. I pulled the car into the service station that overlooked the bridge and the river. We bought three coffees with artificial-tasting milk and took them into the restaurant. We were all so preoccupied with our misery that not one of us remembered that Tim was still wearing his pyjamas (we'd dressed him in those after sorting out his wounds). And choosing the Severn-view restaurant was a particularly bad mistake. The Severn Bridge is a suicide hot spot and pretty soon Tim started talking about how much easier it would be to go outside and jump right off the bridge than spend a life alone without Caroline.

'Didn't I tell you that they were all obsessed with her?'
Cecilia reminded me later as we tidied ourselves up in the
ladies' and prepared for the rest of the drive. 'I'm so glad
I worked it out and got the hell out of there before I got
sucked in too. I feel quite invigorated now.'

'I feel like shit,' I replied.

'You'll get over it. You've had a rough weekend but
you'll be over Hugh before your burns have healed. They
say that it takes one and half times the length of your
relationship to forget it. You've got one and a half months.
I've got nearly two years to get over mine. I don't think it
will even hit me that it's over at all until tomorrow.'

'I suppose you're right. Shit, I suppose we also ought to
be keeping an eye on Tim. He's got four years recovering
to do by your reckoning and we've left him unattended
by a high bridge.'

Tim was indeed still contemplating his navel when we
found him but, thankfully, in the car and not on the bridge.
We set off again. I turned on the radio, but had to turn
it off minutes later when they played 'With or Without
You' by U2 and both my passengers came dangerously
close to blubbing. Half an hour later, we passed the lay-by
where Hugh and I had stopped on our way down to the
farmhouse. I tried not to look too closely but was unable
to miss a pair of my newly bought red knickers which
hung from a bare-branched bush. Hugh had ripped them
off with his teeth rather than bother to take off my jeans
properly first.

I pursed my lips tightly together and told myself that I

should be angry because those knickers cost £12 a pair and not saddened by the memory of Friday night. But it didn't work. Then I opened the glove compartment to look for a map and found the wrapper of Hugh's wine gums.

'So this Hugh and Caroline thing has been going on for a long time?' I asked Cecilia when I thought that Tim might be asleep.

''Fraid so,' Cecilia muttered. 'It's terrible to find out that you were only second best, isn't it?'

Back in London, Julie was flicking through a copy of *Brides* when I walked into the flat. She looked up excitedly. 'Hello, you naughty girl,' she said. 'How was your dirty weekend?' She patted the sofa beside her as an indication that I should sit down. 'Come on, Lara. Spill the beans. What happened? You're back pretty late so I suppose that Hugh decided to keep you in bed for most of the day?'

'Not exactly.' I sat down next to Julie and began to hunt through the remains of the Roses chocolates Andrew had given her for anything that had hazelnuts in it. 'We actually left the farmhouse in the middle of the night but it took ages to get back because we got lost.'

'Oh. You got lost. That sounds romantic.'

'Not really.' I pulled my skirt up to reveal my blistered thighs.

'Christ,' Julie almost spat out her strawberry creme. 'What happened to you? Bondage gone wrong? Don't tell me he's one of those psychopaths?'

'No, he isn't. But Caroline Lauder certainly is. She got a bit jealous of Hugh's intentions towards me last night and poured a pot of coffee into my lap. Then I heard her call me a "mousy little tart" while we were playing Sardines in the Dark and had to leave because Tim knocked Hugh unconscious.'

'Hang on. Hang on. Rewind,' said Julie. 'You were playing Sardines in the Dark?'

'I was hiding in the sitting room with Tim and we heard Caroline rowing about something with Hugh. Turns out that you were completely right about him. He is soiled goods. He's been completely obsessed with Caroline for about a million years and it turns out she's in love with him too. She's called off her engagement to that Tim bloke. I ended up driving him back to his sister's place in London. Hugh stayed in Wales with Caroline.'

'What?' Julie unwrapped a brazil-nut caramel and popped it into her mouth automatically, totally mesmerised by my story. 'She dumped Tim and stole your man? Is this Tim bloke worth having instead?'

'Julie,' I sighed. 'Hugh was never really "my man" and no, Tim is not worth having instead. Besides I'm pretty sure that he's going to spend the next twenty years being as screwed up by Caroline as Hugh is. If there's one thing I've learnt this weekend it's not to bother with complicated men. How's Andrew?'

'Oh, he's simple. But obviously I shall have to ask him to rethink his choice of best man now. I am so disappointed in Hugh, Lara. It would have been so romantic, the best man and the chief bridesmaid. We could even have had a surprise double ceremony.'

'You still might be able to have a double ceremony if you ask Caroline to be your maid of honour,' I said sarcastically. 'But I've had it with men. Your wedding is going to be the last one I ever attend.'

'Don't be like that, Lara. I'll throw you the bouquet.'

'I'll throw it straight back.'

I left Julie to the chocs and went to throw my expensive and useless new clothes into the washing machine, not really caring all that much whether I mixed my colours or put them in on the wrong cycle. My mother phoned to find out how I had got on at my 'country-house weekend' with my new man (she was impressed by anyone with property outside the M25). I told her to stop knitting my trousseau and made a note to ask Julie not to tell my mother anything about my love life or lack of it in the future. But I couldn't face an evening of Julie's wedding plans so I went straight to bed at eight o'clock and gazed at the ceiling for what seemed like four hours.

What did it matter anyway, that Hugh Armstrong-Hamilton preferred Caroline to me? And not only Caroline but this Fiona girl as well? I had a good job and great mates. I did not need my life to be validated by the presence of a man. I did not need someone who was slightly less useful in general than my best girlfriend but who knew how to kiss me in all the right places.

I wondered if Cecilia had ever felt like this.

At about half past eight, Julie rapped lightly on my door

to tell me that I had a telephone call. For a second my treacherous heart skipped in the hope that it was Hugh. It wasn't. Julie didn't recognise the voice, she said, but it was definitely a girl. And quite posh.

'Hang on,' I said. 'I'm on my way.' I dragged myself from beneath the duvet. I know that I had vowed only minutes earlier never to answer the phone again but that rule only really applied to male callers. How much trouble could a girl be? Assuming of course that it wasn't Caroline.

It wasn't Caroline.

It was Cecilia.

'Hello. How are you, Lara darling? Just thought I'd phone to check that you're not crying your heart out all alone in Battersea.'

'I'm not. I'm fine. You sound OK, too. Considering.'

'That's probably because I'm as pissed as the proverbial newt, my dear. Tim and I have been through a bottle of the Old Grouse apiece since you dropped us off at my place.'

'Good idea.'

'Hmmm. We'll probably think otherwise in the morning. Anyway, darling. We were wondering if you'd like to come and join us for supper? We'll get together a bit of a lonely hearts club, shall we? We'll bitch about the ones we left behind and drink until we slip under the table and forget all about them. What do you say?'

'I . . . I . . .' While I was considering my answer, which would probably have to be negative, the front doorbell rang. It was Andrew. Julie let him into the hallway with a giggle and they started to slobber over each other straight away like two rampant cocker spaniels. Less love's young dream than a pair of cannibals breaking a week-long fast.

'Come into my boudoir, Andy Pandy,' Julie was whispering as she dragged him into her room, though not quite quietly enough to spare my blushes.

'I'll come to supper,' I decided instantly. 'Where are we going?'

'La Traviata,' Cecilia announced.

'Christ. But that place is loaded with memories of Hugh for me, Cecilia. Can't we go somewhere a little bit more neutral?'

'No. It's got to be La Traviata. This is about catharsis, Lara.'

'Catha-what?'

'Catharsis. An emotional release. Like squeezing a spot.'

'Oh, right. I see what you mean. I'll be at La Traviata then. What time?'

'Nine o'clock. I've booked the table already. Oh, and by the way. We've decided to wear the clothes that we were wearing last time we went there. To complete the effect.'

'Really?' That meant the fishscale hipsters and Julie's itchy polo neck for me. 'You know what, Cecilia, if I wear that outfit again, it might be just a little too cathartic for my own good. Mind if I come as I am?'

'Lara, I'm afraid I do. This article I have been reading in *Cosmopolitan* says that for the full effect you have to try and recreate the peak of your relationship in every single detail.'

'Funny, I've just been reading an article in *Company*

which says that you should burn everything you associate with the ex-object of your affections.'

'Oh, yeah. We're going to be doing that later as well. In fact Tim has just popped back to his sister's flat to fetch all his photos of Caroline. We're going to have a bitches' bonfire in my backyard. Bring whatever you need to be rid of.'

'I don't have any photographs of Hugh. We weren't really together for long enough for me to collect any souvenirs.'

'Don't worry,' said Cecilia. 'We can lend you some. I've got plenty of photos of him.'

I put down the telephone and seriously began to doubt that I was doing the right thing. Maybe I should leave Tim and Cecilia to it. I hadn't really been with Hugh long enough for it to make me this bitter and twisted, surely? On the other hand, I felt that I had been the catalyst for the Wales disaster and as such, I was obviously important to their plan. Besides, Andy Pandy and Julie-Woolie were getting into full swing now and our flat was just too small for me to be able to escape their passionate displays of affection which left me feeling somewhat out in the cold.

I managed to fight the urge to put on the silver trousers but, at nine o'clock, I was waiting outside La Traviata for the others to arrive.

I saw Cecilia first. Tim shuffled along behind her. He seemed to have lost a foot in height through misery since that morning. This supper was going to be a bundle of laughs, I could tell instantly.

Tim and Cecilia were each lugging huge black plastic bags. 'The mementoes,' Cecilia explained when I asked her. 'In this bag is everything Antonia ever gave me.' She opened the bag and gave me a flash of its contents, which included several books and loads of gorgeous clothes displaying a variety of designer labels.

'And you're going to burn all that?' I asked incredulously.

'Of course I am. Later on.'

I thought of all that DKNY going up in smoke. 'Wouldn't it be a better idea to donate it all to charity?' I suggested. 'That way someone else could benefit from your unhappiness. It seems such a waste. I'll even take it to the shop for you, if you like.' Though not, I was thinking, until I had saved the best bits for myself.

'That's very kind of you but the answer has to be no,' said Cecilia firmly. 'The only way this ritual will work for me is if I know that all traces of my relationship with that faithless girl have been destroyed. Completely and utterly destroyed. Isn't that right, Tim?' Tim nodded forlornly. I noticed that he didn't share Cecilia's manic gleam. 'Anyway,' she said, slightly changing the subject. 'Here's your stuff for the bonfire.' She reached into the pocket of her jacket and brought out an envelope containing two photographs of Hugh, obviously taken at Christmas, I guessed from the tinsel around his head. He looked very sweet and innocent and my treacherous heart couldn't help speeding up just a little at the sight of him. Hidden in my pocket I also had one of the shrivelled blooms from the bunch of flowers he had given me three weeks before. It was pretty desiccated. Ideal tinder.

'Thanks,' I said, taking the photos and putting them into my pocket with the flower. 'These are great.'

'Well, don't get too attached to them. Remember they're for the torch later on.'

I shuddered. Cecilia wasn't reacting to the end of her relationship at all normally.

We walked into the restaurant and were seated at the table where we had first sat together almost three weeks earlier. The maitre d' looked askance at the bin-bags and asked Cecilia whether she wanted him to look after them until we'd finished eating but Cecilia refused. The bags were to represent the missing people at our gathering. She put her bin-bag where Antonia had once sat. Tim's bag represented Caroline. And I put my envelope of photos and the flower on the chair next to Tim's bag to be Hugh.

'Now what did we eat?' Cecilia asked.

I lied and said that I had eaten fusilli as well as the others. This was going to be a ridiculous enough evening without me spilling spaghetti all down my front again. The food came and we ate in silence. Tim hardly touched his plate. I, on the other hand, was pretty ravenous and ate my own plate and the dish that had been brought for the absent Hugh. Cecilia had insisted that we order for them too.

We drank red wine with the pasta and white wine with dessert. Then we washed it all down with as much brandy as we could until I thought I might be about to be sick. Cecilia suggested that we went on to the club they'd been to after the restaurant. I imagined us dancing round the bin-bags and refused. Besides, I argued, Hugh and I had gone straight home that night.

'You're right,' Cecilia conceded. 'And I suppose that this evening is only meant to be symbolic of the past after all. But I'm starting to feel like it's working already. Aren't you? Certainly this bin-bag has been more affectionate towards me than Antonia ever was. How are you doing, Tim?'

Tim let out a gigantic sob and flopped forward into his tiramisu in reply. At that point, the maitre d' decided that dinner was over for us and we had to carry Tim outside, while the management followed with the bin-bags which they deposited with undisguised disdain on the pavement beside us.

Back at Cecilia's house, we trooped straight out into the back garden bearing our burdens. Tim had hardly said a word all evening. In fact, I think that his conversation might even have been limited to saying 'yes' to black pepper. Cecilia had already prepared something of a pyre. The remains of a broken chair were piled carefully in the centre of her little concrete yard, well away from the wooden fence, I was pleased to note. She got out her gold-plated Zippo and touched a flame to a piece of newspaper that was sticking out from beneath the wood. It had been a dry evening and the flames were quickly licking up the chair seat and reducing the newspaper to dust.

'You first,' she said to Tim. 'Put all your memories of Caroline on to the fire. It's time to say goodbye to it all.'

SECOND PRIZE

Tim opened his bag and began to empty his mementoes into the flames one by one. Photographs. Letters. Even a pair of exquisitely engraved gold cufflinks still in their velvety box. Then Cecilia followed suit. All that DKNY. (I tell you I could have wept. Julie, doubtless, would have grabbed a fire-extinguisher and told her to go to marriage guidance.) Then finally it was my turn, with my shrivelled carnation and two solitary photographs. Pictures of Hugh taken before I had even met him. It was more than a little spooky and I felt a right prat.

'Let's say goodbye to the things that have bound us,' Cecilia was saying with her arms raised high in the air. I hoped she wouldn't try to set up a chant. 'Now that they are gone, we can start afresh. New lives! New lives! New lives!' She'd had far too much brandy at the restaurant. Tim wiped his nose disconsolately with the back of his hand and turned to go inside.

'Is that it?' I asked, praying that it was.

'Yes,' said Cecilia. 'I suppose that is it. We just leave it to burn right down now. I'll gather the ashes up and throw them into the Thames tomorrow to complete the cycle. Fancy another drink? I think I've got Southern Comfort somewhere.'

Julie and Andrew would probably still be awake and making an exhibition of themselves, so I decided against my better judgement that I might as well follow Cecilia inside. Tim was already sitting in a comfy chair. His glazed eyes were staring straight ahead as he automatically tipped Southern Comfort into his glass, then brought his glass to his mouth, emptied it in a single gulp, then filled it up with alcohol again.

'Save some for us,' said Cecilia, wrenching the bottle from his hand.

'Is he going to be OK?' I asked.

'He will be after the next stage,' assured Cecilia.

'What's the next stage?'

'Well, according to this here guru in *Cosmopolitan*, first you have to go through rejection. Then you have the replacement stage.'

'Replacement?'

'It's exactly as it sounds. You see, Tim is a very physical person. That's what he's going to miss most about his relationship. But as soon as he knows he can satisfy his bodily needs elsewhere, the memory of Caroline will begin to fade into the background until she's nothing but a ghost. That's the advantage I have over Tim. I know that Antonia isn't the only woman for me. I know that I can find everything I had in her elsewhere.' She looked at me slightly too meaningfully for comfort.

'Really,' I muttered. 'Well, I'm not sure I'll be able to replace Hugh so quickly. It took me three years to find him after my last romantic disaster. It's a good job I'm not a very physical person, I suppose.'

Cecilia poured another slug of Southern Comfort into my glass and moved a little closer to me on the sofa. 'Oh, but you are a very physical person, Lara. Really you are,' she murmured hotly into my neck. 'In fact, I think that you're physical enough for both of us. Remember yesterday in

Wales when you comforted me in the sitting room? Then, at dinner in that tight black dress of yours. I couldn't take my eyes off you. You were the most attractive woman in the room.'

'I was?'

'Yes, you were. Hey Tim, come over here and sit on the other side of Lara. We've got to finish the exorcism.'

'What?' I spat.

'Let's complete the process of sealing this period of disaster by planting the seeds of a new beginning for us all.'

'I don't know. Gosh, is that the time already?' I looked at my watch frantically. 'I really should be going.'

But Tim had already risen from his chair with slightly less animation than the average zombie and crossed the room to sit beside me. The sofa was a bit crowded now. It was only a two-seater in the first place and though he wasn't nearly as big as Hugh, Tim was no mere slip of a thing. Squashed between him and Cecilia, pinned to the seat with trepidation, I folded my hands in my lap and wondered how soon I could make a polite getaway.

'Isn't this nice?' said Cecilia.

I smiled as though I was wearing nipple clamps. Then Cecilia reached across my lap and picked up one of Tim's hands. To my horror, she dropped it to land lifeless on my thigh. Tim tipped his head on to my shoulder and sat there sniffling while Cecilia dropped her own head on to my other shoulder and took my right hand between both of hers. Then she began to trace a finger over the lines on my palm, tickling me with definite intent.

'We could begin the healing process right now, Lara,' she whispered. 'All three of us. Here on the sofa. What do you think of that?'

'Surely we should have a proper period of mourning first?' I suggested desperately.

'Why waste time?'

I was just thanking my lucky stars that Tim would be neither willing nor capable to join in and thus I only had Cecilia to deal with when there was an urgent hammering at Cecilia's door.

'Leave it,' she purred. 'They'll go away.'

'No, no,' I insisted, leaping to my feet. The knocking continued, getting faster and faster. 'They sound like they've got something really important to say to us.'

They had. I opened the door to a panting, red-faced man. 'This your house?' he asked.

'No, it's hers,' I pointed towards Cecilia, as I tried to slip past him and out into the night.

'Well, tell her her bloody fence is on fire.'

I managed to slope off while Cecilia and Tim were sobering up very quickly as they waited for the fire brigade to arrive to put out the conflagration. I have never been so grateful for a change of wind direction as I was for the one that blew that bonfire on to the fence. As they say, 'it's an ill wind . . .' The next day, when I told Julie what had happened, she said that she was pretty disappointed in me for not hanging around to check out the talent. According to her, a fireman was almost equal to an officer in the RAF in pulling terms.

CHAPTER TWELVE

At work the next morning, I noticed that people were treating me as though I were a piece of fine bone china. Though I had been absent from my desk for almost a week, my boss didn't even ask to see a doctor's note. Apparently, it was obvious from my appearance that I had not been at all well. Maureen kept me constantly supplied with cups of herbal tea to flush out my system and wouldn't let me stand at the photocopier, deciding that my mysterious illness was overriding her varicose veins, which usually gave her priority over any seated work.

Joe flitted around me with a peculiar air of guilt, as though it was his fault that I was in such a state, since he was the last person to have seen me in full health. He had obviously told Maureen about the mystery man in the taxi and on one occasion, when I got up to make my own herbal tea for once, I heard her saying, 'You don't think it's something to do with him, do you?' in the hushed tones that suggested terrible abuse.

I appeared suddenly behind them and they shut up. 'It was just diarrhoea,' I assured them.

By the following Monday things were pretty much back to normal. My in-tray was full again with sheets of notes and sarcastic memos. Malcolm told me a ridiculous joke. I told myself that things weren't worse than before, they were just the same. This time next year, Hugh Armstrong-Hamilton would be nothing but a memory. Some posh bloke that I met at Julie's engagement party. The best man at her wedding.

Oh God. The best man at her wedding. That thought lurched into my brain with increasing frequency as we neared the Big Day. I imagined an afternoon of torturous embarrassment. He would be bound to bring Caroline, of course, now that they were an item. She had been bad enough when she didn't have him. Now I wondered how much of a bitch could she be when she had the upper hand.

Two weeks after the Wales débâcle and I was still sulking like a child who'd dropped a jammie dodger in the dog's bowl. Julie had had enough of it. When she found me in front of *Home and Away* munching through a family variety box of biscuits for the tenth night in a row, I think she realised that it was time to take action and yank me back into my old self.

'Come on,' she announced on the second Tuesday. 'We're going out. Tonight.'

I protested. It was eight o'clock. And I was already in my pyjamas. But Julie was having none of it. She frog-marched me to the bathroom and instructed me to stand under the shower slathering myself with various expensive potions until I felt good enough to be civil again. While I did that, she ransacked my wardrobe and laid out an outfit on my bed. She chose the short black dress. The very one I had been wearing when Caroline poured boiling coffee over me. I protested on the grounds that it was laden with memories and then that I didn't have any sheer tights to go with it, but Julie had already thought of everything and produced a run-free and barely-worn pair of her own fifteen denier.

'I don't want to go out,' I told her again. 'I just want to stay inside and eat biscuits for the rest of my life.'

'Don't be so ridiculous. So you've been chucked. Haven't we all at some point in our lives? And since you had only known him for three weeks and been snogging him for less than two of those, I hardly think you're entitled to an extended period of mourning.'

'Cecilia said that it takes one and a half times the length of a relationship to get over the end of it,' I protested. 'So that means I've got another whole week before my mourning's done.'

'Rubbish. I got over Hugh really quickly.'

'You never went to bed with him, did you?'

'No, but you forget that I had lusted after him for almost a year. And I think that twelve months of painful infatuation counts for a lot more than a full-blown fortnight.'

'I suppose it might do in your case,' I admitted. 'But you had someone to get over him with. At least Hugh had the decency to introduce you to the love of your life before he dumped you.'

'Exactly.'

'Oh no.' The penny dropped. 'Julie, where did you say we are going? I am not stepping a foot outside that door if you're trying to set me up on some ridiculous blind date.' I started to pull the dress off again. 'I refuse to be set up. If that's your plan, you can just leave me here with the biscuits or find yourselves another chief bridesmaid for your wedding.'

'We're not going to meet up with anyone,' she said smoothly, helping me to zip the dress back up. 'It's just going to be me and you, going for a drink and a bit of a gossip just like old times. No reason why we shouldn't look our best though, is there?'

'Then where are we going?'

'Nowhere too special.'

'Good, because I can't afford too special since I wasted all that money on stupid Hugh-impressing outfits.' I gazed mournfully at one of the mud-ruined pumps which was still sticking accusingly out of my waste-paper basket.

'Don't worry,' said Julie. 'It's my treat.'

Julie's treat? Now that was very suspicious. 'I don't believe you're not up to something,' I told her once more.

'Lara.' She crossed her heart. 'I do understand that you're not ready to get back into the scene again yet and I appreciate and respect that. Honestly I do. Love on the rebound is really bad news, anyway. When you've been dumped by the man of your dreams, the next one to come along can only ever seem like second prize even if he's actually rather fantastic. You have to make sure that you've flushed all the debris out of your mind and regained your self-respect before you start again.'

'Thank you,' I muttered. 'I'm glad we agree on something. But I'll have you know that I'm not that hooked up on Hugh Armstrong Hamilton. I do still have my self-respect. It's just that ... it's just that, you'd feel shitty too if you'd gone through what I went through that weekend in Wales. I don't think a medieval torturer could have invented worse.'

'Are you going to put some make-up on?' Julie asked, inspecting my reflection critically in the mirror. 'Because for someone who's not too upset about things you've got some pretty impressive circles under your eyes.'

'Oh, right. Thanks for that.' I dug out my ancient tube of Hide-the-Zit in natural orange.

'And you need some lipstick. You can't wear that dress without lipstick, you know. It's far too formal to go bare-faced.'

'Julie, can't I just slip into something a bit more casual if we're only going for a drink? Putting this dress on requires the full performance and you know how mascara just makes me want to rub my eyes so that I end up with it smeared all down my face before we even get to where we're going.'

'No wonder,' she said, picking my five-year-old mascara out of my filthy make-up bag between finger and thumb and eyeing it with undisguised contempt. 'How old is this stuff, Lara? I take it you do know you're supposed to replace your mascara every three months or so.'

'I thought that was just a marketing myth.'

'Lara, you must have had this mascara all through that terrible bout of conjunctivitis you had. And you wondered why it took so long to clear up? Ugh. Disgusting.'

I shuddered at the thought.

'Look, skip the mascara, OK? Just slap on some lipstick and let's go. We're late already.'

'Late? What are we in a hurry for?' I tried one more time to catch her out. 'I thought you said that it was just going to be you and me.'

'It is. It is,' she blustered. 'But I don't want to miss happy hour.'

I knew that we weren't just 'going for a drink à deux' when Julie ordered a cab to take us into town instead of suggesting that we walk round the corner to the Lavender Bar which was our usual haunt for a girls' night out. The cab pulled up outside Harvey Nicks and we took the lift up to their bar and restaurant on the fifth floor instead. I had been there only once before, with a girl from work. It was while I was temping at a City bank in the Easter vacation before my finals. This friend and I had been propositioned at the bar by a couple of Arab gentlemen who obviously thought that we were working girls in another sense altogether.

I had been disgusted by their attentions, but Shameen,

who was also an impoverished student working in her holidays to supplement her grant, had tried to persuade me to take them up on their offer. I caught the bus home without her. By the beginning of the new term, Shameen had traded in her bicycle for a brand-new Volkswagen Golf GTI and a mobile phone.

As Julie and I walked into Harvey Nicks now, it was clear that nothing much had changed since that terrible night when I took the moral high-road that didn't lead to the end of my overdraft. Every head swivelled towards the door as it opened to check out the new blood coming in. As I looked steadily at the polished floor while Julie ordered our drinks, I could sense eyes boring into me from every direction. Is she, or isn't she? they seemed to ask. I hope my outfit didn't scream yes!

Despite the fact that the evening was meant to be 'her treat', Julie didn't pay for the first round of drinks. The bill was left instead to a burly contract builder standing to the side of her who peeled fifty-pound notes off a wad at least thirty thick. Julie simpered, to make him feel a little better about having picked a couple of duds to gain the benefit of his attentions. We weren't after any builders that night.

When we had finished our first drink and been bought two more (this guy was very hopeful), Julie excused us and we found ourselves a table in the corner of the room. The builder tried to maintain eye-contact with Jools all the while and kept raising his glass and blowing air-kisses.

'A fool and his money,' Julie hissed through her Nutrasweet smile. 'Seen anyone you like yet, Laz?'

'What?' Was that the idea of coming to this place? 'No. I haven't,' I snarled. I had been too busy trying not to make eye-contact with an elderly man at the bar who had synthetically straight teeth and a very badly fitted wig.

'Never mind,' said Julie. 'I'm sure someone will be along soon that you'll really really like.'

'Julie, what's with the optimism? What do you know that I don't?' I asked suspiciously.

'Er, nothing.' But at that very moment, my question was answered. Julie got up from her seat and gave an excited little wave. Oh, surprise, surprise. It was Andrew, still in his suit, straight from work. And with him, another suited guy who was barely my height with curly, dishwater-coloured hair and thick round glasses. Obviously, he was mine for the night.

'Andrew, what a surprise!!' Julie shrieked. 'What are you doing in here?'

'Just passing by, my darling,' he said as he kissed her on the cheek. 'Never been in here before so we thought we'd pop up in the lift and see what all the fuss is about. It's good to see you, Lara. I heard you'd been unwell so I didn't expect you to be out again so soon.'

'Oh, spare me!' I moaned. 'I know that this is a set-up, Andrew, as, I'm sure, does your friend.'

'Oh, yeah. Sorry, Lara. This is Simon Mellons.' Dishwater-boy stepped forward and offered me a tentative hand. I shook it hard to let him know that there was to be no messing. 'Simon works in my office with me.'

And with Hugh, I inferred sadly.

Suddenly, I remembered. This Simon was the dweeb from Julie's engagement party. I hadn't recognised him because he'd changed his hair from a sad indie-boy bob to a sadder short back and sides. And the glasses were new too.

Andrew disappeared to get more drinks since for some reason the builder suddenly seemed to have lost interest in buying for me and Julie. Julie squeezed along the seat to allow Simon to sit next to me. He smiled at me and asked my name again. As if he didn't know, I fumed. As if Andrew and Hugh hadn't run a tombola in the office to find out who would have the honour of being paired off with me tonight.

I continued to fume like a damp firework for about five minutes as I wondered what Hugh had said about me. 'She's a nice girl. Pretty fast. And doesn't make too much fuss when you want to get rid of her afterwards.' Well, I wasn't going to play along with their game. It may have suited Julie to be set up in this way but it didn't suit me. No way was I going to settle for second prize.

Andrew returned with the drinks. A Kir Royale to replace my orange juice. They were trying to weaken my defences. Get me pissed and I'd be happy with just about anyone, eh? Once upon a time perhaps but not tonight.

Julie was asking Simon plenty of mundane questions

to get the conversation started. How long have you been at Partridge Skelton? Which part of London do you hail from? Have you got a nice car? What are your intentions towards my best friend?

I briefly explained my role at Hartley and Hartley for the second time that evening and Simon nodded enthusiastically. I had heard that people nod twenty times faster than usual when they're not really interested in what you're talking about. Simon asked what drove me towards working in personnel.

'I like people,' I told him flatly. At that moment it couldn't have been further from the truth. I thought longingly of the variety box of biscuits I had left behind. Of watching all the soaps I had videoed that week in one big veg-fest instead of trying to make this ridiculous small talk. Julie and Andrew had moved closer together now and were whispering endearments into each other's ears while simultaneously trying to give Simon and me space to better acquaint ourselves. Simon's glasses had steamed up since coming in from the freezing cold outdoors and he wiped them clean with a crumpled handkerchief that looked as if it had seen two world wars since its last wash.

'I usually wear contacts,' he explained.

'Yes, I didn't recognise you with the glasses on.'

'Not sure if they suit me. It's quite nice in here though, isn't it?' he said banally.

'Mmm.'

With the Kir Royale drained and the conversation

reduced to nods and strained closed-mouth smiles, I decided that it was time to excuse myself to the Powder Room. But I didn't find it. Instead, I jumped straight into the lift and didn't stop until I was out on the pavement again and heading back towards Battersea on the number nineteen bus. Maybe I was being ungrateful of Andrew and Julie's efforts but I felt sure that Simon would be just as relieved that the nightmare had ended as I was.

I thought about him briefly on the bus home. Very briefly. He wasn't as ugly as he could have been, I supposed. He had no obvious tics, physical or verbal. His dress sense was OK, though you can never get a proper sense of a man's fashion habits until you've seen him out of his work-gear at least twice and Simon had already blotted his copybook on that count with the lime chenille. I excused my churlish behaviour with the thought that Simon definitely had a Lacoste polo shirt lurking somewhere in his closet. And Mickey-Mouse boxer shorts. Perhaps even a Tasmanian Devil tie. I would have bet good money that he had a degree in computer science and that he liked to go clay-pigeon shooting at the weekends. Yes, I had him taped. I was almost grateful to Julie for organising the date as I inserted my key into our front door. Tearing Simon to pieces had made me feel almost human again.

Now where were those chocolate biscuits?

They were being handed round in the sitting room.

'What? How come? What are you doing here?' I asked in frustration. Simon, Andrew and Julie were lined up along the sagging sofa in front of a taped episode of *Friends*.

'We came back in Simon's car,' Julie informed me triumphantly. 'You should have told me you were feeling ill, Lara. We would have brought you home straight away.'

'Huh?'

'Lara's been suffering from terrible bouts of nausea ever since she came back from India,' Julie elaborated. 'We think it might have been the stuff she took to prevent malaria.'

'What?' I'd never been to India.

'Yes. Makes her memory flicker on and off sometimes as well. Sit down, Lara. I'll fetch you a cup of tea to make you feel better.' She patted me in a show of false consideration and froze me to the armchair with angry eyes.

Simon smiled sweetly at me again. I hoped in some ways that he had fallen for Julie's ridiculous story because sitting there as he was, so shyly and stiffly on our sofa, I almost thought that perhaps he didn't deserve to be hurt just because Hugh had squashed me.

'Whereabouts in India did you go?' he asked me politely.

'Oh, India?' I silently cursed my flatmate. 'She's always getting that wrong. It was Turkey, not India.'

'I didn't think you needed to take malaria precautions for Turkey.'

'No? Well, that's probably because you don't. My doctor got it all wrong too. Terrible really, isn't it? Now I'm always feeling sick and what for? For absolutely nothing. That's what.'

'You should sue.'

'Yes. Maybe I will.' I wondered if I could bring a case against my flatmate for setting me up with her fiancé's friends and causing permanent psychological damage to them and me both.

Julie returned from the kitchen holding a bottle of well-chilled Chardonnay. 'No tea tonight I'm afraid because we seem to have run out of milk,' she told us. 'Anyone for a glass of this instead?'

We didn't have enough glasses. Several had been broken at Julie's engagement party, so I had a Bertie Bassett mug of white wine. By the time I'd finished it, I thought, I'd be able to do a pretty good impression of someone suffering from nausea.

CHAPTER THIRTEEN

'So what did you do before you became a Merchant Wanker?' I asked rudely, as I lolled in the armchair three hours and three bottles of Chardonnay later like a rag doll without its stuffing. 'I suppose you studied computers or something boring like that.'

'No,' said Simon. 'I studied French and Russian literature actually.'

'Oh.' I was surprised.

'But I ran up so many debts that I simply had to go into the City when I graduated. I like the finer things in life. Champagne. Fast cars. Academia may have satisfied me more intellectually but there was no way it was going to cover the Moët et Chandon.'

'So you decided to get shallow?' I sneered. He had blown my computer science theory but I sure as hell wasn't going to let him off lightly yet.

'Not really. But right now I do need the money, for several reasons.'

'Like what? To pay for clay-pigeon shooting week-ends?'

'Never lifted a gun in my life.'

'Skiing holidays in Verbier?'

'I can barely control my feet as they are, let alone attached to two-metre-long sticks on ice.'

'Yachting?'

'I get seasick.'

'Polo?'

'I'm allergic to horses.'

I was running out of posh things that he might have in common with Hugh that I could hate him for but I was sure as hell not going to let myself start liking him.

'I've heard that you're a keen squash-player?'

Now he was calling my bluff.

'Squash?' I was confused for a minute, then I remembered. That bastard Hugh must have been talking about me again unless Julie had told Andrew about my pathetic lie. 'Well, I used to play a lot of squash,' I lied. 'Until I started getting these attacks of nausea.'

'That really is so terrible. The last thing you want from a holiday is to come home with some debilitating condition that stops you from doing the things you like best.'

'Quite.' I thought of the blisters and bruises I had picked up in Wales which had almost stopped me from sitting comfortably in front of the television. 'These days, I think going away from home is just too dangerous.'

'You could go to a health farm.'

'Why?' I snarled. 'I'm not fat.'

'No,' Simon sighed. 'No, of course you're not fat. I didn't mean that you should go for your figure, I meant for your general health and well-being.'

'I'm perfectly well, thank you.'

'Never mind.'

'I bet you go to health farms,' I tried once more to catch him out.

'No, I don't. I can't afford to. Like I said, I'm saving up.'

'For what?'

'I'll tell you another day. Do you want some more of this?' He went to refill my glass.

'If you're trying to get me drunk so that you can seduce me, it's not going to work, you know.'

'Lara, you're already drunk. There's no trying about it.'

I rearranged myself on the armchair defensively, but my legs suddenly seemed to have become too long to tuck beneath me neatly. I flicked my head back to get my hair out of my eyes and it took more than a few seconds for my focus to come back. I was absolutely pissed, but I told him once more, forgetting that I had already mentioned the fact, 'I'm not drunk.'

'As you say. What time is it now?' Simon asked. 'I should probably be going.'

I peered at the clock on the front of Julie's stereo with its numbers just slightly too small to be read by the human eye. 'Gosh,' I said. 'It's almost four in the morning.'

'I thought it was earlier than that. Talking to you certainly makes time fly.'

I blushed. Or maybe it was just an alcohol flush. He wasn't the only one who hadn't noticed time passing. Had I actually been enjoying talking to this bloke? Or rather, trying to push him into a fight?

'I ought to go.'

'No,' I said suddenly. 'You've drunk way too much to drive. You'll have to stay here until you sober up. Until tomorrow morning. You can sleep on the sofa and Julie will iron your shirt when she gets up. She always does Andrew's. I'll just get you a pillow from my room.'

I stood up but hovered for a moment by the door as though his gaze was holding me still. Then he took off his glasses and rubbed at his eyes. 'Yes, thanks. That would be lovely.'

I brought him the bottom one of my two pillows which was the one I figured would be less likely to smell of hair-grease. Simon hugged it to him and breathed in deeply. 'Mmm,' he murmured. 'Delicious. What is that perfume you wear?'

'I don't,' I told him, embarrassed. 'Unless you count roll-on Mum.'

'Then it must be pure you. Eau de Lara.'

I smiled nervously and skittered off to bed.

'Eau de Lara?' No one had ever commented on the way I smelled before. At least, not in a positive way. My younger brother had called me 'Smelly'. That Simon was a strange bloke. He had blown all my first impressions of him out of the water. French and Russian? There was something supremely sexy about a man who could handle his foreign languages. I rolled over to face the wall and closed my eyes over a vision of his face. Eau de Lara? I drifted into sleep and woke myself up seconds later with a huge snore. My bedroom door was ajar. I crept out of bed and closed it tightly. I snore like a wart-hog and for some reason, it suddenly mattered that Simon didn't yet know.

'So what do you think?' Julie collared me after work the next day, when I had a hangover the size of Birmingham and the 'Eau de Lara' comment had totally worn off. 'Did you and Simon get on well after Andrew and I went to bed?'

'If you mean, did we find lots of things to talk about then yes. If you mean anything else, then mind your own business.'

'If you don't tell me, I shall find out the truth through Andrew anyway.'

'Not if Simon is a gentleman which I am inclined to believe he is.'

'Oh, yeah. He's a gentleman all right. Andrew was telling me all about him yesterday. Simon wanted to be an academic but he gave it up to work in banking when his grandmother became ill so that she can get private medicine.' My jaw dropped open. And I had been so nasty about his ambitions. 'It's terrible really. He must feel like he's sold his soul to the City but his parents died when he was young and she's the only family he has left . . .'

I wasn't listening to Julie's prattle. Instead I thought about Simon, bravely donning a pin-striped suit and ploughing all his wages into BUPA.

'. . . When a man does something like that for his grandmother, you can rest assured that he'd really care for you. He's accepted his responsibilities so early, not like those guys who just want to go on playing with their fast cars and fast women until the girls they go after start to say "sod off, grandad" instead of "yes please".'

'Yeah. It is good of him.'

'And he's been single for absolutely ages. Hasn't had time for romance what with working so hard and looking after his grandmother but now he's got her a place in this fantastic convalescence home, he thinks he's just about ready for love.'

'Yeah, but I'm not.' I shut down the image of Father Teresa. Coming from Julie it was bound to be more than slightly exaggerated anyway. In reality, he had probably just given his grandmother a lift to the chiropodist to get her corns done. 'Julie,' I continued, 'you can't just get a piece of paper and write a list with your single girlfriends on one side and single men on the other and expect them to pair up and cop off just like that.'

'He liked you,' she said defensively.

'Yeah, and I liked him. It's just that he's not very dangerous, is he?'

'Dangerous? What do you mean dangerous?'

174

'You know.'

'No, I don't. Honestly, Lara. One minute you're complaining that your tryst with Hugh Armstrong-Hamilton nearly killed you, then, when I bring you someone who'd treat you like a princess, you want someone to treat you like shit again. You're impossible, Lara. You're as bad about men as you were about trying on those fantastic silver trousers I made you buy. You should give him another chance. You liked those hipsters second time around, didn't you?'

'Yes, but I haven't worn them since.'

Julie ignored me and prattled on. 'Anyway, he's coming round to dinner tomorrow night. I'm doing my vegetarian Stroganoff and no, you're not doing anything else because I know as well as you do that you haven't got anyone else to do it with.'

I laid down my fork and threw up my hands in despair. 'Julie. No way! You don't have to fix me up just because you're getting married next month. I will survive without you, you know. I'm not like a dog. You don't have to find me a new owner before you go.'

'You need a man, Lara. It'll calm you down. Otherwise you'll start taking in stray cats and talking to yourself in little squeaky voices while you feed them, pretending that they're talking back to you.'

'There's nothing wrong with taking in stray cats,' I muttered defensively. 'They're a lot less likely to leave you in the lurch than any man I've ever met.'

'But they can't be your escort to my dinner party.'

*　　*　　*

Julie was right. I had no choice but to be at her hastily arranged soirée with a hastily arranged date. I racked my brains all that next day at work for someone I could spend the evening with but everyone I knew was either attached or unbearable. And even the unbearable ones were unavailable that night. I asked Joe if there was a pub quiz we could go to but he just looked at me awkwardly and said that he'd already arranged to do something else. Hardly surprising really, after the way I had left him stranded on the steps last time.

Maureen said I could go along to the bingo with her if I was desperate for something to do.

Not that desperate, I said to myself. The bingo would have been fine. But hearing about Maureen's iffy water-works all night? Thank you but no. So I was scuppered. I grouchily bought a bottle of wine on my way home from the office. White. Oak-aged. Cheap. Julie had taken the afternoon off work to have her wedding dress fitted and so she had already begun to cook by the time I got home. The smell of her vegetarian Stroganoff wafted downstairs to the street outside the house. Her cooking was almost worth enduring this torture for. But only almost.

'Oh, white,' she said, taking the bottle from my hands. 'Specially selected for Safeway? That's nice. You'd better go and get changed, hadn't you? The boys will be here any minute and we're dressing up tonight to make it extra special.'

'You don't look very dressed up,' I commented, taking in her jeans.

'Yes. Well, that's because I'm cooking,' she told me as she ground some pepper into the pan. 'I'll get changed when I'm sure that I won't get splashed any more. Hurry up, you've just about got time to have a shower before they come.'

'Have you been talking to my mum?'

I stood under the hot shower and mused about the evening to come. There was no point blaming Julie. She was only trying to be nice. It was I who needed to change. I needed to be more assertive. I needed to tell her that I could sort out my own love life without her intervention. I was, after all, almost twenty-six years old. I had a responsible job and I was thinking about getting a pension plan. I could look after myself. In fact, it didn't really matter if I never met another man in my life.

'Lara?' there was a knock at the bathroom door. It was Julie. 'Lara, can you hear me in there? I've just had a call from Andrew. His car's broken down so I've got to go and fetch him from his house. Simon's coming here straight from work. Will you keep an eye on the Stroganoff and let him in when he arrives?'

'Can't Andrew get a cab?' I asked. I didn't want to get out of the shower yet and I certainly didn't want to have to be responsible for the well-being of Julie's Stroganoff. I would be bound to burn it. And what's more, I didn't want to have to make conversation with Simon on my own.

I heard the door slam. Damn. It was too late. Julie was

already gone. I got out of the shower reluctantly and dripped all over the newly cleaned floor. That would piss Julie off.

'We're dressing up?' I sneered, as I pulled on some fairly clean jeans. 'Well, they can dress up as much as they like but I just want to be comfortable.' I tugged a tatty red sweater over my head. It had a mark on the front where I must have spilled some toothpaste and forgotten to wipe it off. I dabbed at it furiously and unsuccessfully for a while with a damp cloth. Then it was time to check the cooking. Faintly burnt smells had been wafting my way while I stroked on some of that ancient mascara that would make my eyes water and, sure enough, when I went to stir the bubbling pot I discovered that the wooden spoon was stuck firmly to the bottom of the pan. I stirred it anyway, until big black chunks of the stuff that had been burned to the bottom began to float to the top. Extra flavour, I hoped, and planned to ply Julie with drinks so that she wouldn't notice.

It was then that I discovered that it didn't matter whether I ruined the dinner or not. I found a hastily scribbled note, addressed to me, tucked under the salt and pepper pots. 'Dear Lara,' it said. 'Really hate to do this to you but one day you'll see that it was all for your own good. I'm not coming back tonight. Simon arriving at eight. Crème caramel in the fridge.' I screwed the note up and hurled it into the pedal bin. How could she? How could she do this to me? I looked at my watch desperately. Ten to eight. Simon would have left his place in Pimlico already. There was no way I could cancel now.

I took the ruined Stroganoff off the heat and sat down at the kitchen table in despair. The bottle of white was already open, so I took a huge swig. And another. And another. And washed it down with some Virgin vodka that had been chilling in the freezer since it escaped consumption at the engagement party by being hidden in the cistern of the loo. Simon didn't even have the decency to be on time. By the time he finally did arrive, almost an hour later than expected, I had finished off the vodka completely. I stood up to answer the door and almost fell straight back down.

'Wow, Lara. Are you OK?'

I lurched out through the open door. 'I'm fine, I'm fine. Come on in.'

'Sorry I'm so late. The traffic was terrible over Chelsea Bridge. As usual.'

'S'OK,' I mumbled. 'Been having quite a good time on my own anyway. Fancy a drink?'

'No thanks,' he said, rattling his car keys. 'I'm driving. Remember?'

'That's OK, then. All the more for me.'

He had bought me some flowers. Once again, the house was full of bouquets from Andrew to Julie so I had to use the bathroom bin. I forgot to put any water in it this time though. If he noticed that I had forgotten, Simon didn't say. It wasn't until six months later that it dawned on me he probably thought I was throwing the flowers away.

'It was really nice of you to invite me round like this,' Simon began hesitantly while I was dealing with the flowers. His glasses had steamed up when he stepped into the warm kitchen and now he was wiping them clean with the corner of his jacket. 'When Andrew passed the message on at work,' he continued, 'I was really pleased.'

'What message?'

'That you wanted me to come over tonight. It was really nice of you to ask.'

'I didn't ask you,' I said flatly as I slopped the Stroganoff on to two plates. 'Julie did. I was set up. Again.'

'Oh.'

'Doesn't matter though,' I slurred, putting a plate down in front of and nearly straight down the front of Simon. 'It's nice to have company, isn't it? Even if you didn't ask for it yourself.'

'I had no idea that was the case. I'll leave if that's what you'd prefer.'

'No, no, no. I was only joking,' I assured him, leaning across the table to take his hand and dragging my sleeve through the Stroganoff as I did so. 'It's lovely to have you here, Simon. Honestly. Honestly it is.'

'Are you sure?'

'Yes. I'm sure. Hasn't Julie told you? I'm simply gagging for a shag. Whoops.' I clamped my hand to my mouth theatrically. 'I'm not meant to say that, am I? I'm meant to be playing all hard to get and mysterious until you're hooked. I always get that bit wrong.' Simon smiled stiffly.

'But then, since you've been to see me twice this week already, I assume you can't be getting all that much of it yourself.'

'That's not why I've come here,' Simon told me defensively. 'If it's any consolation, I'm just as fed up of this business of being set up with a date as you obviously are. I wouldn't have come this evening if I'd known that it was Julie's idea and not yours. I do have my pride, you know.'

'So do I!' I said enthusiastically, jabbing the air with a fork and spattering myself with yet more Stroganoff. 'Exactly, Simon. I have my pride too.'

'And one of the reasons why I was so happy to come here tonight is that I thought that you and I were thinking along the same lines. You didn't want to make a grab for me the other night and I didn't want to make a grab for you. I appreciated your reserve.'

'Oh, yes. I've got lots of reserve,' I agreed emphatically.

'And we had an interesting conversation, I seem to remember.'

'Of course, we did. Very, very interesting.' Though I couldn't remember a word.

'Er, Lara,' Simon asked nervously. 'Are you going to put that fork down? You're getting Stroganoff everywhere. All over your lovely jumper.'

I put the fork down in my half-eaten dinner and looked at it forlornly. 'Doesn't matter,' I told him. 'It's only an old jumper anyway.'

'But it suits you.'

The jumper wasn't actually that old. I had bought it for the Wales weekend. I had actually been wearing it when I got thrown off that bloody elephantine excuse for a horse. Suddenly, through my drunken haze, I was vividly reliving that humiliating moment and the ones that followed after. I could actually feel my bottom lip quivering as I recalled the bruises and the stone that went through the knee of my jeans. I knew I was about to cry.

'Oh, Simon,' I exploded into my wineglass. 'Why does it always happen to me? Why me? Why do I always have to meet the men who are only interested in one thing? When am I going to be the girl that someone actually wants to set all others aside for and settle down with?'

'Are you that desperate to settle down?' Simon looked surprised.

'No,' I whined. 'Of course I'm not desperate to settle down. But it would be nice if someone would ask me from time to time. Everyone thinks I'm just a good-time girl . . . but I never seem to be the one having a very good time!'

Now Simon had put his fork down too.

'Nobody loves me,' I snorted.

Simon took my hand across the table. 'Would you like me to get you a glass of water or something?' he asked. 'You look like you've had quite a lot to drink and I promise you that things will look better when you've sobered up. They always do.'

SECOND PRIZE

'I am sober now.' I slurred in my defence.

'No, no. You're not really,' Simon said kindly. 'Look, I shouldn't have come over tonight. Things like this always end in disaster. I'll help you wash up this mess and then I'll be on my way home.'

I blinked up at him. He was already heading towards the pedal bin with the remains of his Stroganoff. I knew that I had let it get pretty badly burnt but he really had taken barely a mouthful.

'No,' I squeaked. 'You don't have to do that. Leave the plates by the sink. I haven't even got the garlic bread out of the oven yet. Please, Simon. Stay. Come over here and talk to me. I just need someone to talk to.'

Simon sat down again and folded his arms on the table in readiness for a debate.

'Not in here,' I said. 'Let's go through there and sit on the sofa. It's more comfortable.'

'OK.' Simon got up again and followed me through to the sitting room. If I hadn't been seeing two of everything at the time I might perhaps have noticed that he didn't look particularly comfortable as I snuggled down next to him on the sofa and began to blub into his shoulder.

'I must be completely hideous or something,' I said as my opening gambit. 'That's why nobody wants me.'

'No, Lara,' Simon replied by rote. 'You're beautiful. You really are.'

'Then why didn't you want to jump on me when you met me? You said you didn't want to jump on me?'

'Because,' Simon explained patiently, 'I thought that

would have been a little too forward for you. I know you're a sensitive girl, Lara. Not the type who's after a quick feel-up on the settee.'

'Really? Could you tell all that the other evening?'

'I could tell when you left the bar so suddenly. I thought, here's a girl who doesn't deserve to be messed around. She's been hurt too many times before and she deserves careful handling. I wouldn't have followed you back here at all that night if Julie hadn't been so insistent. She was being forward for the both of us.'

'The stupid cow.' I buried my head further into Simon's shoulder, getting green chenille up my nose. 'I'm sorry I was so rude to you the other night, Simon. I mean, I thought that you were really nice and everything. I was just angry at Julie for trying to get me involved with someone new so soon after I'd been hurt by that bastard.'

'I suppose you mean Hugh?'

'Yes.'

'Forget him.'

'Forget him? That's easy for you to say. I'm having to think about joining the Foreign Legion.'

'What was so special about him? Andrew told me that you'd only known him for three weeks or so.'

'But they were a very intense three weeks. Besides, it's not Hugh personally. It's the symbolic nature of the whole thing.' I surprised myself by managing to get those words out in my state. 'That kind of thing always happens to me.'

184

'What kind of thing?'

'Falling in love with someone who's in love with someone else and getting a series of physical injuries in the process of finding out. Look.' I pulled down the waistband of my jeans to show him the purply-yellow bruise which was still visible above my panty-line. 'I got that falling off a horse.'

'What's that got to do with Hugh?'

'I wouldn't have been on the horse in the first place if I hadn't been trying to impress him.'

'Lara, Hugh Armstrong-Hamilton is pretty unimpressable. Take it from me.'

'I thought he liked me.'

'I'm sure he did.'

'But not enough.' I screwed up my eyes and sniffled into Simon's shoulder. He was wearing a familiar aftershave which only made things worse. Not the same as Hugh's, thank goodness, but the same as Guy's, the bloke prior to Hugh who had thrown me over for his best friend Toby.

'It won't always be like that,' Simon cooed. 'I promise. One day you'll meet someone who really loves and respects you but before that happens you've got to start loving yourself. If you tell yourself that you don't deserve to be hurt then you probably won't be. And likewise, if you can't ride a horse, don't pretend that you can.'

'You sound like Julie,' I sniffed. 'Except that she advocates getting back on to the horse straight away to conquer your fear of it.'

185

Simon laughed. 'And I was meant to be the next horse, eh?'

I was snuggling my half-awake face into Simon's neck early the next morning when the realisation hit me that there was a man in my bed. A man in my bed! A man with no clothes on. I sat up carefully, trying not to wake him. Excitement turned to mild disappointment when I remembered exactly who he was. No, forget mild disappointment. Excitement turned to abject horror.

It was Simon. Simon of the thick glasses and dishwater-coloured hair. Simon of the vol-au-vent spat out on the mantelpiece at Julie's engagement party.

Fragments of the previous night's conversation drifted back into my aching mind.

'I'm not the kind of girl who wants a one-night stand.'

Had I said that?

Had I just had one?

I was on the side of the bed nearest to the wall. Pinned in by his unfamiliar body. I tried sliding under the duvet and exiting the bed via the bottom but it was useless. Simon stirred and slung a heavy arm over my waist with a blissful smile.

'Er . . . Excuse me,' I whispered, as I managed to extricate myself at last and slid to the floor. I crawled out to the bathroom on my hands and knees.

In the bathroom, I checked for damage. Neck first. No love bites, thank goodness, so no clues there. But I was naked. That had to mean I'd done something. But

I couldn't remember. I couldn't remember! People had always talked about alcohol induced, memory blackouts but this was the first time I'd ever had one.

Perhaps we had just slept together platonically, I told myself rationally.

No, said the irrational part of my brain. We couldn't have done. I would definitely have put my pyjamas on if that were the case.

I could hear Simon stirring, getting out of my bed, walking out of my room, walking towards the bathroom. I slammed the bathroom door shut quickly and locked it while I formulated a plan. There weren't even any towels to hide my nakedness in the morning light thanks to my lifelong habit of leaving damp ones in the bedroom. My mother always told me that no good would come of my sluttishness.

I briefly considered wrapping myself from head to toe in toilet roll.

Simon knocked gently on the bathroom door.

'Morning, Lara. Can I make you a cup of coffee while you're in there making yourself more beautiful?'

'Er, no,' I squeaked. 'I don't drink coffee in the mornings.' The truth was that I didn't want to give him the slightest excuse to hang around. But my refusal obviously wasn't going to stop him having one. I heard the kettle being filled. Simon was whistling the melody of a dance-tune from the charts. I heard him switch on the radio. The arrogant pain was making himself at home.

After almost twenty minutes of listening to him being

domestic, it dawned on me that he was going to hang around in my kitchen until he could say goodbye face to face.

If I didn't get out of the bathroom soon, I would be late for work so I fashioned a kind of bikini with two rounds of toilet roll around my bust and four rounds wrapped around my bum. When I emerged, Simon looked at me quizzically for a nano-second, then burst out laughing.

'What?' I snapped. 'What's so funny? I just ran out of towels.'

To make things worse, he was clad from head to toe in shirt, suit and tie.

'I think there's a towel on the floor in your bedroom,' he told me between guffaws. 'I'll keep my eyes shut while you go and fetch it.'

'Yes. I think you'd better,' I sobbed. I turned on my heel and fled for my room. The scratchy pink bikini bottom ripped apart and drifted to the floor as I did so.

'You'd better go,' I shouted from my bedroom door. 'I'm not too good with people in the mornings.'

'No kidding,' I heard Simon mumble. There was the sound of a chair scraping across the kitchen floor. Footsteps. The front door opened.

'I'll see you soon, I hope,' he called.

'Yes. Great.'

'Maybe over the weekend?' he added hopefully.

'I'll call you, yeah? I'll let you know.'

'OK.'

The front door closed behind him. I didn't leave my

188

room until I heard the sound of a car starting in the street below. Once I was certain that he had left, I discarded the tissue paper bikini and drank black tea naked at the kitchen table. God, I hated myself that morning. I also hated my body. I especially hated my messed-up ideology.

I was a disaster zone. I had only allowed myself to break down in front of Simon because I had assumed that I would never have to see him again after my outburst. But – oh, it was such a cliché – I had obviously blurted out my tale of woe and then fallen straight into his manly arms for comfort. How many times had I read about the perils of such a situation in *Cosmopolitan*? At least enough times to get me through the final of *Mastermind* with 'Things not to do when you're on the rebound from a broken love affair' as my specialist subject.

And why is it that you can see these things so clearly only once you've done the dreadful deed and got a splitting hangover?

I had to drag myself into work. The first call of the day was from Julie, of course.

'Hi, sweetheart,' she trilled. 'And how was the Stroganoff?'

'I left you some to choke on.'

'Hey!!' Don't be like that. I was only trying to be helpful. Anyway, when Andrew drove me past the flat on the way to work this morning I couldn't help noticing that Simon's car was still parked just two doors down the road. At seven o'clock. So you can't have had that bad a time.'

'I can't remember what kind of time I had, that's the problem.'

'What do you mean, you can't remember? You don't think you . . .' Julie gasped. 'You didn't, Lara, did you?'

'I really haven't a clue. When I woke up we were both naked . . .' Maureen raised an eyebrow at me across the office. 'I mean, we both bared our souls naked to each other . . .'

'Oh, I see,' said Julie, catching on quickly. 'You can't talk because you're in the office and someone's listening in, right? Never mind, I'll call Andrew now and get the full story from him. They can talk about anything in their office. Honestly, the conversations we've had during office hours . . . You wouldn't believe. Bye bye. I'll see you tonight.'

'Julie! Wait!!' I cried. 'Don't call Andrew.' But she had already hung up. I knew she would be calling Andrew straight away and that Andrew would doubtless know everything by now. I imagined Simon giving a blow-by-blow account of the evening complete with details that I didn't even know myself and with Hugh Armstrong-Hamilton sitting right opposite him while he did it.

At that moment, Joe walked up to my desk to give me a folder of figures I had been waiting for all week. 'Hope you found something to do in the end last night,' he said guilelessly. 'Sorry I couldn't come out with you.' Maureen, who had obviously gathered by feminine intuition and big ears that I had indeed found something to do and was regretting having done it, called out, 'You should have come to the bingo with me, Lara. It was a good night, last night. I won twenty-five quid.'

'Congratulations,' I smiled stiffly and turned back to my computer. But I couldn't work. I knew that I wouldn't be able to concentrate at all until I had put the nagging questions about what really happened out of my mind. With shaking fingers, I picked up the phone and began to dial Simon at his office. I knew the number off by heart of course, since he shared an office with Hugh.

'Partridge Skelton and Partners Ltd.,' trilled the receptionist.

'Er . . . yes. Can I speak to Simon . . . er, Simon . . . er.' It suddenly struck me that I couldn't even remember Simon's surname. 'Oh, forget it,' I blustered. 'I'll call back later on.'

I put my fingernails straight into my mouth and began to massacre them. They had grown just about a millimetre since Wales. I had never felt more stupid in my whole sorry life as I did right then. I could feel my ears burning as the whole of London talked about me. I was sure I could.

I couldn't possibly wait until that evening for Julie to return from work late and fill me in on my misdemeanours so I forced her into an early lunch. We met at the sushi place with a revolving food bar in Liverpool Street Station. On the condition that it was my treat, worse luck. Julie piled her plate high with the little dishes, colour coded from expensive to 'Oh, my God, you could feed a family of six for a week on that'. Fortunately, I didn't really feel like eating. I just sipped a Diet Coke and probed.

'So, did you and Andrew have a nice chat this morning?'

'Mm-hmm,' she nodded, mouth full of raw tuna.

'And did Simon get into work on time?'

'Uh-huh.'

'Great. And did he say whether he had a good evening or not?'

'Yep.'

'Did he?'

'He did.' She gave me a conspiratorial smile.

'Oh, God. Did he go into details?'

'He might have done.'

'Don't might me now, Julie,' I snapped. 'Did he go into details or not?'

She looked at me through knowingly-lowered eyelids, taking intense pleasure in my sheer agony, no doubt. Julie was supposed to be my best friend, but at times like this I wondered whether she had an evil twin.

'Julie, don't keep me in suspense about this,' I pleaded. 'I think I have a right to know what I did with my own body last night.'

She was trying to stifle a giggle, I could tell.

'Julie,' I whined. 'I'd tell you straight away if it were you in my position. You know I would.'

'And I would tell you straight away if I had anything

to tell you. Since when have I been able to keep a secret, Lara? I'm afraid that the fact is, I know nothing because Andrew knows nothing. Simon obviously knows something because apparently he was sober as a judge last night, but he's not telling anyone anything. As I said last week, it looks like you've found yourself a gentleman there. Good show.'

'That is of little comfort to me right now,' I moaned. 'I woke up naked, for heaven's sake. He was naked too. How can he possibly be a gentleman if he took his clothes off in front of me?'

'So? You were in your single bed, Lara. It gets hot in there if you keep your clothes on.'

'But what was he doing in there in the first place?'

'You'll have to ask him that when you see him again. That's the only answer. Mind if I go for another one of these?' She picked up a lump of fish on a dish that designated it was worth approximately twice its weight in gold. I shrugged. The day couldn't get very much worse. Not even if my credit card exploded from the strain of that lunch. Not even if a can of Diet Coke was found secretly to contain six hundred calories per sip.

'Well,' I sighed. 'I guess I never will know what happened because I'm never going to see him again.'

'What?!'

'You heard me. I'm never going to see him again. I can't possibly. I've made such a fool of myself. One minute I'm sitting on the sofa saying that I've been badly hurt and I'm not to be messed with. Next thing I remember I wake up with a naked man in my bed, which plainly suggests that I did allow myself to be messed with after all. I think that the only way I can deal with this is to forget it ever happened and that means forgetting Simon . . . oh, Simon whatever-his-name-is.'

'Mellons,' said Julie helpfully.

'Exactly. And that,' I replied, 'is now classified as more information than I need to know. And I'm never going to drink again either.'

'What about at my wedding?'

'You can have them make my Buck's Fizz with lemonade.'

Julie didn't push it and neither, thankfully, did Simon, once Andrew had passed the message on. Funny thing was, though, I found that I was kind of put out that he didn't make more of an effort to make me change my mind. It sort of suggested without words that I wasn't worth the bother.

Julie switched her attention, reluctantly, from my love life to her own wedding, which was creeping up fast. In fact, it was now less than a month away.

Thankfully, I had just about managed to persuade Julie that we really couldn't use her future sister-in-law's bridesmaids' dresses by saying I had heard that peach was an unlucky colour and offering to pay for the replacements myself. My credit card had barely recovered from the Welsh débâcle and the sushi deal but I was still determined to look my best when I followed Julie down the aisle. Particularly if Hugh was going to bring that witch Caroline along. I wanted her to be aware that she had Hugh only because I wanted her to have him. I was not some 'mousy little tart' but a gorgeous, generous woman who didn't want to stand in the way of true love. If, I sniffed, that was what it really was.

So, the bridesmaid's dress that I chose was an empire-line affair in deep burgundy velvet which went far more successfully than peach puke with my light brown hair. I had also made sure that the skirt wasn't cut like a puffball. Julie could have milkmaid sleeves to her heart's content but I wanted to look like a woman in control, not one who had just lost her sheep, when the dreaded day finally dawned.

I stayed off the booze and worked like a demon as the last weeks ticked away. I stopped reading articles in women's magazines about how to catch a man and switched instead to the mind-expanding *National Geographic* with its pretty pictures of large fish. I was determined to recover the calm, collected Lara who stayed out of trouble. The one who drank cooking wine, burned vol-au-vents, and had not met Hugh Armstrong-Hamilton and fallen hopelessly and stupidly in love.

Julie's hen-night was held at our flat four nights before the wedding. First, our old schoolfriend Martina entertained us with a selection of dildos she had brought from her place of work. (She was a manageress at an Ann Summers concession and to think, as my mother frequently sighed, that she had been Head Girl of St

Mary's). Then I burned a load of vol-au-vents and we got out of our heads on Chardonnay (OK, so I said I wasn't going to drink but this was a special occasion) while we waited for the entertainment to arrive.

One of Julie's work colleagues had suggested that we get a travelling tarot-card reader in to read all our fortunes, but fearing that this might be just a little serious for some of the guests, I had booked a stripper as well as a contingency plan. He arrived before the tarot-card reader and so I had to secrete him in my bedroom until we were ready for him. As it happened, he went on while I was having my cards read in the hall. From the way Julie was shrieking, I guessed that he must have been quite good.

Madame Francine said she found it quite difficult to concentrate on the spirit world in the face of all that hilarity, but finally something started to come through – just as Julie and the stripper crashed into the hall, en route to the kitchen to 'get something to eat' before he went home.

'What can you see?' I asked excitedly. 'Promise you won't tell me anything really terrible, will you?' She remained silent for a moment which was the worst thing that could have happened after my saying that. I had asked her not to tell me if she saw something bad and so obviously she found that she couldn't tell me anything at all.

'You are looking for love,' she told me finally in her rich Eastern European accent.

'I'm not actually,' I replied indignantly. 'I've decided to give love up for the moment.'

'That's as maybe. But it hasn't given up on you. I see much happiness coming your way,' she sighed. 'And it will come from someone you don't expect to return your feelings.'

'Really? Have I met him yet?'

'Yes, you have met him.'

My mind went into overdrive. I had already met him and I didn't expect him to feel anything for me. It had to be Hugh. It simply had to be. I tried to press her for more details but she said that the giggling coming from the kitchen was making it almost impossible to get through to the other side.

'When will it happen?' I asked her frantically, before her connection with the spirits was lost forever.

Her lips began to form a word but at that moment Julie decided that it was her turn to see into the future. Madame Francine half closed her eyes again so that you could see only the flickering whites. 'Infidelity,' she intoned ominously. 'I see infidelity all around.' (Well, Julie was sitting on Antonio the stripper's lap while the cards were being dealt.)

'Whoops,' Julie giggled. 'That doesn't bode well for a new bride.' Fortunately she was too drunk to take it seriously and then Madame Francine blew all her credibility by saying that Julie was going to have a son within the next year.

'Not until I've been to the Caribbean, I'm not,' said the

girl who had a special database on her computer so that she could check whether or not she had remembered to take her pill.

For the rest of that evening, I played Madame Francine's words over and over in my mind. Antonio said he liked us all so much that he would do another strip for free but I was pretty disinterested. His deeply tanned muscle only reminded me of that evil horse in Wales. Instead I was desperately doing a mental scan of my diary, working out how much time I had left until the wedding and whether one hundred sit-ups a day could make a difference in less than a week.

'Hey, lady. Want to help me get out of these pants?' Antonio was gyrating his pelvis right in front of my face.

'Er, no thank you,' I muttered, utterly mortified. So Martina did the honours instead. With her teeth.

'What's wrong with you?' Julie whispered. 'He's got a cock like a horse.'

'Don't talk to me about horses,' I said.

CHAPTER FOURTEEN

The day of the wedding came. I had not yet seen Hugh for weeks but I knew he was in town. He had had to miss the wedding rehearsal because of pressure of work apparently. Julie was most distressed by his absence, thinking that everything would go wrong, but I assured her that while Hugh didn't know what was good for him as far as women were concerned, he was an intelligent enough man to remember to bring the rings and what he had to do with them. I, on the other hand, quickly forgot which way I was meant to go when it came to signing the register and had to be directed back on course by Andrew's cousin Melissa. Aged five.

Andrew had also invited Simon to the wedding but he sent his apologies, claiming that he had promised to go somewhere with his grandmother. Julie told me that since her operation, Simon's gran wasn't going anywhere and he had obviously just turned down the invitation to spare my blushes. I was silently grateful to him, though of course I told Julie that I didn't blush so easily any more and couldn't have cared less if he did come along.

I had come through that month a changed person, I told her. Self-confident, self-sufficient . . . and by myself every night.

The night before the wedding, Julie and I spent our last evening together in our Battersea bolt-hole accompanied by the other bridesmaids and Julie's mother. She insisted on gushing about Hugh and how lucky I was to be the chief bridesmaid and therefore first in line for his attentions at the reception according to traditional wedding etiquette. Julie had obviously neglected to tell her that I had already been there and come back without staking my flag. So I smiled and nodded and I resisted the urge to ask if Hugh was going to be coming to the wedding alone.

We rose early the next day, at six a.m., to give ourselves at least eight good hours to get ready before the wedding, which was to take place at four. A mobile hairdresser dropped in to stick our hair up into neat French plaits and then spent more than an hour pulling tendrils of hair out again for that fashionably tousled look. Julie kept rushing to the loo to be ill all morning. Her mother assumed it was nerves. I suspected otherwise.

'You OK?' I knocked gently on the bathroom door. Julie was inside, trying to retain some of her guts.

'I think so. The door's not locked, Lara. Come on in.'

I slipped into the bathroom and took up a precarious position on the edge of the bath while Julie continued to lean over the toilet bowl. I did what I could to help her out by holding her veil out of the way while she chucked.

'You've been a great friend to me,' Julie began when she had finished hurling. 'I couldn't have got through this whole thing without you. And I'm really glad you made me change my mind about the dresses. You look great.'

'No problem,' I told her.

'Yeah, well I've got a bit of a problem now,' Julie replied.

'What is it?'

'This isn't nerves, Lara. I think this is morning sickness.'

'Shit? Julie, you're joking?'

Julie sat back on her heels and wiped her mouth clean. 'No, I'm not. I did a test yesterday morning.'

'But you can't be pregnant. You're on the pill.'

'I was also on antibiotics for two weeks a couple of months ago. I completely forgot that they cancel the pill out. Listen, if you get through this bridesmaid thing OK, will you promise me that you'll be a godmother to my first child?'

'Of course, I will. Of course.' I hugged Julie close, not caring too much if I messed up our hair because Tanya the Tonger was still in the other room on hand for emergencies.

'God, this is really the end of an era, isn't it?' Julie said a little sadly. 'Lara and Julie, partners in crime. By this time tomorrow I'll be up the duff and married. You're on your own now, kid.'

'Don't remind me.'

'I promise you I'll call the baby Lara if it's a girl.'

'And if it's a boy?'

'I'll think of something. Larry? How about that?'

'Don't,' I winced. 'Julie, do you think we ought to let your mother know that you're pregnant? Just in case something goes wrong today.'

'No way. She thinks I'm still a virgin.'

'You mean to say you're not?' I said sarcastically.

'Well, I'm wearing the outfit now. Let Mum keep her illusions for today.'

'Best start your first day as a wife with a lie, eh?'

'Not to my husband!!!' she said in mock outrage.

'Have you told him about the baby?'

'No, he might think I've done it to trap him.'

We laughed. Then Julie grabbed me for a hug again, almost knocking me into the bath as she did so. When she pulled away, I noticed that she was crying just a little bit. I grabbed the cotton buds and tried to minimise the damage to her make-up.

'Are you sure you're OK?'

'Yeah, yeah. I'm just crying because I'm so happy. I'm so happy that I'm going to marry Andrew. You can't begin to understand quite how much I love him, Lara.' Or how much he loves you, I thought as I touched up her mascara. 'It's like I always thought it would be. Like a bloody fairy tale. A dream.'

And I was on a countdown to a nightmare.

One of the smaller bridesmaids yelled from the sitting room. 'The best man's here. He's got some of the corsets. We sent too many over to the groom's house.'

'Corsets?' I asked.

'I think she means "corsage".'

I let the junior bridesmaid sort the flowers out, though it was probably my job. When I heard the door slam behind the visitor, I stood on the toilet seat to peer out through the bathroom window. Hugh was just getting into a car, driven by the groom of course. He looked stunning. Immaculate in his morning suit. The last time I'd seen him he had been dripping blood down the front of his trousers after Tim had punched him in the nose. I told Julie what I was thinking.

'Well, if he gives you any trouble today, he'll have another bloody nose. Best man or no best man.'

'Thanks.'

'Besides, I think you'll forget all about Hugh Armstrong--Hamilton when you meet Andrew's cousin James. He's very single. Just your type.'

'Julie,' I hissed. 'Please. Not today.'

'How long have we got?' someone in the sitting room asked.

'Fifteen minutes before the car comes for the brides-maids and the bride's mum. Then another ten minutes for the bride's car.'

Julie took a deep breath and exhaled so that her fringe blew up out of her eyes. 'When he says "any just impediment",' she asked me seriously, 'you do promise not to bring up that squaddie from Brighton, don't you?'

*   *   *

So at ten minutes past four, traditionally late, Julie walked down the aisle towards holy bondage with Andrew. I swear she couldn't have been more nervous than I was as we took those few small steps through the church. She bore her latest secret serenely as she played the virginal bride. I just tried to concentrate on keeping her train from beneath my feet. And I also tried not to scan every pew in that damn church for Caroline Lauder.

Hugh didn't even turn around when Julie reached the altar. I took her bouquet and stepped aside as I had done at the rehearsal, repeating over and over in my mind 'I must turn to the left. I must turn to the left.'

It was as I was turning to the left that I caught sight of her. In the second row of the congregation on Andrew's side, sitting right behind Andrew's mother. Her china-doll face was obscured by the brim of a neat felt hat but she was instantly recognisable none the less. She wore a woollen suit almost the same colour as my dress. I was so distracted by the sight of her that I forgot to look where I was going and got the heel of my shoe caught up in the vast embroidered silk train of Julie's fabulous gown.

RRR-Rip.

The vicar cut short his opening speech and all the congregation focused in horror on the back of Julie's dress. She turned around slowly to see her fabulous skirt hanging away from the rest of the dress at the waist, revealing the exotic French knickers and suspender set that only her new husband was intended to see. I froze where I was standing, my foot still guiltily pinning down the train.

First a gasp of horror spread quickly through the assembled guests, then there was silence as almost everyone suppressed the natural urge to laugh. Julie was still looking at her ruined dress, open-mouthed with surprise. I took my foot off the train slowly. She tried desperately to pull the skirt back up to cover her behind. I couldn't help her. I was mortified into a statue. Instead Andrew and Hugh bustled around behind her and I was sure that Hugh shot me a look that said 'That's just typical of you. You clutz.'

I gazed down the church towards the doors. They seemed to be so far away. Though the church was huge and now echoing with laughter, suddenly there seemed to be not enough air. I could barely breathe or suppress my rising panic. Thrusting the bouquet back into Julie's hands, I made a dash for the outside world. The run to those doors seemed to take forever and the laughter was like gunshots in my ears as I ran. But finally, I made it out of there and I slumped, red-faced and ready to die, on the wall that surrounded the graveyard. I knew I had ruined Julie's day and worse, I had made a fool of myself, once again, in front of Caroline Lauder. The only consolation was that my mother had missed the scene because she and my father were on a senior citizens' bargain break in Majorca.

The service obviously went ahead, because no one came outside to find out what had become of me. I hid behind a tombstone as I watched the bridal party stream out of the church into the weak December sunshine for the photographs. Julie's dress had been pinned together with the fastener from somebody's kilt. She scanned the graveyard while the photographer tried to shuffle the group into some kind of order. I knew she was looking for me but I didn't dare show my face.

I slunk out of my hiding place only as the bride and groom finally headed off for the reception in a sparkling limousine. The best man and his consort had followed them in the car that was reserved for the bridesmaids. Julie's mother was the first to collar me when she spotted me trying to make my escape.

'What happened to you?' she asked. 'What did you think you were doing running off like that? Julie's ever so upset that you won't be in the pictures.'

'I'm sure she doesn't want to have to remember the girl who ruined her wedding day every time she looks at her photo album.'

Mrs Whitgift looked at me pitifully. 'You didn't ruin her day, love. That dress wasn't sewn together properly anyway. I told her she should have let me do it instead of buying it straight from the shop. But would she listen? Would she bingo! Always been headstrong that girl. It wasn't your fault that dress fell apart. Maybe she'll listen to her mother next time. Now, you'd better tidy yourself up a bit and come with us to the reception.'

'Actually, I was thinking I might go straight back to the

flat. I don't think I can stand the embarrassment of the reception.'

'Nonsense, Lara. You're Julie's chief bridesmaid, even if you did manage to miss the ceremony. And if you go home now, you'll mess up the seating plan.'

So I reluctantly folded myself and my stupid dress into Mr Whitgift's Mini Metro. I'd mess up the seating plan? I could think of at least two people who wouldn't care. If I wasn't there, then Hugh would be able to sit next to the divine Caroline while he delivered his devastatingly witty speech.

When we arrived at the hotel where the reception was being held, the bridal party were standing outside, posing for a last shot while the manager of the hotel flapped about like a turkey two days before Christmas, instructing everyone that no confetti was to be thrown on to the flowerbeds. Julie raised her eyebrows when she saw me and beckoned me over. Hugh handed me a box of confetti.

'Mind you don't have someone's eye out with that,' he said as he did so.

They were not the first words I had dreamed of him uttering when I imagined our meeting after all this time apart. Not, 'Lara, you look wonderful'. Not even 'How have you been since I broke your heart?' I looked resolutely ahead and threw my confetti with everyone else. Then I took my place in the bridal party line-up and prepared to be kissed by dozens of people I didn't know as they filed into the hotel to take their places at the dining tables.

CHAPTER FIFTEEN

The reception seemed interminable. Though I had to sit next to Hugh in my capacity as chief bridesmaid, he barely talked to me, preferring instead to confer his attentions on Andrew's fourteen-year-old cousin, Tiffany, who had stepped into the breech when I fled the church in embarrassment. She gazed into Hugh's eyes as though he were the most perfect specimen of man ever to walk the earth. I wanted to warn her about the evils of the opposite sex before it was too late but with her armpit-long legs and her glossy blonde hair, she probably wasn't going to grow up to have the problems I had been faced with since adolescence anyway.

Soon it was time for the speeches. Andrew and Julie's father made the traditional cracks about gaining a ball and chain and not losing a daughter respectively. And then it was Hugh's turn. Hugh stood up and ruffled a huge sheaf of paper which he had somehow secreted in his jacket pocket. The guests looked aghast at the thought of a speech so long. But then Hugh tossed all the paper up into the air except for one densely scribbled-upon sheet. The crowd laughed with relief, though I reckoned he still had a good fifteen minutes' worth on that one page.

While he spoke, I took the opportunity to scan the room for Caroline. She was sitting two tables away from the top table with a group of people I didn't recognise. She had taken off her hat so that I could see just how perfect her hair was beneath. Her freshly reapplied lipstick shone prettily in the candlelight. I remembered Hugh's comment in the car as we drove to Wales. About how pretty I had looked in the candlelight at La Traviata. But that was back in the days when I still had hopes that I would one day be sitting in Julie's place. Caroline grinned throughout Hugh's speech and even clapped when he made an especially good joke. She was the picture of a devoted girlfriend. She looked so very much in love.

'And thanks of course are due to Lara . . .'

I looked up at Hugh at the mention of my name, his eyes were glittering wickedly. 'For livening up what might otherwise have been a very dull service with her impression of Bucks Fizz's winning performance at the Eurovision Song Contest.'

A tidal wave of laughter and applause rushed around the room. I reached out to take a sip of champagne to calm myself down until the moment passed and managed as I did so to spill it all over my front. The laughter seemed to get louder and louder until I thought my eardrums were going to burst. There were two options: run or hide. I figured that I'd already run once that day, so I slid down on my seat until I was beneath the tablecloth. The guests continued to roar because they thought I was just trying to be funny. But once I was underneath that tablecloth, I burst into hot angry tears and I didn't come back up again until the attention had been diverted from me by the cutting of the cake.

After dinner, the banqueting hall was cleared for the wedding disco. Julie summoned me up to her room to help her freshen herself up for the next flood of guests to arrive. It was the first time I had had the opportunity to talk to her since stepping on her dress in the church. I felt horribly guilty as I made sure that the safety pins holding the skirt to the bodice were still fastened tight.

'I'm really sorry,' I muttered. 'I just can't believe how clumsy I was. I ruined your big day, didn't I?'

Julie turned to face me as fast as her vast skirts would allow.

'You must really hate me now,' I mumbled.

'Lara, don't be stupid,' Julie said matter-of-factly. 'You didn't ruin the day. In fact, you probably made it. Weddings are always stupidly tense but your accident with my skirt, well, it made everyone laugh and it gave people something to talk about while they waited for the photographs to be taken. I just wish that you'd been in them.'

'I'm sorry. I couldn't face everybody after that disaster. Especially not Hugh . . .'

'Hmmm. Well, it's me who should be sorry about him. I had no idea that Andrew had said Hugh could bring her

211

along.' She spat 'her' out. 'And in that ridiculous hat? Did you see it? She was trying to upstage me, I swear. So it was a good job that you upstaged everyone. And spilling your champagne down your front when Hugh made that comment during his speech! That was so funny. You're such a good sport, Lara.'

'No. I'm just clumsy.'

Julie laughed as though she didn't believe me. 'Listen, we'd better go back downstairs again now. You've got just one more duty, I'm afraid. You'll have to dance with Hugh to get the other guests going.' I groaned. 'It won't take long. And I'm sure Caroline will cut in as soon as politely possible. Hey, Lara, don't look so pissed off. You were like that at my engagement party. After tonight you'll never have to see Hugh or Caroline Lauder again. And I promise that it'll be you I'm going to throw my bouquet to.'

'Great. I probably won't be able to catch it.'

CHAPTER SIXTEEN

Julie and Andrew took to the dance-floor first. Andrew had never been what you could call fleet of foot and I was strangely relieved to see him make almost as much of a mess of the hem of Julie's skirt as I had. As the first song ended and the assembled guests clapped the happy couple through a lap of honour, I saw Hugh approach me from the corner of my eye. I waited until he was right upon me before I acknowledged his presence. Then I tried to smile as though I was pleased to be asked to dance. Thrilled even.

'How have you been?' he asked as he held me uncomfortably close and we whirled across the floor. Hugh was an expert at dancing of course. 'I'm sorry I haven't seen you since that débâcle in Wales. I had a hell of a time getting back to London in time for work the next day, I can tell you.'

'I'm sorry,' I told him. But I wasn't. 'So,' I ventured. 'Things worked out then? Between you and Caroline?'

Hugh made a noncommittal noise. 'Yes. Well, within

reason. She's had a bit of trouble since that night. With Tim. He just doesn't seem to be able to accept that things between them are over.'

Now that didn't surprise me. Even after the bonfire at Cecilia's house.

'He just keeps pestering her. In fact, she's going to see him one last time tomorrow, while she's in London, in an attempt to persuade him to give up the fight.'

'I always liked Tim,' I said controversially. 'He seemed like a decent bloke to me.'

'Yes, but decency doesn't get you any place these days.'

'No. Obviously not.'

We had been around the dance-floor three times now and amazingly Caroline still hadn't cut in though the floor was beginning to fill up with a cross-section of generations all doing a variation on the waltz. Or rather a waltz-like shuffle.

'You can dance with Caroline now, if you like,' I told Hugh to save myself the humiliation of being usurped once again.

Hugh looked over my shoulder. I knew that he was scanning the room for her, just as I had been. 'No.' He obviously hadn't spotted her. 'I'd like to dance with you for a little longer if that's OK with you. Or have you got your eye on someone you'd like to sweep you off your feet?'

I laughed bitterly. No, I'm in his arms already, I thought sadly.

'You're a wonderful dancer, Lara,' he murmured appreciatively as the tempo speeded up.

'Yes, I had lessons.'

'Instead of horse riding, eh?'

I frowned into his shoulder. Why did he have to bring that up? Why couldn't he just make irrelevant small talk and keep all references to our disastrous encounter out of it. 'I'll never forget the way you looked when you came back from that hack. You were so red-faced. You even had a bit of straw sticking out of your hair.'

And do you remember what we did next? I wanted to ask him. Do you remember the walk to the top of the hill and the kiss we shared as we looked down on Caroline's farmhouse? But before I could do anything so obviously champagne-fuelled and silly, we were interrupted by a tap on Hugh's shoulder.

'Mind if I cut in, mate?'

'Not at all.' Hugh stepped back immediately.

Another set of arms wrapped themselves around my body and another crotch pressed itself far too closely against my skirt.

'You look gorgeous in that dress, sweetheart. I'm the groom's uncle. Uncle Randy.'

'I'm Lara,' I told him politely, as I watched Hugh disappear again.

'Yes, I know who you are, love. I've been asking Julie about you.'

I glanced across the floor to see her giving me the thumbs up.

'Did she tell you that I'm a lesbian?' I tried.

'Ha ha, very funny that.' He pressed his pelvis closer against mine and much to my horror, the music began to slow down.

I briefly escaped the attentions of Andrew's Uncle Randy (his real name and very descriptive it was too) by pretending that I was desperate for the loo. Unfortunately, he offered to wait for me to come back so I told him I'd meet him by the buffet. Of course I had no intention of reappearing before he got bored.

As I walked out into the lobby, I could hear shouting in reception. I didn't bat an eyelid at first because it's the kind of thing that happens at weddings, isn't it? People do start shouting once the champagne has run out and the groom's Auntie Mary has run off with an usher from the bride's side. But on my way back from the ladies', a visit which lasted at least ten minutes to give Randy the hint, I was surprised to find that the unfortunate fracas was still in full swing. The hotel staff were obviously trying to eject somebody and this time I couldn't resist getting a closer look on the pretence that I might be able to help. It was then that I noticed Caroline, standing by the reception desk with her fist stuffed into her mouth as if she was about to scream.

And the man that the receptionist was trying to eject was Tim. Her ex-fiancé Tim!

'Let me in,' he shouted. 'I just want to speak to her. Her, over there.' He jabbed a finger in Caroline's direction. 'That woman.' Caroline was obviously distressed but remained sickeningly glamorous with it.

SECOND PRIZE

'She's asked us not to let you into the hotel, Sir, and as one of our guests, I'm afraid that her wishes must take priority over yours.'

'Just let me talk to her. You've got to understand. We were going to get married today too. Me and her. If she hadn't run off with that bastard first.'

Caroline covered her ears.

'That bloody rich bastard. He doesn't love her. He just wants whatever someone else has. Just let me talk to her. I've got to stop her from doing something stupid like marrying him.'

The hotel staff had stopped manhandling Tim now and he was standing patiently on the hotel steps while they waited for Caroline to respond to his accusations. She was sniffling. There was no saving her mascara, which started to run down her cheeks like lines drawn on wallpaper by a bad toddler with a crayon.

'Caroline, please,' Tim pleaded. 'Just give me one more chance to talk it over. If you're really convinced that Hugh loves you after that, I promise that I'll never come anywhere near you again.'

The hotel staff looked to Tim, then to Caroline again. I could see that they were firmly on his side. He seemed such a nice chap and it was so romantic wasn't it? Bursting into a wedding reception like that? If only the feckless girl in question had been the bride herself, then their night would have been complete.

'Madam?' asked the manager.

Caroline bit her lip dramatically.

217

'Please.' Tim dropped to his knees in front of her.

'Oh OK, let him in. Let him in. But I want someone to stay outside the door of my room in case he tries anything funny.'

Tim stepped inside. The doorman gave him a friendly punch on the arm. The receptionist looked delighted. Tim looked slightly unsure. He was a lot thinner than when I had last seen him. His cheeks stuck out like razor blades. His eyes were just dark hollows now. Oh, if only someone had loved me like that, I thought. Loved me enough to give up cheeseburgers and kebabs until I promised him my undying affection. I watched from a distance as Caroline and Tim retreated to the room that she was doubtlessly sharing with Hugh and much as I disliked her, I liked Tim enough to think it was my duty to make sure that Hugh was kept out of the way until Tim had given it one last try.

Leaving the lobby straight away, I danced up to Hugh where he was jigging near the disc-jockey with one of the smaller bridesmaids on each arm.

'Having a good time, Lara?' he asked.

I nodded.

'Don't suppose you've seen Caroline on your travels?'

I shook my head.

'I can't think where she could have gone to. I haven't seen her in hours. Perhaps she's in her room, nursing an early hangover. She was really necking that champagne earlier on.'

'She'll be OK,' I reassured him.

'Well, you're probably right but I suppose I'd better go and check anyway. There'll be hell to pay if she has got a headache and I don't make sure that she's got everything she needs to get rid of it.' That sounded about right for the prima donna that she was.

'No, Hugh.' I took his hands and kept him firmly on the dance-floor. 'Leave her alone. She'll be fine. Honestly. And if she needs an aspirin there's always room service.'

'Yes, for most people that would be comfort enough. But you don't know Caroline like I do, Lara. She needs very personal attention. Believe me.'

And two thanksgiving services on a Sunday, I thought. I suddenly realised that my charms were not going to be enough to keep Hugh from her side. Perhaps I should try to be a little more physical. I crushed myself up against him and wrapped my arms around his waist. He looked very surprised. 'Lara, what have you been drinking?' He tried to gently prise me away from his chest.

'Champagne mostly. But I just thought it would be nice to get close to you. Shall we have just one more dance? We probably won't meet again for a very long, long time.'

'I've got to see if Caroline is OK,' he insisted. He broke away from me easily when he applied just a little force.

'No, don't,' I grabbed his arm and pulled him back into the fray. 'Stay with me.'

'Lara. I've got to go.'

'Hugh, you mustn't.'

We started a tug-of-war with his arm acting as the

rope. There was no way that Tim would have finished presenting his case to Caroline yet. I had to keep Hugh on the dance-floor until it was safe for him to go upstairs. I was tugging him back so hard that I didn't notice the amused circle forming around us. I was hanging on like a bulldog. Hugh only got away because his jacket sleeve ripped clean off.

Hugh looked at the severed arm of his morning suit with a mixture of amusement and disdain. 'Making a bit of a habit of this clothes ripping thing aren't you?' he snarled, as he tried to pull the sleeve back up to his shoulder. 'Do you have any idea how much this jacket cost? It's Yves St Bloody Laurent. I'll be sending you the bill, of course, you clumsy little fool.'

Hugh stormed off in the direction of the reception. He seemed far angrier than someone whose only problem was a ripped sleeve. Perhaps something had clicked in his brain and he'd realised that I was protecting someone from something and wasn't just desperate for his body. I skittered after him in my high heels, still pleading with him all the way up the stairs to Caroline's room.

'Let's go and get some coffee,' I begged. 'We can ask the people in reception to make it for us. We could sit in the public lounge. We haven't really talked in such a long while.'

'Lara.' He flicked me off his arm. 'Go back downstairs, will you?'

'I want to get to know you better,' I whined. But it

was too late. He had spotted the unarmed guard of the night-porter outside Caroline's door.

'Is my girlfriend in there?' he asked the man. 'What is going on?'

The night-porter blanched. He had been listening out for funny business exactly as Caroline had requested and he knew only too well what funny business was going on now.

'Let me in there,' Hugh rattled the door handle. 'Caroline, are you in there? Open the door at once.' But she didn't move quickly enough. Within seconds, Hugh had the door off its hinges. We stood back as the dust settled. Tim must have presented his case very well indeed, since Caroline was beneath him and smiling on the bed.

The night-porter and I were terrified. We stepped back against the wall. There seemed to be no way that this little scene couldn't end in bloodshed.

'Hugh! No!' Caroline was shrieking. 'Stop him!!!! Stop him before he does something violent.'

But Hugh stepped silently into the room and silently gathered up his own clothes as though Caroline and Tim weren't even there. 'Make sure that this room gets put on her credit card,' was all that he told the night-porter, then he walked back down into the lobby, dignified to the last.

I caught up with him in reception just as he was asking the receptionist about the possibility of being accommodated elsewhere. But the hotel was fully booked. As Julie had often told me, her wedding was to be the wedding of the century and thus everyone was staying overnight at the hotel from the bridal couple to the maiden aunts.

'I'm sorry, Sir.' The receptionist could offer no solution.

'I've got twin beds in my room,' I ventured, tugging on his intact sleeve. 'You could stay in there if you like.'

Hugh looked at me sadly. He had dropped a sock on the floor and I bent to pick it up. All those thoughts of bloody revenge I had had while driving back from Wales seemed pretty stupid now. I could see that Caroline had hurt Hugh far more than he had hurt me. She couldn't have caused much more damage if she had stuck a knife straight through his heart.

'Thanks, Lara,' he said in a whisper. I lent him my room key and went back into the dying embers of the disco to give him some space while he sorted himself out.

It had reached that point in the evening where Julie was ripping off her suspenders and throwing them off the stage to the people waiting below. When she saw me, she waved like crazy to attract my attention. Then she grabbed the mike off the DJ and said, 'Now I'm going to throw my bouquet.' I reached up half-heartedly as the roses and ribbons sailed towards me through the sky. Julie was a good aim but unfortunately, I'm not such a good catcher. I missed it the first time and had to pick it up off the floor. Luckily, Andrew's sister informed me that still counted as far as the tradition goes.

SECOND PRIZE

By this time, news of the débâcle upstairs had filtered down to the wedding party via the hotel staff. Andrew threatened to punch Tim's face in for being such a cad until Julie reminded him that he hadn't been that chivalrous when Hugh was a cad to me. No one knew where Hugh had gone. I thought that for his own sake, I would keep my mouth shut. The last thing he needed was a string of 'well-wishers' wanting to see the wreck of the best man.

When the hotel staff started to sweep up around us, I shuffled back to my room, sharing my concerns about Hugh's whereabouts with Andrew's mother as we passed in the corridor but not letting on what I knew.

I opened the door to my room as quietly as I could. Not even a creak. Inside, it was dark but I could just about make out the shadow of Hugh on the far bed silhouetted by the floodlights in the hotel garden. He was snoring. At least he hadn't topped himself.

I crept across the room into the en-suite bathroom. But when I went to turn on the light, of course I discovered that it was connected to a loudly whirring fan. I switched it off again as quickly as I could but it was too late. Hugh had already woken up.

'Caroline? Is that you?'

'No,' I said. 'It's Lara.'

'Oh.' He didn't sound too impressed. 'What are you doing in here?'

'It's my room.'

'Shit.' The penny dropped. 'Of course it is. Shit, shit, shit.' He shouted so loudly that the last shit shook the flimsy wardrobe doors.

'Careful,' I whispered. 'My flatmate's, new mother-in-law is on the other side of that wall. If you want to shit, you'll have to go in the bathroom and turn on the fan. Then she won't be able to hear you.'

'Sorry.' Hugh sat up in bed and clutched at his head. 'Christ, my head hurts,' he moaned. 'What's been going on? Please tell me I'm going to wake up in a minute and find out that today has just been a dream.'

'I'm afraid not,' I said. 'And there'll be pictures to prove it.'

That started him off. 'Yeah, pictures of me and Caroline playing the happy couple before he turned up. I should have known that she was encouraging him.' Hugh thumped the bedside table. 'No bloke in his right mind would have clung on for as long as he did without some sort of encouragement.'

'You did. Andrew told me that you carried a torch for Caroline for three years.'

'That was different. God, I ought to go round to that room right now and knock his bloody head off. If only I wasn't seeing double. I'll probably knock off the wrong one and end up with my fist in the wall.'

'You know what I always say. Things will look better in the morning.'

'No, they won't.'

'Oh well. Your head will feel better in the morning at

least.' I perched on the side of my bed and started to undo my complicated strappy shoes.

'What are you doing?' Hugh asked.

'I'm getting ready for bed.'

'You're sleeping in here too?'

'Yes. Of course I am. As I said, it is my room.'

'Oh, I'm sorry,' Hugh sighed. 'I forgot. It's just that . . . what if Caroline finds out that I spent the night with you?'

'She's hardly in a position to complain, is she?' I protested.

'She was very jealous of you when I brought you down to Wales, you know.'

'Well, she hardly need have been jealous then. You chucked me after our second shag.'

'Yes, but I spoke very highly of you to her first.'

'That is a comfort,' I said sarcastically.

'She thought that you and I had a chemistry between us. That's why she spilt the coffee on you. Remember?'

'How could I forget? I still bear the scars.'

'If she knew I was spending the night with you she would go up the wall with jealousy. There's no way she would believe that it could all be totally innocent.'

'Well, it is,' I said flatly and not without disappointment as I slipped under the sheets with my bridesmaid's dress still on. I folded my hands over the top of the covers like a medieval statue on a tombstone and closed my eyes. I was beginning to regret my act of altruism already. I should have known that he would go on about Caroline all night long.

'I can't believe I didn't see it coming,' he moaned.

'Look, Hugh,' I was unusually snappy. 'I know that you've had a very nasty shock but I have had a long day on my feet and right now I would really like to get some sleep. If you want to know the truth, I knew that Caroline wouldn't be any good for you from the moment I met her. She wants everyone to love her and goes after the ones that get away with a vengeance. She was always going to go back to Tim. If not now, the moment he found someone to replace her. It's exactly what she did with you. She thought that you might fall for me and so she stepped in to make sure that you didn't. She doesn't care about you or Tim, she just can't stand the fact that one day you might meet someone you like more than her. There. I've said what I wanted to say. Goodnight.'

Seconds later, the reading light above Hugh's bed flicked on and he stared across at me. I pulled the sheets up defensively.

'I'm sorry, Lara. I've been so selfish. Of course you must hate Caroline after all that business down in Wales. If it's any consolation, if Caroline hadn't said yes to me that night, I would have liked to make a go of something with you.'

'What?' I spat the word at him. 'You would have made a go of things with me if Caroline hadn't wanted you? No, that isn't a consolation, you arrogant sod. It's never a consolation to know how narrowly you missed first prize.

SECOND PRIZE

Not that I would have wanted you if you'd crawled back to me on bare knees across a field of hot gravel. You might think I'm desperate but I'll have you know that I can pick and choose too. And a lot of men would pick me over Caroline Lauder any day of the week. At least I'm a proper woman, not like some lipstick picture drawn on the front of an ironing board. I read only last week that men who like small tits are latent homosexuals anyway.'

Hugh looked at me aghast. I probably should have let it end there but I was just getting into my stride and I was nowhere near finished with him.

'It was a real eye-opener spending that weekend in Wales with you and your friends. They've got everything they need. Money, money and more money. And they're all so bored with their privileged lifestyles that they have to keep themselves occupied by messing other people's lives up. You're a bunch of sad, incestuous posh twits. I'd never share a man with my best friend.' (That wasn't strictly true but Julie and I hadn't been aware that we were sharing Peter Hamilton until we both turned up to meet him from his Saturday job at WH Smith's one afternoon. And that was when we were in the sixth form.)

'That's why the aristocracy have got such funny faces,' I continued vehemently. 'You're all inbred. No chins and big noses. And that's just the girls. Hugh Armstrong-Hamilton, I wouldn't want you if you were the last man on this earth and if you're so afraid of Caroline Lauder thinking otherwise, though I assure you she's probably not thinking of you at all right now, I'd be very happy to sign an affidavit to prove it.'

'Have you finished?'

'I think so.' I gathered up my bedclothes and carried them through into the bathroom. 'Now, I'm going to sleep in the bath so that I don't have to listen to your snoring.'

'Do I snore?' Hugh cried plaintively as I locked the bathroom door shut.

'Yes,' I shouted. 'Like a pig.'

The next morning, when I emerged from the bathroom, aching like mad from spending the night in the bath, Hugh had already gone. Not even a note to say thank you for sharing the room, though under the circumstances I suppose I shouldn't have expected that. I took off my bridesmaid's dress, of which I was now becoming quite fond, and packed my bags in readiness to leave. As I was checking out, Andrew was leaning against the reception desk looking hollow-eyed from lack of sleep. He told me that Julie was just saying goodbye to her parents before they embarked on their three-week-long honeymoon in the Maldives.

'Did you . . . er, did you . . . ?' I began.

'See Hugh this morning?' Andrew finished the sentence for me. 'Yes, I did. I saw him and Caroline in the car park.'

'Were they arguing?'

'I couldn't hear what they were saying from where I was standing, but it looked as though they were being pretty civil actually.'

'I thought as much.' Though I couldn't remember much of what I'd said to Hugh I knew I'd said some pretty mean stuff but now I didn't feel quite so bad. What was it that Caroline had? To have fully-grown men fighting over her like boys in the fifth form? Laying one guy one night and another the next as if it was as uncomplicated as plain snogging between teenagers. I guessed I'd never know since now that Julie's wedding was over, I would never see Hugh again.

'Do you think they'll stay together after last night?' I asked.

Andrew shrugged. 'Don't ask me about relationships. I don't understand what makes two people stay together at all.'

'What? Not even you and Julie.'

'Yeah, well.' Andrew straightened himself up. 'That's easy. What we've got is love.'

Julie floated down the stairs then, looking resplendent in her eggshell-blue going-away outfit. 'Ready, Mr Tolson?' she asked.

'Ready, Mrs Tolson,' he replied.

Julie leant forward to kiss me goodbye. As she did, she whispered, 'Christ, this waistband is getting tight.' Then the waiting taxi honked its horn from the car park and they disappeared on their drive to Heathrow.

CHAPTER SEVENTEEN

S o, as Julie had said as we sat on the floor in the bath-room, we had reached the end of an era. Fortunately, she had very generously paid her share of the rent on the Battersea flat for two months after her wedding so I didn't have to think about moving out straight away while I got used to the new hole in my social life.

After the trauma of sharing with girls who never did the washing-up all through college, I had decided that the best bet would be to look for a new place rather than a new flatmate. So in the first instance I trawled the local estate agents, becoming increasingly despondent as they showed me around places which would cost me most of my take-home pay but which would not give me enough room or light to keep some of my favourite pot-plants.

I changed my mind about moving and decided that I would try to look for a housemate again after a letting agent tried to persuade me that a bedsit with a shower and toilet right in the middle of the single room would provide great humidity for my ferns. It suddenly became very clear that the lovely flat Julie and I had shared was well worth putting up with a nightmare housemate for.

Besides which, they didn't necessarily have to be a nightmare, did they? I put an ad in the local newspaper and got fifteen interested calls on the first day. I made a list of the people who sounded nice and made appointments for them to visit that evening at twenty-minute intervals. I was very hopeful, I told my mother when she called to see how I was getting on, that I wouldn't even have to run the advert again. Some of these people sounded lovely. I was sure I would be spoilt for choice.

Of course, it was a different matter altogether when they actually turned up at the flat. Later that night I put a line through everyone on my list who had turned out to have dodgy facial hair, an unhealthy interest in serial killers or a job in accountancy. That left me with one girl, who admitted to having a pet rat, and another who was a bit too much of a Sloane for my taste. But since I had heard that rats don't have bladders and therefore pee indiscriminately the whole time I plumped for the Sloane and I called her to let her know that she could move in straight away. She thanked me very nicely but said that since visiting my place the night before she had decided to move in with her boyfriend after all.

Of course. She'd moved in with her boyfriend! What a surprise! It was what everyone my age seemed to be doing. Cohabiting. Even Joe at work had suddenly sprung a mystery woman upon us at the Christmas party. By Twelfth Night, they were sharing his bijou place in

Clapham South and, no doubt, his Saturday spot by the fishing pond.

The end of the second month crept inexorably closer. I placed my advert in the paper three more times but the quality of applicants just got worse and worse and worse. The most hopeful candidate turned out to be a rock drummer with his very own drum kit. I also turned down a born-again Christian with an anti-abortion handbag and an interesting actuary who was doing OK until he told me about his ingrowing toenails over tea and biscuits.

I was getting pretty desperate. I called Julie on the off-chance that after a month of married life she might have decided that she wanted to keep on a pied-à-terre now that she had moved out to Croydon. She couldn't afford to of course. Had I seen the price of baby buggies, she asked? But, she added comfortingly, she thought Andrew might know someone who was looking for a room.

'You must be joking?' I said, when she told me who that someone was. He had been staying with them since the lease on his flat ran out. 'Simon Mellons? No way, Julie. Absolutely no way. Besides I'm not sure he'd want to live with me anyway after that disastrous date we had.'

'Andrew's already asked him and he says it's a great idea as long as it's OK with you. Which it will be of course, since you don't have much choice,' she added smugly. 'Besides, you can use the fact that your night together was a romantic wash-out to your advantage,

Laz. At least you know he won't bother to come creeping into your room in the middle of the night.'

'I don't know,' I whined. 'I really wanted a girl. Boys are so smelly. They leave their trainers on the sofa and belch and fart all over the place and never bother to clean their teeth.'

'You can train them out of all those habits.'

'But why should I have to? Why can't I live with someone who is already house-trained?'

'You could always call back that actuary with the ingrowing toenails. Or what about that nice religious girl? She'll ban you from having men in the house altogether.'

'Yeah,' I snorted. 'And what a difference to my scintillating love life that would make.'

'Do you want me to tell him he can move in or not?' Julie persisted.

I thought about the extra three hundred or so pounds I would have to find every month otherwise. I hadn't done much overtime lately.

'OK,' I said grudgingly. 'But we'll have to have a trial period.'

'He says exactly the same.'

The cheek of it, I fumed, as I enjoyed my last night alone in the flat. He was moving into my space and yet he wanted a trial period? I already regretted having given in to Julie but I knew at this late stage there was little else I could do. At least I knew what Simon's hobbies were. So there would be no nasty surprises there. But did I really want to live with someone who had once groped my tits and knew that I didn't shave my bikini line? I imagined hanging out my intimate washing and seeing him study it surreptitiously, knowing exactly how I filled out that bra.

I called Julie to tell her that it was all off.

'I was just going to call you,' she trilled before I could get the words out. 'Simon's back already. We've loaded his stuff into the cars and we're going to drive round right now.'

'What?'

'Yes, right now. He says he can't wait to get shot of us love birds. It should only take us about half an hour to get to you now that the traffic's died down.'

Julie hung up before I could protest. I slumped on to the sofa and began to chew my knuckles. The only thing I could do now was make the trial period so horrendous that he simply had to leave. I would start by not bothering to wash up the collection of dirty plates I had been saving all that week.

Ring. Ring.

I leapt across to the phone, praying that Simon had had a change of heart and that Julie was calling to let me down gently. But it wasn't Julie. She was still en route. And suddenly it appeared that she wasn't the only visitor I was going to have that night.

'Who is it?' I asked irritably.

'Don't you recognise my voice?'

Amazingly, I hadn't at first. But after a nano-second I

realised that it was Hugh Armstrong-Hamilton. I swallowed my rising panic and said, 'Of course. How are you?' in a remarkably level voice.

'I'm fine. And you?'

'Fine, fine. Just awaiting Armageddon again.'

'What?'

'I've got a new housemate moving in tonight.'

'Of course, Simon Mellons.' Christ, the City grapevine was effective. 'But why do you sound so worried about it?' Hugh continued. 'I hear that you two get on very well.'

'Not in that sense,' I told him hastily. 'Anyway, what can I do for you?'

'Actually, I was just phoning to say "thank you" for that night at Andrew and Julie's wedding. I know it's a bit late for me to be calling to say all this but I'm sure you'll understand that I wasn't exactly seeing things rationally when we were last together.'

'What do you want to thank me for? I was completely horrible to you.'

'Well, I can't say it didn't hurt at the time, but in retrospect I can see that everything you said about me and Caroline was true. I am a snob. She is a snob. And our whole snobby relationship was a disaster.'

'Was?'

'Was.'

Why was it, I wondered, that Hugh always seemed to know everything about me and yet Andrew had carefully neglected to mention that Hugh and Caroline had split up over the Tim-thing after all.

'When?' I asked, trying to sound as if I wasn't actually that interested.

'Just about a week ago, believe it or not.'

Wow, so he had given her quite a chance after her *faux pas*. Almost a month and a half.

'Who?' I asked.

'Mutual, I suppose.'

Not quite as good as him having chucked her but infinitely better than vice versa.

'So, it's over then?' I said banally.

'Dead as a dead thing.'

'You must be very upset.'

'I'm not doing too badly considering. Listen, I was wondering whether I could pop round and see you tonight. I'm in the vicinity.'

Damn, I thought. Why couldn't he have turned up last night? Julie, Andrew and Simon would be arriving any minute and I would be expected to help lug boxes up the stairs.

'Things are going to get busy here pretty soon,' I told him sadly. 'As I said, Simon's moving in tonight.'

'I'll give him a hand. Please can I come round?'

'Oh, I don't know.' I looked at my reflection in the tiny mirror on the mantelpiece. I had been planning to wash my hair all evening but never quite got round to it. When Hugh saw me again I wanted him to find me looking like a goddess not the *Sesame Street* grouch. On the other hand my copious body odour and unshaven armpits might prevent me from doing anything too stupid if Hugh was as gorgeous as I remembered. 'Oh, all right then,' I conceded. 'But you'll have to take me as I am.'

'I wouldn't have you any other way.'

The old charmer, I thought, as he put down the phone and the doorbell rang almost simultaneously. Julie and Simon must have driven like Damon Hill and Schumacher. But it wasn't them. It was Hugh.

'How?' I gasped, frantically smoothing down my hair.

'I called from just over there,' he said, pointing to the telephone box which stood right opposite my block. He must have been pretty sure that I'd give in. I smiled what I hoped was a wry smile and stood aside to let him in.

'It's changed a bit in here,' he commented as I ushered him into the sitting room.

'Yes, I got rid of those terrible Monet reproductions as soon as Julie went down the aisle. And now I'm just waiting for everything to change again.'

'You look very well,' he said, taking my hands and looking so deeply into my eyes that I couldn't help but blush. 'Radiant, in fact.'

'Thank you. So do you.' I wriggled my sweating hands free.

Damn, damn, damn, I thought as I put on the kettle. He was just as lovely as I remembered, despite his broken heart. He certainly seemed to have taken splitting up with Caroline better than Tim had. And though the sensible part of my brain reminded me that I didn't want to do anything with him, I began to wish that I had shaved my armpits so that I could turn him down elegantly if I got the chance.

'So,' I said, returning with two mugs of tea. 'What have you been doing, since I saw you last? Tell me all the gossip.'

'Caroline's gone back to Tim.'

'Oh. I thought that was what had happened that night in the hotel.'

'Oh no. We made it up again after that. She promised that seeing Tim that night had just confirmed that things were over. Obviously, they weren't. Tim's a persistent bastard.'

'Go, Tim,' said a little voice in my head.

'But it was useless anyway. Caroline was never the girl for me. I was blinded by the way she looks, the way she treats you as if you're the only other person in the world. Until the next "only" person comes along. I need someone more down to earth than that,' he said and looked straight at me.

'Well, I could have told you that,' I replied, hoping I didn't sound too triumphant.

'Why didn't you? Why didn't you try harder to hang on to me, Lara?'

'Hugh,' I exclaimed. 'I hardly felt like I had a foothold before you told me where to go.'

'But there was definitely something between us that we should have worked on. You gave up so easily, Lara.' He reached across the coffee table to take my hand. 'You could have pulled me back from the brink.'

What? My heart was thundering in my chest. This was the last thing I had expected. Hugh squeezed my fingers. My cheeks burned. He got up from his seat and put one knee on the coffee table so that he could reach across to kiss me.

Brrriiing!!

Crash!

The doorbell was ringing. I leapt to my feet. And Hugh collapsed through the cheap plyboard coffee table all at the same time. I left him dusting himself off as I went to open the door. When Julie walked in I just rolled my eyes in the direction of the sitting room and she mouthed 'Oh, my God'.

CHAPTER EIGHTEEN

There followed a truly crazy fortnight. Hugh seemed determined to make some serious amends. We went back to La Traviata. The maitre d' looked at me somewhat askance but I didn't explain why. The next night we went to a concert at the Royal Festival Hall. It was Fado, a type of Portuguese folk music in which passionate old men and women sing operatically about fishwives over a Gypsy Kings'-style beat. Then we went to the ballet and watched a rather avant-garde piece from China, which was all nose-flutes and men in white loincloths standing very very still. But I had a great time. It didn't matter whether Hugh took me to see an incomprehensible ballet or a boys' own war movie, I wasn't interested in what was going on up on the stage or screen. As long as Hugh held my hand, I could have watched paint dry and written a two thousand-word critique extolling its virtues.

I hardly saw Simon at all for his first two weeks in the flat. I would dash in from work, get showered, get changed and grab a new pair of knickers just in case I didn't make it home that night. The sex, of course, was as great as I remembered it had been when we briefly tried the concept out all those months before. Hugh would call me at work to tell me that he thought I was beautiful and longed to hold me in his arms. I didn't care that I could hear Andrew snorting with laughter in the background.

On our next date at La Traviata, at the table which was almost becoming our own, Hugh took my hand across the garlic bread and whispered that he thought he loved me.

'No,' he added quickly, 'I don't think I love you. I know.'

I almost fainted. I grinned all the way back to the flat that night and continued to grin for another week. I told Julie, who was still finding time in her busy schedule of eating coal and flicking through baby catalogues to dish out advice. She reminded me that words were just words and that before I went all mushy what I should really be looking for was a gesture of commitment, since anyone could talk about love. I was disgruntled for about five minutes but the next time I picked up the phone, I had that gesture to give me the green light when Hugh uttered those simultaneously dreaded and longed for words.

'I'd like you to meet my parents.'

Of course, Julie, being pernickety, thought it was a bit early in our relationship for something as serious as that. But I thought she was just jealous because Andrew had kept Julie away from his mother for as long as he possibly could. In the end, Julie had to read up on her future

mother-in-law in *Who's Who* and transpired to bump into
her at a meeting of her local W.I. Julie's mother-in-law
was the daughter of a baronet or something similar. Titled
but brassic. Not even the title had been passed on to
her son.

Hugh's parents weren't in *Who's Who* (Julie had checked
long before this development) but I suspected that they
would still be a good deal grander than any prospective
parents-in-law I had met before. Thus far I had had pretty
good luck with boyfriends' mothers. They seemed to like
me. They could probably imagine me capably putting
their grandchildren's nappies on the right way up or
something like that. It was just the boyfriends I had
failed to convince that I should be allowed to become
a permanent fixture.

Anyway, it was bad enough having to think of an
outfit for the nerve-racking meeting. (Julie was her usual
amount of help, i.e., not much.) But two nights before
the dreaded event, Hugh nearly made me pop my clogs
when he called to ask me what I was going to cook.

'What am I going to cook?' I repeated incredulously.

'Yes. We talked about this, didn't we, sweetums?'

'No, Hugh. We did not.'

'Oh, well. Pasta's fine. I'll just have to tell them that
you're a career girl who doesn't have time for cuisine.'

For a moment, my image of Hugh almost lost its glossy
veneer. The second he put down the phone I was on it
again to Julie. I had five minutes of feminist rant before I
asked her what on earth I should make for these people.

I had thought that Julie was a marvellous cook, one who would have all the answers, but she assured me that what I thought was marvellous would be considered rather rustic by the likes of Mr and Mrs Armstrong-Hamilton. There was going to be no getting away with mousakka or Stroganoff. It was going to have to be roast swan . . . Or chicken at the very least.

I had to have a day off work just to think about it. I was up to my elbows in back issues of *Good Housekeeping* nicked from the launderette when it struck me that there was one person who could definitely help, much as it would be asking for trouble to admit it to her. That person was my mum.

'His parents?' she shrieked. 'Well, who is he for a start? How come your father and I haven't met this young man yet? How come you haven't even mentioned that you have a new boyfriend and now you're cooking dinner for his parents?'

I made excuses like mad and promised that I would insist on a return match chez my mum and dad the very next Sunday. This news mollified her for about three seconds.

'And why are you doing the cooking?' my mum asked, momentarily finding the feminist hat she had abandoned when she found that it didn't go with any of her outfits. 'Can't this boyfriend of yours open a tin for himself?'

'It's not going to be a matter of opening tins, Mum,' I said, full of trepidation. 'I was hoping you might be able to tell me how to, I don't know, how to roast a chicken or something?'

There was a succession of motherly tuts.

'I don't know, Lara Fenton. I let you off far too lightly when you were growing up, my girl. I let you tinker about with that Girl's World learning how to do your eyeshadow rather than help me get the dinner and now you're twenty-five years old and you've never even roasted a chicken.'

'I've never needed a whole chicken before. You can get ready cooked portions at M & S these days.'

'In my day we didn't have M & S to rely on,' she shrieked. 'In my day, we knew how to make our own gelatine by boiling a calf's foot and stripping out the ligaments.'

I winced. 'Let's forget any recipes that need that though, Mum. Can't be too careful with BSE.'

At the other end of the line, I could tell that she was already flicking through her well-thumbed Elizabeth David. 'At least they're not vegetarians,' she was muttering. 'Can't make anything but mush and pasta if they won't eat a bit of meat. Chicken. Chicken. Where's the chicken? Ah. Here it is. Have you got a pen ready?' She spieled out a recipe for roast chicken with a honey glaze that sounded more like an experiment for degree-level biochemists. I took the instructions down dutifully in my rusty shorthand, learned when a woman at a temp agency told me my psychology degree would be worthless without it.

'That's great, Mum. Thanks. I'll let you know how it goes.'

'Hang on a minute,' she said ominously. 'What are you doing to go with it? You can't just serve a chicken up on its own, you know.'

'Oh. I don't know. I'll do roast potatoes or something. I'll have a look round M & S tomorrow.'

'M & S!!! M & S!!! Sheesh, Lara!!! No wonder you're nowhere nearer getting a mortgage. You're spending all your money on ready-peeled spuds.'

'I'm a busy career girl, Mum. I haven't got time to work wonders in the kitchen like you do.'

Something had obviously flattered her. 'No. I suppose you're right. And we're very proud of your career ambitions, your father and I. Honestly we are. But a woman has to be a Jill of all trades to get on.'

(She meant to get a husband.)

'I'll tell you what, Lara,' she continued. 'Just once and once only, your mother will come to the rescue. I'll cook your special dinner for you.'

It was like being given £500 to spend at Harvey Nichols. 'Will you really?'

'I will. It will give me a chance to see what this new man of yours is like.'

I might have known there would be a catch.

'Oh, Mum,' I tried to wheedle my way out of it. 'It's really sweet of you to offer. Really. But Hugh's kitchen is so small. I'm sure that now you've told me what to do I'll be able to manage on my own.'

She had an answer for everything, especially since she had spent £200 on a comprehensive set of plastic microwave-safe, refrigerator-proof kitchen bits and bobs. We would be able to cook the dinner at her place and then transfer it all, in the back of the Metro, to Hugh's. Brilliant. That meant I was going to have to endure an afternoon of Cook with Mother punctuated by 'Isn't it about time you started thinking about a pension', and I still wasn't going to be able to get out of introducing her to Hugh either because I had no transport of my own. And what's more, I just knew, knew with every fibre of my body, that my mother would conspire to hang around in Hugh's kitchen until she met his mum and dad too.

I felt so sick with the anticipation of that evening that I bore the 'Mrs Davenport's daughter has a mortgage and an endowment plan' speech all the next afternoon without complaint. I wasn't going to need a mortgage or a pension. I was going to be dead by morning.

'But Hilary,' said Mrs Armstrong-Hamilton to my mother, when we had warmed the last of the julienne potatoes. 'You can't just go home now that you've done all this work. You must stay and join us for dinner. I'm sure that there's enough to go round.'

My mother didn't look at me. Good job, because as they say – if looks could kill.

'No, really I mustn't,' she said coquettishly as she buttoned up her mac. 'I should be getting back to my

Dudley. You know how these men are, Annabelle. They can't make a cup of tea for themselves half the time.'

'Then tonight he must learn to fend for himself,' said Hugh's mother, sweeping Mum into the dining room. 'I believe in teaching independence to everyone in my family. Girls and boys.' I pondered on the pretty appalling job she was making of it. Hugh, despite the promising start he had made with lunch in Wales, had since seemed disinclined even to wield a tin-opener over a can of baked beans and his father looked as if the only independence he was after began in a 'D' and ended in 'Vorce'.

'Do you mind if she stays?' I whispered to Hugh as he helped me get the chicken out of the oven.

'Not at all,' he replied, through lightly clenched teeth that spread in a fairly realistic smile when we carried the chicken to the dining-room table.

I couldn't eat a thing, even though the chicken looked delicious when it was carved and on my plate in front of me. My mum and Hugh's mum swopped pleasantries about the youth of today, ram-raiding and joy-riding and such. Hugh's father said nothing. Hugh said nothing. I was going to say nothing unless someone said something to me first.

'So Lara,' Mrs Armstrong-Hamilton turned her attention to me when she had finally finished expounding her views on the reintroduction of boot-camps. 'Hugh tells me that you read psychology at university?'

I nodded, praying that she wasn't going to ask me anything too difficult while my mouth was still full.

'Is it true what they say?' she continued. 'That people get into psychology because they have something wrong with themselves?'

Instantly, the rapport that had been building between my mother and Mrs Armstrong-Hamilton dissolved.

'No, they do not,' my mother exclaimed. 'People get into psychology because they're interested in helping other people overcome mental illness. You couldn't be a good psychologist if you were mad yourself, could you, Lara?'

'No, Mum,' I began.

'Well,' said Mrs Armstrong-Hamilton. 'I'm only repeating what's been said to me. My GP tells me that it's a load of bunkum, this analysis business. He says that the only cure for these people who say they've got emotional problems is a dose of good hard work.'

'I think you'll find that's a rather old-fashioned view,' said my mum.

I couldn't believe I was listening to my mother in defence of the psychologist. She'd been heartbroken when I first told her that I wasn't going to be a lawyer. Or even a teacher. A sensible job.

'And that's also the kind of prejudice that makes it difficult for psychologists to go about their valuable work,' Mum continued. 'We all have to learn to move with the times.'

Mrs Armstrong-Hamilton was about to protest.

'More wine, Mummy?' asked Hugh. It was the first useful comment he had made all night.

'I'm sorry, Annabelle, but I won't have anything said against modern psychologists,' my mother could not be stopped.

'Oh God,' I said suddenly. 'I can smell burning, can't you? Come on, Mum. Come and help me rescue dessert.'

I had thrown her off her stride. 'Dessert?' she said quizzically.

'Yes. It's burning. Can't you smell it?'

'Oh, yes. I can smell it too,' added Hugh, improvising like a pro, twitchy nose and all.

'But it's crème caramel,' said my mother. 'How can it be burning? It's in the fridge.'

'In the fridge? Oh, my God.' I leapt to my feet and dragged my mother to hers. 'I thought you were supposed to warm it up in the oven. Come on, Mum. It'll be ruined.'

Thank heavens I managed to persuade her that I was just as stupid as she had always suspected. By the time we returned from discovering that the crème caramel was still safely in the fridge, the conversation was back to boot-camps, which Annabelle thought were a very good idea for the poor, and though the atmosphere around the table was two or three degrees lower than it had been earlier on, at least the cutlery was only being used for eating.

After his parents had left for their posh hotel, Hugh sat alone in his sitting room, smoking a fat cigar, while my mother and I did the washing-up. We packed the Tupperware boxes away one inside the other like Russian dolls. Hugh didn't appear until the last of the drying was done. He looked tense.

'Thanks for everything,' he muttered, as though he didn't really mean it.

'Well,' said my mother chirpily. 'I'm going to take these boxes downstairs while you two young love birds say goodbye. I'll beep the horn when I'm ready to go, Lara.' I rolled my eyes. That had ruined my chances of staying the night.

Mum disappeared. Hugh looked at me for a moment before saying, not thanks for being such a trooper, but 'I don't suppose you could lend me two hundred quid?'

'What for?' I asked, surprised. He earned about four times as much as I did.

'Just got a few cashflow problems this month,' he replied.

'Well,' I said. 'I don't have it now. I could get it out of the cashpoint tomorrow and give it to you tomorrow night. I hate to ask, but how long a loan is this likely to be?'

'Oh, not long at all. Listen, I've got a better idea. Why don't you give me your card and your pin-number tonight. Then I'll get the money out on my way to work tomorrow morning and have the card couriered back to you just as soon as I get into the office.'

It didn't sound like such a great idea to me but I had a feeling that I wasn't exactly the golden girl in Hugh's eyes at that moment and I was eager to reinstate myself

CHRIS MANBY

in his heart whatever it took. Besides, if you couldn't trust the person you were sleeping with who could you trust? I handed the card over. My mother beeped from the Metro outside.

'I've got to go, Hugh. Thanks for having me and Mum around tonight. Your parents are really nice people.'

Hugh saw me outside. As soon as my mother and I had driven far enough away from Hugh's for waving to be futile, she said, 'Well, I don't think much of his mother. Bit snooty, don't you think?'

'Yeah, Mum.' It was rare that she and I agreed about such things.

'Thinks she can lord it up just because she's got a bit of money, she does. Well, that doesn't make you a better person. Remember that boy at your college who could fart the national anthem? And his father was in the House of Lords.'

'You're right, Mum. You're right.'

'I know I am. But,' she continued, ruining the moment. 'It's the man himself that you marry, isn't it? Not your in-laws.'

I sighed. 'Don't go buying a hat.'

'He's ripe for the picking, Hugh is,' Mum continued regardless. 'He needs a woman's touch about that flat for a start. He hasn't got anything on the walls. Not a single picture. And when I went into the bathroom . . . Well,' she tutted, 'that line around the bath could support a new species of coral . . .'

*   *   *

I went to bed that night with a vague but persistent feeling that the spell had been broken again. I was sure I had seen the love leak out of Hugh's face as he prodded at the crème caramel and told me that he'd always hated eating things that wobble. I had replied in a whisper that my favourite strategy was to lick things that wobbled until they got hard. He had just looked at me, witheringly, as I went bright red when his mother asked what we had been whispering about.

I called Julie for a post-mortem but Andrew told me that she was already in bed nursing the bump. Simon was still up. I could hear his television through my bedroom wall but I could hardly talk about my love life with him, could I? Why would he understand?

CHAPTER NINETEEN

I wasn't expecting Hugh to call me ever again but the next day he did ring. Up until that moment, I had clean forgotten that he had borrowed my cashpoint card.

'I don't know what happened exactly,' he told me. 'I opened up my briefcase to get out some papers on the Tube on the way to work and I suppose it might have fallen out then.'

'So you haven't got it?' I asked.

'Of course I haven't got it, Lara. That's what I've been trying to tell you. You'd better get on to your bank and cancel it. But wait until after lunch, just in case it turns up again. Don't want to get yourself into any unnecessary hassle.'

Maureen told me that I was an idiot to let anyone know my pin-number, even if I had met his parents. But I did as Hugh asked me and when, after lunchtime, he told me that he still hadn't found my card, I called up the bank and reported it missing. They reminded me gravely that since I had ignored all their nice glossy leaflets about card insurance, I would have to pay an excess if the card had been used by someone else.

I thanked the telephonist profusely but largely ignored what she had to say. After all, if someone had found my card and was going to use it they would have to know my pin-number, wouldn't they? Or be very good at copying my signature which I had made deliberately difficult when opening my post office savings account at the age of nine and a half.

I called Hugh to let him know that I had cancelled the card. Not that he needed the information, but he hadn't suggested when we would next be meeting up and I couldn't settle back down to my work until I had a date in my diary to look forward to.

'Can I call you later tonight? I haven't a clue how this week's going to pan out yet,' was his terse reply.

I put the phone down and spent a black five minutes, sure that this was the end. Then I spent a slightly greyer five minutes, thinking that everyone was entitled to feel moody and that Hugh was probably being snappy with me because he felt guilty about losing my cashpoint card. Talking of which, I hoped I would see him that night because I would need to borrow back some money if he had taken any out before the disaster.

'Has anyone called?' I asked Simon that night even before I said 'hello'.

'Don't think so.'

'Are you sure? Not even Hugh?'

He shrugged his shoulders.

SECOND PRIZE

The next day I called Hugh at his office and he claimed that he had indeed phoned but that it must have slipped Simon's mind to tell me. We didn't arrange a date for that evening because Hugh said that he was busy but would call me when he thought he might have a night off. He didn't mention the money and I felt too embarrassed to say that I needed some. I went out and bought an answerphone that lunchtime with my overburdened credit card.

I had thought that the little white answerphone would be a great investment. Never again would I miss a call because my housemate couldn't be bothered to write a message down or pass a message on. But pretty soon I'd had the machine for two weeks and no one had left a message. More importantly, Hugh hadn't left a message. Every night I would come home to find that the message counter was still not flashing up a figure. Every time I saw that little green zero, it made me quite distraught.

I had given up calling Hugh at work because his secretary would always head me off with a tale about meetings or lunch. I was starting to get desperate. He hadn't returned a single call since the day my cashpoint card went missing. What was going on?

Since I'd been promoted, or rather moved sideways on to a project that was harder and 'more prestigious' but not reflected in my salary, Simon was sometimes beating me home. It was possible that he had listened to the messages before I got back and then accidentally erased them.

'Simon,' I asked as he was settling down with a microwave

macaroni in front of *Animal Hospital*. 'Have you had any messages on this machine yet?'

He shrugged. 'Nope. Don't think so.'

'It seems bizarre that no one has left us a message in almost two weeks.'

He nodded.

'Not a single one. Perhaps it's not working. I'll just try pressing this button here.'

I pressed the 'play' button. The machine whirred into life, rewinding and winding its tape until it got to a part which had been recorded over.

'Hi, Lara. It's Hugh. Been calling you all week but you're obviously too annoyed at me to call me back. Look, I'm sorry, a thousand times sorry that I didn't call last week. Can't we get together tonight and try to make things right again?'

I stared at the machine as if I was hearing the voice of a ghost.

'There's a message from Hugh,' I exclaimed somewhat hysterically. 'You didn't tell me there was a message from Hugh.'

'I didn't know there was one. Perhaps the flashing light that tells you someone has called doesn't work.'

'You might be right. I'll have to take it back to the shop tomorrow. But I'll just get Julie to call me first. See if she can get through.'

'Don't bother her now,' Simon said. 'She's probably got her feet up. She'll be eating coal and pickle sandwiches or something.'

'Well, if I take the machine back to the shop and there's nothing wrong with it, I'll look a right idiot, won't I? I'm going to call her.'

'Hang on.' Simon got to his feet and began to scrabble about in his briefcase. 'I'll call you from my mobile. That do you?'

He called. The answerphone whirred into action. He recorded a message. The message counter flashed.

'It's flashing now,' I said accusingly.

'Must have mended itself.'

'Yes,' I was unconvinced. 'Either that or it was working all along and someone tried to erase Hugh's message before I got to hear it,' I said pointedly, poking my head round the door into the sitting room where Simon was just putting his mobile phone away. 'You knew I had a message, didn't you? And you chose not to tell me?'

Simon continued to pick at his macaroni cheese.

'Didn't you?' I persisted.

'Look, Lara. What does it matter if I did know Hugh called you? The man's a creep. He's no good for you and you shouldn't let yourself get involved with him again. You'll be making a big mistake if you do.'

'I think I'm big enough to make my own mistakes, thank you.'

'Yeah, I've been watching you do that ever since I met you.'

'What's that supposed to mean?'

'Lara, Hugh treats you like dirt. You're just someone to pass the time with while Caroline won't play ball. He doesn't care about you. At best, he wants to use you to make Caroline jealous but I think he's probably using you in other ways as well.'

'That's rubbish. You don't know him like I do,' I said defensively.

'I work with him, Lara. Believe me, you don't know him like I do. I have to listen to him talking about you at work as though you're some stupid little schoolgirl who can't get over a crush. He's using you. That's all. Using you while Caroline continues to mess him around.'

I felt strangely cold as Simon told me these things. 'What exactly does he say about me?' I probably shouldn't have asked. 'Tell me, Simon. I have to know.'

'He says that you call and pester him all the time. That he can't get away from you and that he wishes he'd never started things with you. But then, on the other hand, he says that you're just too good in bed to pass up altogether if Caroline isn't in town.'

'What?'

'You should be flattered. He says that Caroline's useless.'

I had a sudden, nauseating image of a gaggle of men in pin-stripes and red braces gathered around Hugh's desk to hear the latest instalment on Hugh's love life including Lara Fenton's favourite positions and proclivities. And to make matters worse, two of those men listening were men that I knew. My best friend's husband and my housemate. How could Hugh be so cruel?

'You are pulling my leg, aren't you?' I said when I had

collapsed into the comfy chair by the window. 'You are having a laugh with me?'

'I only wish that I was,' said Simon. 'I know how you did it in that chair for a start.'

'Oh . . . you . . . you . . . You can't do.' I picked up a half-empty coffee mug and hurled it across the room at Simon, narrowly missing his head and totally ruining a reproduction Matisse which was leaning against the wall awaiting a new frame. 'Now look what you've made me do!!' I followed the mug with a couple of cushions.

Simon got up calmly and walked into the kitchen. 'They were right. It is always the messenger who gets shot.'

I sank back down into my chair and gazed at the coffee stain on my picture and on the wall. He had to be wrong. He had to be. Simon had probably just made a lucky guess that I had done it in that chair at all. After all, if Hugh didn't want to see me, he wouldn't have called begging forgiveness for neglecting me while he had to work late, would he? If he just wanted sex there were plenty of places a man as good-looking as he was could find that.

I dialled his number. No reply. The answerphone clicked in after three rings. I called him at work. His secretary told me that he had left the office at five. So much for working late. After almost a fortnight of kidding myself that everything would be OK if I gave him enough space, I was gripped with a sudden rush of panic that twisted my guts. Perhaps he had been lying to me.

I had to call Julie and find out if she'd heard the same story from Andrew.

'Oh hi,' she trilled. 'I'm just getting Andrew to make me a beetroot and marzipan sandwich.' I nearly gagged at the thought. 'How's tricks? How's Simon?'

'Fine,' I lied. 'I couldn't ask for a better housemate. He's very frank and honest. Talking of which, if you'd heard that Hugh had been saying terrible things about me you would let me know, wouldn't you?'

'Such as?'

'Such as private and personal information about things I may or may not have done in the privacy of my own home.'

'Oh, you mean what you did on that chair?' I blanched. 'Honestly, Lara, you're such a wench. I don't think I'll ever be able to sit in that armchair again without blushing, though if the baby carries on growing at this rate, it's unlikely that I'll ever fit in that chair again anyway.'

'Thanks. Enjoy your sandwich.' So Simon had been telling the truth. Still sitting in that stupid chair, I began to shiver. It was as though I had been stripped of all my clothes and in more than one way, I guess I had.

Simon appeared with a plateful of sandwiches and offered me one. I took a big bite but the cheese and pickle tasted like stale ash in my mouth. 'Did you call Julie?' he asked. I nodded. 'And she told you exactly the same things I did, didn't she?' I nodded slowly.

But there was worse to come. 'Why do you think he didn't call you for two weeks, Lara? It wasn't because you were a bad cook, or because he felt bad about losing your cashpoint card. It certainly wasn't because he was working late. It was because Caroline was in town. "Sorting her head out".' He used his fingers to make little inverted commas in the air. 'She's gone back to Wales now. And so Hugh thinks he'll just pick things up where he left off with you. It's like you're his town house and she's his place in the country.'

I spat the unchewed remains of my sandwich back out on to my plate.

'He said that they'd split up for good.'

'Really? He told me that Caroline had asked if they could have a three-week cooling-off period. I guess she just didn't cool off.' He flicked on the television as if to indicate that he didn't want to talk about my disastrous love life any more. On a new dating programme, the giggling girls in the audience were invited to vote for the men they liked best from a panel of ten. The ones they liked least were being pushed backwards into a bath full of gunge.

'And what exactly was wrong with him?' the presenter asked one of the girls who had passed the death sentence on a chap with highlighted hair and a pink Ralph Lauren shirt.

'He was way too slimy, wasn't he?'

'Yeah,' her friend chipped in. 'He's the kind of bloke who would tell you that he loved you and then say exactly the same thing to your very best friend the next night.'

'That's your problem,' Simon said wisely, as he wagged a finger at the television screen. 'You actually like a bit of slime.'

'Thank you, Simon,' I hissed. 'I think I know what my problem is now. And you're really enjoying my agony, aren't you?'

'On the contrary, I'm only telling you what Hugh's like because I don't want you to get hurt. Better that you know now than let him juggle you with Caroline for months and months before she makes her mind up. Unless you want to be the other woman, of course.'

'I do not. I'm nobody's second best.'

'Then start acting like you aren't, will you? Honestly, when Hugh says jump, you say "how high". You weren't like that with me and I respected you for it.'

'Oh, yeah,' I sneered. 'I wondered how long it would be before you brought that up.'

'What?'

'Us. You and me.'

'Only to illustrate you in a positive light, Lara.'

'I really dented your delicate male pride then, didn't I?' I began to rant. 'By turning you down like that? I bet you thought you were giving the performance of your life that evening.'

'What?'

'Really going for it. You even took your socks off.' I held the neck of my blouse together prudishly at the memory, or rather the 'unmemory' of that evening, as I swore at him.

Simon's mouth began to twist upwards in a quizzical smile. 'At least I can remember what actually happened, Lara. You'll be relieved to know that I didn't really "go for it" that night. If I wanted to shag something with no reflexes whatsoever, I would have bought myself a blow-up doll. They don't answer back. Or get the wrong end of the stick entirely.'

'I have not got the wrong end of the stick,' I protested.

'You have,' he said calmly. 'You always do. Someone says one thing to you and you go off and interpret it in your own sweet way. You wouldn't believe what Hugh has been doing to you if he confessed it to you himself.'

I left Simon to his sandwiches and made a beeline for the phone. I called Hugh again. His number rang and rang but no one picked up the call.

Two days later I got a letter from him, saying that he thought he might still be on the rebound from Caroline and so we had better call things off.

'Coward,' Simon hissed when he saw the note. 'If I thought you wouldn't take it the wrong way, I'd go out and smash his head in for you.'

I couldn't let it finish with a letter of course, so I dressed myself up in my best Friday-night clothes and, fighting against my better instincts, I caught a taxi round to Hugh's. He was in, surprisingly, and even more surprisingly, he let me in too. When I asked him why we had to finish, why we couldn't carry on in a more frivolous kind of way perhaps, he quoted some book called *Girls Who Like Men Who are Boys* or something like that. Apparently we needed a 'cooling-off period' to see whether what we had was just desperate passion in the face of his loss, or real love. The words 'cooling-off period' were like expletives to my heart.

'You see,' he said as he bundled me out of the door again. 'It's for the best, Lara. And it isn't necessarily the end of everything. I'll call you in a month or so.'

'Will you?' I asked pathetically.

'Of course I will.' He kissed me on the forehead and hailed a taxi simultaneously.

As I waved goodbye and the taxi sped around the corner, I was sure I saw another cab draw up outside Hugh's flat, to disgorge a long-legged girl with very familiar dark hair. I cried all the way home, then locked myself in my room and cried again until I felt like I had nothing but a hollow space inside.

How had things gone so horribly wrong so suddenly? I couldn't believe that Hugh had been waiting for Caroline to have him back all the time he was with me. It wasn't possible that the man who had told me that he loved me in La Traviata was lying. I racked my brains to see whether there had been a clue, just one teensy weensy little hint that should have made me run the other way when Hugh turned up on my doorstep again after Julie and Andrew's wedding. I could think of nothing. And the night when Simon revealed all, Hugh had wanted to see me. The letter had arrived two days later without Hugh ever having known that his cover was blown. Or was that the case at all?

CHAPTER TWENTY

The honeymoon period for me and Simon was definitely over. In fact, I felt like my honeymoon period with life was over. The night after Hugh and I said goodbye for what seemed like forever, I decided that it was time to tackle Simon about being more than a little slack when it came to doing his share of the chores. I was at the kitchen sink when I decided to mention it, up to my elbows in soap suds as I scrubbed away at the scrambled eggs that he had eaten for breakfast.

'Of course I do my share of the housework,' he said, putting two mugs on the draining board as if that proved it. 'You're still pissed off with me about the whole Hugh thing, aren't you? In fact you're taking it out on the entire male race.'

'I am not. This is a separate matter altogether. I don't believe you've touched the floor mop once since you moved in.'

He touched it right then, like a kid playing tag. I didn't see the joke.

'And what about the bathroom? The loo brush isn't just for decoration you know.'

'I know,' said Simon. 'But I think I might be allergic to that stuff you put down the toilet. It makes me come out in red blotches.'

'Sitting on the toilet while you read an entire Jeffrey Archer novel is what makes you come out in blotches.'

'I meant on my hands.'

'I've got some Marigolds.'

'OK, then,' said Simon, shuffling a pile of official-looking papers pointedly to let me know that my triviality was keeping him from his work. 'Just to please you, I'll do it now. Then will you give me some peace?'

While I was standing back in amazement, he delved into the sink and whipped the dishcloth out of the water.

'Where are you going with that?' I shrieked as he rushed into the bathroom. 'That's the dishcloth!' In the time it took me to dry my hands so that I wouldn't drip water all over the freshly mopped hallway floor, he had smeared the cloth around the bath and was using it to wipe around the rim of the toilet as I walked in.

'What on earth are you doing?' I almost contracted a stomach bug on the spot. 'You can't use the dishcloth on the toilet, you idiot.'

'Why not? I used it last time.'

'Tell me you have never cleaned the toilet before. Please tell me?' I begged him.

'See,' he said proudly. 'I've cleaned it loads of times and you've never even noticed.'

I felt faint and more than a little queasy.

'Don't you know what lives in the toilet?' I asked him.

'Crocodiles?' He thought we were going to have a bit of a laugh about this obviously.

'If only. Maybe it would have got you by the wrist while you were being so stupid. E-coli!!! E-coli lives down the toilet, you fool.'

'What's that?'

'It's something that lives in poo,' I shrieked. 'It's a germ. It can make you go blind or deaf or something.'

Simon laughed. 'Don't be stupid, Lara.'

'Me, stupid? How can you say that I'm stupid when you've just wiped the loo seat with the cloth that I use for washing up the dishes. No wonder I've had stomach cramps ever since you moved into this flat. You could have killed us both. As it is, I'm going to have to burn that dishcloth and it was brand new this week. What else have you used in here?'

'Nothing.'

'Don't lie to me, Simon. Not now.'

'Well,' he began innocently. 'I couldn't find the loo brush last week so I used that bristly one you've got for when you curl your hair.'

'OhmiGod.' I slumped on to the side of the bath. 'OhmiGod. I might be able to forgive you if you swear to me that you're lying.'

'I swear I never lie.'

I went to get up and punch him, slipped on the bath

mat, fell backwards into the bath and cracked my head on the wall. I couldn't have been out for long because when I came round he was still laughing.

I called Julie straight away and told her the story. She agreed that she had never heard anything quite so terrible in her life but when I asked if she thought it was a chucking out offence she told me fondly that she never let Andrew anywhere near the housework because he would doubtless have done something similarly stupid.

'Yes, but you're married to him.'

'All men are big children, Lara,' she reminded me. 'You just have to put up with it.'

I'd heard that the huge rush of hormones you get during pregnancy does funny things to your brain but I had thought until now that it was just a myth put about by jealous men. Or perhaps Julie was a Stepford wife.

'I'm kicking him out,' I said firmly.

'Lara,' Julie said in her voice of reason. 'Don't you think you're being just a little hasty over this. I mean we're talking about one misused dishcloth, not the revelation that he's a serial killer or something like that. Are you sure you're not still just a little bit angry over what he said to you about Hugh? Or about the fact that Simon told you he didn't actually sleep with you that night you blacked out? I reckon that's probably dented your pride just a little no matter how relieved you're pretending to be.'

'No, Julie,' I exploded. 'I am definitely not suffering from dented pride. I am, however, probably suffering from beriberi and botulism. Oh, why did you have to get married on me, Julie?'

'Because Andrew and I make the perfect team,' she cooed. Yuk!

'You mean,' I interpreted, 'you both go out to work all day and then you come home and wait on him hand and foot like he's a baby, even when you're getting to be the size of a barrage balloon with a real one.'

'Lara, I don't know why you're choosing to get angry with me,' she said sniffily. 'I didn't use the dishcloth round the toilet bowl. And for your information I do not wait on Andrew hand and foot. He always makes the tea first thing on a Sunday morning. Besides, it's nice to do something for other people from time to time.'

I could see Julie was short on sympathy that night. She probably fancied a charcoal sandwich.

'Anyway, darling,' she continued. 'I'm sorry to have to desert you mid-rant but I've got to check the chicken's properly basted.'

'But you don't eat chicken, Julie.' She had made a stand about factory farming by dressing up in a chicken suit and handing out leaflets about battery farming during our fourth year at school.

'I know, but Andrew does. He needs to watch his nutrition.'

He certainly did. Julie was eating for two now but Andrew had always done so.

Simon had obviously heard most of my conversation with Julie. When I put down the telephone, he was standing right behind me with the Marigolds still on. He closed a yellow rubber clad hand around my mouth.

'It's the phantom Marigold killer!' he intoned. I would have shrieked but as I said he was holding my mouth so I had to resort to giving him a sharp elbow jab in the goolies instead.

'Not very funny,' I said as he rolled on the carpet in agony.

'Likewise.'

'I'm sorry,' I said, not meaning it in the least.

'I was coming to say sorry too, about the toilet thing. I didn't think you'd get so upset. But then I heard you slagging me off to Julie.'

'You deserved it. I won't be able to use anything in that kitchen now until I've boil-washed the lot of it. I can't trust a single thing in there to be germ-free.'

'In that case, let's go to a restaurant.'

'What?'

'Let's go to a restaurant for dinner. My treat. You've obviously had a hard day. And I promise we won't go anywhere that reminds you of Hugh.'

'That shouldn't be hard,' I sniffed. 'He only ever took me to that crappy Italian place. Urgh. I don't feel much like eating anyway, since the only thing I can smell at the moment is that disgusting rubber glove.'

'Smells a bit like a condom, doesn't it?' said Simon, sniffing his fingers gingerly.

'I didn't know you had ever come across one of those?'

*   *   *

SECOND PRIZE

We went to the King of Burgers as I couldn't make my mind up between Indian and Chinese. After we'd stuffed down a couple of flame-torched quarter-pounders, we walked back to the flat. Simon linked his arm through mine.

'Am I forgiven?' he asked. 'After all, I have just bought you dinner.'

'Yes. And knowing that place, the burger probably had more E-coli in it than the loo seat. You are forgiven however. And you're also forgiven for breaking the news to me about Hugh. I was just being stupid as usual. Love not only makes you blind. It makes you deaf and dumb as well.'

'I'm sorry you had to find out the hard way,' he told me earnestly. 'And I suppose I should have told you earlier. It was difficult having to listen to Hugh saying all those terrible things about you and knowing that you thought he was the best thing since Pop Tarts.' Simon suddenly spluttered into a balled-up hanky.

'What's up?' I asked suspiciously.

'Oh, nothing.'

'Don't try to tell me it's nothing again, Simon. What are you finding so funny now?'

'It's just that Pop Tart thing,' he admitted foolishly. 'That's one of the names Hugh used to call you in the office, because he says you only take a couple of minutes to heat up.'

I shook Simon's arm free of mine straight away. 'Suddenly,' I snarled, 'you're unforgiven again.'

'It was he who said it, not me,' Simon pleaded. 'You weren't a Pop Tart when I met you for the first time. That time you were more of a Ice Pop.'

'Simon, you're really not making this any better. Take off your glasses, in case I have to hit you.' I was finding it hard not to cry again. 'Honestly, you men are all the same. You think that women and their emotions are one big joke for you to have hours of fun with. You don't understand how your stupid one-liners can cause us so much pain.'

'Oh, Lara.' He stopped me on the pavement and fumbled in his pocket for a balled-up serviette. 'I didn't mean to upset you.'

'Not only has Hugh been unspeakably rude and vicious about me,' I continued. 'He also owes me two hundred quid.'

'Two hundred quid?'

'Yeah, he borrowed my cashpoint card before he lost it.' It was the first time I had mentioned the incident to Simon because I had known what he would say next.

'Well, that was pretty stupid of you.'

'I know. And not only am I two hundred quid down on the money he owes me, the next person to pick up my card cleared the account out and it looks like I'm going to be liable for it.'

Simon looked at me seriously. 'Your card was used after Hugh lost it?'

'Yeah.'

'And the person who picked it up used it to get money out of a cashpoint?'

'Yeah. And now I can't even ask Hugh for the money he owes me back because I'm too embarrassed to ever speak to him again. And I'm going to go overdrawn when I have to pay my rent.'

'No, you won't,' said Simon, wiping the tears from my cheeks with the burger bar napkin and depositing a smear of ketchup in their place as he did so. 'I'll sort your rent out and I'll ask Hugh to give you your money back.'

'You would do that for me?'

'Yeah. But you get to clean the bathroom until Christmas, if I do.'

'Sounds like as fair a deal as I'm ever going to get from a man.'

'So, do you give me permission to act as your bailiff?'

I nodded and sniffed. 'Yeah. But keep it quiet, won't you? If Andrew finds out about this he'll tell Julie and Julie will tell my mother and my mother will march round to Hugh's with a frying pan to sort him out.'

'She would?'

'She gave my ex-boyfriend a black eye when he tried to gatecrash my eighteenth birthday party with his new bird on his arm.'

'Cool mother.'

'I was mortified at the time.'

'My grandmother would probably have done the same. Before she got . . .' Simon hesitated. 'Before she got ill.'

'I'm sorry.' I looked at the floor.

'It's OK. She says she's done pretty much everything she wanted to. Seen most of the world. Had hundreds of lovers. I think she would have carried on living like a playgirl forever if she hadn't found herself lumbered with me at the age of fifty-five.'

'Sounds like an amazing woman.'

'She is. You'll have to come and see her with me some time.'

'I'm not meeting any more mothers or grandmothers until I have an engagement ring on my left hand,' I announced.

'Well, don't hold your breath for one from me,' spluttered Simon.

'Dream on. Do you think I'd be desperate enough to say yes if you asked me?'

'You've got getting settled down on the brain, Lara.'

'I have not. Right now I'd be quite happy to be single for the rest of my life. It's everybody else. Nobody seems to think a girl can get by without a man. Well, I'm going to prove you all wrong. I'll die a spinster and a happy one at that . . .'

Suddenly, he kissed me. Right on the lips.

I pulled myself free and stumbled backwards with shock. 'What did you do that for?'

'It was the only way to make you shut up for a minute.'

'Well, don't do it again.'

'Don't worry. I won't. Besides you didn't shut up long enough for me to say what I wanted to say, anyway.'

'What did you want to say?' I snapped as I wiped my mouth dry. 'I can shut up for as long as you need.'

'I just wanted to say that you're special, Lara. You're the most special girl I've ever met.'

I blushed.

'I don't mean it in a sexual way, of course.'

'Well, good,' I huffed. 'Because I wouldn't want you to. I don't think I ever want a man to think about me in a sexual way again.'

By now we had reached the flat. We watched the end of a film about a woman torn between two lovers and then went our separate ways to bed. Men are so strange, I thought as I mused over the damp patch on the ceiling which the landlord would never repair. No wonder it was difficult to communicate with them. They didn't have the ability to communicate at all. Fancy Simon kissing me like that to shut me up.

Yeah, fancy Simon just kissing me like that . . .

CHAPTER TWENTY-ONE

M y mother called me at work the next day, fractious that she hadn't heard from me in over a week. I pointed out that if I had been murdered she probably would have seen it on the news. Funnily enough, she didn't find that thought a comfort at all.

'So what have you been doing with yourself?' she probed. 'I expect you've been spending all your time with that lovely Hugh chap. Julie tells me it's going well.'

'When did you last speak to Julie?'

'A couple of weeks ago now.'

'Huh,' I snorted ironically.

'Got a cold, darling.'

'No. I just don't like the thought of you gossiping about me to my friends, Mother,' I admonished. On the other side of the office Maureen was suddenly all radar, ready for a fight.

'We weren't gossiping, darling. But if you're never in to pick up the phone to talk to your dear old mother whose only joy in life is to hear what her darling daughter is doing . . .'

'You could have left a message on my answerphone, Mum. I would have called you back straight away if I had known you were going through one of your empty nest phases.'

'I can't talk to that thing. Besides, when I telephoned last night I wasn't even sure that I'd got the right flat. There was a man's voice on it.'

'You know who that is. It's my new flatmate Simon. I told you about him.'

'Not in any great detail.'

'There isn't much detail.'

'I'll have to ask Julie. But anyway, your flatmate wasn't in last night either.'

'I know. He was out with me.'

'Oh.' How was it that my mother always managed to invest such meaning into that single syllable? 'Doesn't Hugh mind about that kind of thing? Your father would have been terribly jealous if I'd been out with another man while we were courting.'

'It's none of Hugh's business, any more.'

'Tell that to him.'

'I'd be glad to. If only we were speaking.'

'You haven't broken up with him, have you Lara? He was such a catch.'

'You didn't like his mother.'

'I know but she'll be dead in a few years. And she'll leave him the estate. Why haven't you tried to make things up with him again? What did you fall out over? I know you can be headstrong, Lara. Sometimes you have to back down to keep the peace in a relationship.'

'It wasn't my fault. Hugh's got someone else.'

'Oh.' That shut her up.

'Yes. And I'm sure his mother thinks that this other girl is the best thing since sliced bread.'

'Well, just let her try to say that to me. After all the effort you made for him. I could tell he hadn't been brought up properly when he left us to do the washing up.'

'Yeah.'

'So where did you go with this other chap last night?' Thank heavens she changed the subject.

'Simon took me to the King of Burgers,' I explained. 'For doing his share of the housework ever since he moved into the house.'

'Well, it's not very romantic. But then romance isn't actually that good a basis for a long-term relationship according to this new book I've been reading. It's called *Perfect Love for Life*. I know how busy you are, Lara, so I thought I'd read it for you and pass on the most important tips. Where does he come from, this Simon chap?'

'He could come from Mars for all I care. Before you say another word, Mum, he is not going to be my perfect love. He's my housemate. Why do you have to try to fix me up the whole time?'

'You're my only daughter, Lara. I want to know that you'll be cared for when I'm gone.'

'Richard Branson's started a pension company for that.'

'Have you found out about his scheme?' my mother asked hopefully.

'No,' I said.

'Then I'll have to continue to hope that you find a man who has.'

'Mother. I don't need a man in my life.'

'Men are like diamonds, Lara,' said my mother philosophically. 'You have to polish them up and create the right setting before you can really see their true value sometimes.'

'Mum,' I sighed. 'All the men I meet are more like lumps of coal. Anyway, since splitting up with Hugh, I've decided that I've given up on the lot of them and I'm going to become a lesbian.'

Before she could protest, I put the phone down, so that I could get on with some work. Then I took it off the hook again straight away so that she couldn't call me back in indignation. But my mother may as well have been in the room with me, since Maureen was staring at me, goggle-eyed, as if my frizzy hair and smart suit were about to fall away leaving me with a crew cut and dungarees.

'Can I help you, Maureen?' I asked pointedly.

When I figured that mum had probably had enough time to calm down, I put the telephone receiver back in its cradle. It rang again almost instantly. But this time it was Julie.

'Lara,' she screeched. 'I've just had your mother on the phone. She is going crazy. She says that you're becoming a lesbian and we need to get one of those doctors who rescue people from the Moonies to come round and sort you out before it's too late.'

'What? With a damn good seeing to, I suppose?' I said drily. 'Take no notice of her. She's insane.'

'But I have to take notice of her when she calls me up in the middle of my breathing exercises.' Julie had begun her antenatal classes. 'It's not good for the baby, hearing all that angst. Can't you calm her down somehow?'

'Not unless I marry Prince Edward. Honestly, Julie, I just told her that I've split up with Hugh but now she's heard Simon's voice on the answering phone and she won't be happy until I admit that we're living in sin and not simply sharing a dishcloth.'

'Oh, yes. The dishcloth. Did you throw him out over that?'

'No, I forgave him actually. He took me out to dinner.'

'He did? Where?'

'To that King of Burgers place you started avoiding as soon as you knew you were pregnant. The one where we saw the cockroach that time.'

'Well, it's not exactly romantic. But then romance . . .'

'Julie, don't say it. It didn't need to be romantic because we were just going out as friends.'

'Friends?' She repeated the words as though she were my mother, hearing from my lying adolescent mouth that I hadn't been smoking when I was caught behind the chemistry lab at school.

'What did you mean by that?' I snapped.

'Mean by what? Oops, sorry Lara. I've got to go. When you're this far gone the baby really pushes down on your bladder and sometimes you've just got to run for it before you have an accident . . .' she slammed the phone down.

'That's slightly more detail than I need to know right now,' I told the silent receiver.

Maureen strolled up to my desk and deposited a neatly typed memo in my in-tray. I didn't need to read it.

'It's from the top,' she informed me. 'Says that all telephone calls will be monitored from the beginning of next month to make sure that we aren't making too many personal ones.'

Great. I wondered who had initiated that and looked daggers at the back of Joe, who was probably making idle chit-chat on the Internet with an ornithologist from Idaho who called herself 'Aria, goddess of the skies' even as Maureen spoke. I would have to get my mother put on-line, I thought. Though with her technophobia she would never be able to get much of a conversation going . . . Hey! What a fantastic idea this Internet thing was.

Funny thing was though, much as I was prepared to deny it, by the time I was ready to leave the office that evening, I was actually looking forward to getting back to the flat for the first time in ages. I was actually looking forward to seeing Simon. To having a chat about my day with someone who didn't automatically launch into a monologue about how much more dreadful their day had been before I could even get the words 'Maureen' and 'mother' out. Someone who would tell me that being without a man was better than being shackled to one who thought that foreplay was something to do with golf and that fidelity should only be applied to sound systems.

Yeah, I thought. Simon was actually a very good listener. Almost as good as a girl. And he was quite funny too. In fact I would have to get him to write some of his jokes down so that I could take them into work and impress Malcolm.

I stopped at the shop on the corner of our road and bought a bottle of nice red wine to surprise him with. Perhaps I would even cook something for the pair of us. No. I suddenly remembered that I couldn't cook. Perhaps we could call out for a pizza.

I was whistling as I turned the key in the door, looking forward to an evening with all the advantages of male companionship without the ultimate betrayal that always seemed to accompany the limited joy of having sex with a member of the half of the species that doesn't believe in cunnilingus.

'Lara, I've got a bit of a favour to ask you.'

Simon had brought cream cakes home with him and I was already halfway through an éclair and looking forward to opening the wine. But I should have guessed that this patisserie came with strings attached when he asked me, 'I was wondering what you were planning to do tomorrow evening.'

'Oh,' I brightened. 'Nothing really.'

'Oh,' said Simon. 'That's a pity.'

'Are you going to invite me out somewhere?' I asked coquettishly, wondering if he needed me to play his stunt girlfriend at a fabulous City dinner and missing the worried look in his eye altogether.

'Not exactly. But I was kind of hoping that you would have something to do because I was going to ask you to be out of the flat tomorrow evening if you possibly could. It's just that I want to cook dinner for someone.'

'Someone?' I replaced the half-eaten éclair on my plate. 'And you don't want me to be around, right?'

'Well, it might be a little bit awkward that's all. I want to make a good impression. I want her to feel really relaxed.'

'Her?'

'Yes, it's one of the girls from the desktop publishing department at work. Her name's Valeria, I'm sure I must have mentioned her.'

'You haven't. But she sounds exciting,' I added gamely.

'She is exciting,' he sighed. 'She's Spanish actually. And I don't think I've ever met anyone so beautiful in my entire life.'

'Oh.'

'I couldn't believe it when she said that she would have dinner with me. I was expecting a knock-back. After all, you know what my track record with women has been like.'

'Yes,' I tried to laugh.

SECOND PRIZE

'So what do you think?'

'I'll think of something,' I said valiantly. 'There are a couple of people I could go out with tomorrow. It's just that I was planning to have a quiet night in. Washing my hair or something. You know. Girl's things. Never mind. I should make the effort to go out more often anyway.'

'Oh,' Simon's face brightened. 'That's really good of you, Lara, but don't go to too much trouble will you? I mean, if you have to stay in tomorrow, then you have to stay in. It is your flat too, after all.'

Yes, I thought, and you still haven't finished your probation period in it. Suddenly feeling a little less beneficent, I shut myself away in my bedroom without mentioning the wine on the pretence of having some work to do. Once I was behind closed doors the worrying began.

Even though he had given me the option, I knew that I couldn't stay in and play gooseberry to Simon and his señorita. Where was I going to go?

Friday nights, as Julie had told me all those months ago when I tried to get a date out of Hugh, were the nights that all the best people had booked up for months beforehand. I had really been looking forward to a night in, as well. That selfish, selfish flatmate of mine. Why couldn't the cheapskate take her out to some nice restaurant? It then dawned on me that to make things worse he probably wanted me out of the house all night as well, not just until the pubs closed. He wouldn't like it if I wandered in just as he was about to make his big move.

Didn't she have a place they could go to? Surely I had right of primogeniture, being the first of the two of us to live at that address. I called Julie. She and Andrew were going away to a country hotel for the whole weekend, making the most of their limited amount of freedom left before the sleepless nights set in.

In desperation I got out my address book and flicked through it. There were names in there of people I had learned to count with. Most of the numbers were out of date. Some of the numbers I hadn't called in nigh on thirteen years. It was a disturbing lesson in what can happen if you don't keep up with that Christmas card list. No doubt if she had been caught in the same situation, Julie would have been choosing between a dozen or so dates by now. I wondered if perhaps I should call her again and ask her to make a foray on to the grapevine for me before she went away. Perhaps she could find an interesting party where I might be able to blend into the kitchen cabinets until it was time to wipe the jelly off the walls?

No. I couldn't call Julie. She and I hadn't exactly been seeing eye to eye lately and telling her that I couldn't find something to do on a Friday night without her help would have been inviting more hideous blind dates for months to come.

I flicked through an old copy of *Cosmo* while I pondered my dilemma. It was then that I happened upon another of those fatuous articles about the joys of being single which are inevitably written by a journalist who has been happily married for three decades. It said that no woman should feel too embarrassed to do things on her own in this day and age. It was no longer unheard of for a woman to walk into a bar on her own. Or for her to go alone to the cinema . . .

I decided that I would go to the cinema. At least in that case any disapproving people wouldn't be able to see me being emancipated because it would be too dark.

I actually did it, too. I marched into the cinema on my own, bought one ticket without apologising and a family-sized tub of popcorn.

Eventually, the film credits rolled and we started to exit the cinema. I tried to keep quite close to the couple in front as they made for the Tube, hoping that to the disinterested eye, it might look as though I was with someone. So much for emancipation. I had been sandwiched between two sets of snogging Italian teenagers and if there is one thing that brings home the horrible sense of loneliness, it is the sound of tongues tangling in the dark when you're not one of the tongues involved. I was not even consoled by my popcorn.

Now it was well after eleven. The pubs were closed. And I couldn't bear to sit through another showing of *Independence Day*. The only way I could possibbly stay out now would be if I went to a club and I was not going to go to a club on my own, no matter how desperate Simon was to get off with Valeria. No matter what *Cosmo* had to say about emancipation and independence. Simon had had six hours. I figured that if he hadn't managed to get her safely into his room yet, he would never manage it. Tough shit, Simon, I thought. I was going home.

I let myself into the flat and crept through the darkness of the hallway to the sitting room, taking care not to make any noise that might spoil a romantic moment.

It was pretty dark in the living room so I flicked on the light.

It was then that I realised that Simon hadn't quite yet scored. A woman who must have been a panther in a past life was stretched out fully across the sofa. She sat up suddenly. Simon was nowhere to be seen, though one of my CDs was in the player and my wax-candle model of Notre-Dame, which I had been saving intact since a memorable sixth-form trip to Paris, was ablaze. They had even had the cheek to crack open my bottle of Bourbon.

'Who are you?' the pantheress asked with a sneer as she quickly buttoned up her fitted black shirt so that it strained across her Wonderbra. She seemed unnecessarily rude for a visitor. 'I asked who you are?' she said again when I didn't reply.

I looked at my belongings, being used as props in Simon's big love scene, felt suddenly quite inexplicably angry, and told her, 'Actually, I'm Simon's girlfriend.'

'But Simon says he doesn't 'ave a girlfriend,' she exclaimed with surprise.

'Well, he would say that wouldn't he?' I said flatly. 'We've been living together for almost three years.'

'Oh.'

'This is typical of him. I go away for just a couple of days and I come back to find that he's trying to replace me . . .' I couldn't stop myself. 'Still, if you're into a threesome . . .'

Valeria was out of the flat long before Simon came back from the all-night garage with the packet of fags she had asked for.

'What are you doing here? Where's Valeria?' he asked when he found me sitting in her place on the sofa.

'She had to go home suddenly,' I said, screwing the top back on to my Bourbon before carefully marking the level on the side with a felt-tip pen.

'Why? What happened?'

'I don't know. I guess those Mediterranean types can be pretty unpredictable sometimes.'

'I'd better call her,' said Simon frantically. 'Check that everything's OK.'

'No,' I covered the phone with a cushion. 'Wait till she calls you.'

'Do you know something I don't?' Simon asked, narrowing his eyes. 'What did you say to her?'

'I didn't say anything.'

'What did you say to her, Lara? If you don't tell me now I shall find out from her soon enough.'

'OK. OK,' I smiled. 'So I might have pretended that I was your girlfriend. I didn't think she'd take me seriously, did I? She didn't hang around long enough for me to tell her the truth.'

'What? You told her that you're my girlfriend! Why did you do that?'

'Because,' I shook my half-empty Bourbon bottle at him. 'And . . .' I pointed at the melting Notre-Dame. 'That candle was really special to me, you know.'

'I'm sorry. I didn't know it was precious to you. I just didn't have time to buy any candles. But what's the whisky got to do with it.'

'It's mine, that's what.'

'No, it isn't,' Simon replied, pointing to the unopened bottle which still stood on a kitchen shelf and snatching the half-finished one back. 'That's yours over there.'

'Shit. Sorry. But that still doesn't make up for the candle, you pig.'

'I would have bought you another shitty candle, you cow. Now you've ruined my chances with the best girl I've ever met in my life. Why didn't you go after her when she ran off?'

'The best girl you've ever met, eh?'

'Yeah. The best,' Simon repeated angrily. 'How long has she been gone?' I shrugged my shoulders. 'Well, I'm going to try to find her. If she calls here in the meantime, you'd just better put her straight about you and me. Christ, Lara, whatever possessed you to tell a lie like that?'

I wasn't sure.

Simon fled in hot pursuit of Valeria, slamming the door behind him. I blew out my Notre-Dame candle and collapsed in a heap on the sofa where Valeria had lain so prettily. I tried not to feel guilty about what I had done. In my opinion, she hadn't actually looked that nice. She had the pinched-up lips of someone who could be quite mean without provocation and she had certainly been snotty enough with me to confirm that view. I predicted that in not too long at all Simon would be glad that I had saved him the bother of going out with her and doubtless being gossiped about in the loos at work.

Besides, if she couldn't take a joke.

The telephone rang.

It was Valeria.

'Is he back yet?'

'Er, actually,' I muttered, 'he's gone out to try to find you.'

'Well, tell him not to come anywhere near me. I was just telephoning to tell him that he's a bastard.'

'Valeria,' I swallowed hard. 'Actually, he's not as much of a bastard as you think. There was a bit of a misunderstanding. I was joking about being his girlfriend. I didn't think you'd take me seriously and rush off.'

'Why didn't you come after me and say that?' She sounded hurt.

'I don't know,' I told her truthfully. 'I guess I thought it would be fun to see Simon's face when he got back from the garage to find you gone.'

'You think that's funny,' she hissed. 'It's a good job I didn't punch him. You should find yourself something better to do than make stupid jokes. How about you get a life of your own?'

'Fine. I will. But I don't know why you're taking it so badly. He's running across London right now to be at your side . . .'

I could hear the buzz of a doorbell in the background. Valeria slammed down the telephone. I guessed that Simon had already arrived at her flat.

Feeling rather stupid and shame-faced, I walked back to the sofa and sat down again to stare at the turned-off television, but at least I now had the house to myself. Unless of course Simon and Valeria decided to trek back across London to pick up where they had left off.

Why had I told her that I was his girlfriend? I asked myself again.

Maybe it was something about the way she was lying there, looking so expectant that had really pissed me off. What right did she have to hang around waiting for love on my sofa when the only fun I got on it these days was hunting for an escaped custard cream that had fallen down between the cushions?

Yeah. I just thought she looked a bit predatory, that was all.

It was nothing to do with the way I felt about Simon. No, nothing at all to do with him. He could have gone out with Claudia Schiffer for all I cared, just as long as she didn't act like my house belonged to her. I curled my feet up beneath me and switched the television on with the remote. On screen, a gilded couple were sharing a lingering kiss on the beach. I switched the television off again.

CHAPTER TWENTY-TWO

'Valeria this, Valeria that, Valeria bloody Valeria.' Whenever I saw Simon, when he wasn't round at Valeria's house, he was talking about her. He had quickly managed to paper over the cracks formed by my joke (pathetic as it was) and now Valeria was back with a vengeance. Simon was talking about spending his Easter holidays in Madrid with her family. He had bought a *Teach Yourself Spanish* book with an accompanying tape and was driving me insane by walking around the flat playing the tape on his Walkman so that I could only hear, *'Para mi, un birra por favor'* three hundred times a day.

I took my problems to Julie, who said that she'd heard Valeria was OK and that I would feel much better when I found someone new of my own. Or was it, she probed, that my heart was actually trying to say I was in love with Simon and I was refusing to admit it to myself. I stated a firm 'no'. It was merely that Valeria came round three or four times a week to make a mess in my kitchen and hog the bathroom for hours while she prepared herself for bed with enough perfume to choke a horse.

Almost four weeks after the first time, Simon came home with cream cakes again. I knew what that meant.

'No,' I said firmly without even looking up. 'I am not going out so that you can have the flat to yourself again. It's the third time you've asked in a fortnight.'

Simon unwrapped a juicy chocolate éclair and floated it past my nose. 'Go on, Lara. You know you want to.'

'Know I want to what?' I snapped. 'Certainly I know that I wouldn't mind eating that éclair. That much is true. But I very much mind having to spend a night out on the streets to earn it.'

Simon flumped down in the chair beside me. 'Please. Please. Please,' he begged. 'It's our one month anniversary tomorrow.'

'One month? Why do you have to celebrate that? Are you afraid you won't make it to two?'

'No, I'm not afraid we won't make it to two. I want to cook Valeria a romantic meal, if you must know. But then, I suppose you've forgotten what it's like to be in love, haven't you?'

I stuffed half the éclair in my mouth even though I had no intention of keeping my half of the bargain.

'You could go over to Andrew and Julie's. Or to some other friend's place. You have got other friends, haven't you?' Simon persisted.

It was like a red belly to a stickleback. 'Yes, I have got other friends as a matter of fact. It's just that after a hard week at work, I sometimes like to flake out in front of my own television in the flat that I pay rent on. OK?'

'I'd do the same for you, Lara,' Simon pleaded, spoiling the effect quickly when he added, 'If you ever managed to be nice enough to attract someone to cook dinner for, that is.'

'Right,' I snarled, shoving the last of the éclair in my mouth. 'You can have the flat tomorrow night. See if I care. I've got dozens of dates that I can take up if I want to. It's just that I haven't really felt inclined to do so before. But tomorrow, I'll let someone take me out to dinner. Someone who's not so cheapskate that he would want to cook me a "romantic" dinner in this bloody grot-hole instead of paying for one at Quaglinos.'

'Who's that?' I might have known that he would ask.

'No one you know.'

'No one who exists, knowing you.'

'Oh, is that what you think, Simon? Well, I'll tell you what, I'll arrange for him to pick me up here, then you can see for yourself whether he exists or not. I think you'll be surprised.'

'I doubt it.'

'You know, your probation period in this flat is nearly up,' I informed him tartly.

'You know, you couldn't afford the rent on this flat without me.'

I snatched the cake box with its remaining two cakes and took it with me to my bedroom. Safely inside, I collapsed on to my bed and stuffed the cakes into my mouth quickly, barely tasting them as they slipped down my throat. Then, feeling like a really fat pig, I passed the obligatory five minutes of self-loathing before I could get back to the business of loathing Simon.

Now I was in real trouble. Dozens of dates? Only if I brought home my desk calendar. And I had announced that my date would be picking me up just to prove how desirable I was. I dug my address book out from beneath a pile of greying bras and flicked through it desperately. The situation was going to be exactly the same as it had been when Simon first brought Valeria home. I would have to pretend that my hot date was meeting me at the cinema and watch three showings of some Arnie film on my own.

The problem of my not-so-hot date was preoccupying me so much when I got to work the next day that I didn't notice that not one of my colleagues was sitting at his or her desk. Instead, they were all crowding around Joe's untidy work-station, and coming from behind the circle of curious bodies I could hear the odd strangled sob.

Maureen emerged from the comfort scrum bearing Joe's mug. 'He needs some sweet tea,' she told me briskly. 'He's had a terrible shock, poor boy.'

'Oh, really,' I asked. 'Did he catch a barracuda on Clapham Common?'

Maureen shot me a look which told me that my levity on the matter in hand was not appreciated. 'It's his girlfriend,' she elaborated. 'Her ex-fiancé turned up at Joe's flat last night and she's decided to get back together with him. Would you credit it? She just packed up her things and left Joe there and then. Didn't want to talk about it.'

'That's terrible,' I muttered.

'He's devastated,' said Maureen. 'Women are always letting him down.' She muttered that barb so that it was barely audible but I knew that she was including me amongst those Joe-deserting Jezebels.

'Must be the only man in London getting a taste of men's own medicine,' I ventured.

'And he doesn't deserve it,' Maureen defended. 'He's a lovely young man and he'll make someone a wonderful husband. Only problem he has is that he's not a bastard.' I was shocked. Maureen never swore. 'Stupid young girls like you and that Linzi only chase after the ones who run away from them the whole time. You don't know what's good for you, you girls. You think that a real man has to act like Sylvester Stallone.'

'It must be the way we were brought up.'

'I reckon it all changed for the worst in the sixties.'

'Well, I wasn't around then, so it can't be entirely my fault.'

'It was Mick Jagger and the Rolling Stones that made the bad boy fashionable.'

'When we all should want someone like David Cassidy . . .'

Maureen ignored me and splashed boiling water on to a teabag in Joe's *Fishing News* limited edition trout mug. 'I'd better get back to him. Tell him there's plenty more fish in the sea.' That was apt.

I made myself a coffee and took up my position at my desk. Joe's period of mourning lasted until lunchtime at which point Maureen passed closely by my desk and hissed, 'I've got to go and get my hair done now. Can you take him for a sandwich, love? There's a good girl.'

Though it had been phrased as a question, it obviously wasn't meant to be one and when I started to tell her that I had an urgent appointment at the post office, she pretended not to hear me.

'Keep him talking,' she advised me. 'But try to steer him off the subject of *her*. Tell him about his good points.'

'Well, that'll keep the conversation flowing until two minutes past one,' I sniffed.

'What?' snapped Maureen.

'I was just thinking that you ought to go on a course or something, to do counselling professionally. You're a natural listener, Mo.' She puffed up with pride as she buttoned up her bright red duffel coat.

'You know, Lara, I think you might be right,' she purred. 'People have often said that I have a natural empathy with those in distress.'

I didn't have anything like a natural empathy for someone as pathetic as Joe after the way I had bravely borne my split with Hugh. I hadn't let out so much as a tragic sniff during working hours. But I knew that if I didn't escort Joe to lunch, getting Maureen to do any more typing for me that week could become somewhat difficult.

'Are you coming to the canteen?' I asked Joe grudgingly

at one o'clock. 'And what about you, Malcolm,' I added in an attempt to find safety in numbers, 'Do you fancy coming too?'

'No, thanks,' said Malcolm, looking visibly relieved that someone else had landed themselves with Joe. 'I'm going into town to look at a new skateboard.'

'I'll come with you,' tried Joe.

'No,' insisted Malcolm, almost pushing Joe back down on to his chair. 'You stay here. You need to get some rest now. Get your strength up.' Malcolm fled the office quickly, giving me a wink as he left, as if that made up for leaving me in peril.

'Worst of it is,' Joe sniffed on to his canteen chips and tinned tomatoes later that day. 'I bought these tickets for a concert tonight and now I've got nobody to go with.'

'Can't you get a refund?'

'Not now I can't. I suppose I could try to sell them on the door but then I might get into trouble for being a ticket-tout.'

'Yeah, I hear it carries a big jail sentence,' I said sarcastically. 'What are the tickets for anyway? Anything good.'

'Yes. It's for an evening of Fado. That's a type of Portuguese folk music.'

'I know,' I said, remembering that joyful evening of singing fishwives I had spent with Hugh at the Royal Festival Hall.

'You know about Fado?' Joe asked excitedly.

'Well, I don't really know much about it, but I have come across it before, yes.'

'Oh,' Joe sighed. 'It's my favourite kind of music. It's so passionate, so haunting, so very sad.'

'Yes. And if you see it on your own, you might end up committing suicide,' I said through a mouthful of bread and butter pudding. Healthy eating was still an alien concept in the Hartley and Hartley canteen.

'Well, why don't you come with me tonight?'

'Er, I've got other things to do.' I lied.

Just at that moment, Malcolm glided into the canteen on his brand-new skateboard, under the disapproving eye of the matrons from personnel. 'Lara,' he yelled from the self-service queue. 'I've just been up to the office. There was a message on the machine from your housemate. He says, have you got a date for tonight or do you want him to call Dateline for you?'

Everyone in the canteen did their swivel-headed best to see whether I was indeed fixed up for the evening. 'Thank you, Malcolm,' I replied gaily through gritted teeth. 'You can tell him not to panic. I've got something to do.' Then I yanked Joe across the table by his tie in what was meant to be a foxy kind of way and said, 'Might just take you up on that Fado after all.' I had decided that if I went to the concert I would at least only have to see the new Schwarzennegger once before I could go home.

As I waited for Joe to pick me up that night, I prayed that he wouldn't think Fado worth dressing up for. I didn't have much time to make myself beautiful since Simon was already in the bathroom by the time I got home from work and he didn't emerge until half an hour before I was meant to go out.

'What *is* that aftershave?' I asked, doing my impression of a fly that's just been blasted with Deet as I staggered into the bathroom.

'It's Egöiste, actually,' Simon sniffed.

'That figures.'

The doorbell rang as I was cleaning my teeth. I wiped the froth off on Simon's dressing gown and ran to grab the door-phone out of Simon's hand before he could invite Joe to 'come on up'.

'Wait there,' I snapped. 'I'll be down in a minute.'

'But you're hardly dressed yet,' protested Simon. 'Surely it would be better if he waited here in the warm while you finish putting on your make-up.'

'I have put on my make-up,' I informed him tartly. It was the natural look as described in that month's *Cosmo*.

'Oh yes,' said Simon. 'Now that you're in the light I think I can see it. The left side of your face is all streaky.'

'Hope your lasagne burns,' was my parting shot.

The Fado was no better than I remembered. In fact, it was the exact same fishwife doing the keening and once again I was struck by the failure of European musicians in general to match the vocals to the tune. The guitars were straight out of *Zorba the Greek* while the vocals were pure *Tosca*. Joe, predictably, understood Portuguese. He snivelled throughout most of the set and when it had finished, he turned to me, all red eyed, and begged me not to leave him on his own until he had recovered from the emotional exertion of the fishwife's tragic song which was about a poor pilchard harvest apparently.

What could I say?

We wandered through Soho until we found a little restaurant where the pasta was matched by pasta prices rather than the GNP of Italy. But Joe hardly touched his penne arrabiata. Instead, he wrung his napkin between his sweaty hands until it was a pile of paper shreds, then he poured salt straight on to the table and began to arrange it into the initials of his recently-ex loved one.

'I don't know what I did wrong?' he said for the hundredth time.

'Sometimes,' I replied, surprisingly wisely for me, 'it isn't a case of having done anything wrong at all. It's just that someone else does things more right for the person in question. Do you know what I mean?'

Joe looked at me blankly.

'I mean, perhaps you were ninety-nine per cent right for her and she hadn't noticed the one per cent which was wrong, but this other chap, well, he was a hundred per cent right straight off.' Joe still stared at me as though I were talking in Dutch. 'Yeah, you're right,' I conceded. 'I don't know what I'm talking about. The fact is, shit happens, I suppose. There's always going to be someone with a bigger car, a bigger chest, longer hair, a nicer house.'

Joe began to bawl. I obviously wasn't doing very well on

the consolation front. 'Oh, God,' I said in embarrassment. 'Joe, how about we get the bill now, eh?'

We wandered from Soho to Trafalgar Square and from there to Embankment. I had thought that a bit of fresh air would do Joe the world of good but it seemed that there was nowhere in this great city where he had not been with that fickle girl of his and every bench we passed, every monument we saw, would spark off an exclamation of 'Cheryl and I held hands on that bench once', followed by at least five minutes of intense and dramatic weeping.

I was tempted to help him push himself off Hungerford Bridge but instead, since I wasn't sure whether that would be manslaughter, I suggested that we get a drink on one of those boats which is permanently moored near the back door of the Savoy. I bought the first round and thought that I would try to cut a long night short by getting doubles. I couldn't leave Joe alone being so unhappy, but if he fell asleep, as he was rumoured to do after enough Southern Comfort, I would have no compunction whatsoever about loading him into the back of a black cab with an address label tied around his neck.

He downed a double Jack Daniels in one and followed it with a fistful of peanuts. Anxious not to let him soak up too much of the alcohol before it took effect, I carefully moved the peanuts out of his reach and claimed that they would be dehydrating. Joe said that he didn't give a stuff if he did get dehydrated. In fact, he wanted to become like desiccated coconut and blow away on the breeze.

'Was she really that great?' I asked him. Stupid question. He began: 'Let me count the ways.'

Joe bought a round. Then I bought a round. I bought rounds until my purse was empty and I had built a pretty respectable pyramid of empty glasses in the middle of the table. I could see three of Joe by now, though that might just have been because I was looking through the glasses. I put the peanuts back on the table and decided that I had better try to soak some of the alcohol up.

'Are you all right, Lara?' I remember him saying. 'You're looking really pale.'

Oh God, there's nothing worse than waking up in a strange bed!

CHAPTER TWENTY-THREE

The first thing I noticed was that I didn't recognise the curtains. They were a seventies'-style floral print with dark brown leaves and orange petals, which reminded me of the curtains we used to have in the caravan we took on holiday until I was fifteen. The real horror of the fact that I didn't recognise the curtains I was looking at right then didn't strike me until I had remembered the make of our caravan. It was an Eldis. And I had loved it, with its curtained-off bunk beds and doll's-house kitchen, until I hit eleven and puberty and the sudden onset of taste struck a dual blow.

Who would have curtains like this in their house? I wondered. Someone cool enough to be ironically kitsch? I doubted it. After all, where would I have picked up someone like that?

There was a gentle knock at the door. The quiet clearing of a throat.

'A-hem, Lara. A-hem. Do you think you could open the door for me? I've got my hands full.'

I clutched the itchy blankets to my naked chest. Suddenly, the memory of my companion of the night before came rushing back to me like a gush of projectile vomit gathering at the back of my throat. I hadn't, had I? Surely not. I couldn't have? No. Not with him? Not even if he had threatened to kill himself if I didn't.

'Hang on a minute, Joe,' I called. My voice was quavering up and down a scale like a choirboy at the end of his career. 'I'll just make myself decent.'

'Decent? Don't worry about that,' he laughed.

I scanned the floor for my clothes, which I eventually found hanging from the back of a chair. I couldn't have put them there. I wasn't that tidy. I offered up one final prayer that I had found myself in the spare room. But my filthy shoes were racked neatly alongside a polished pair of man-sized brogues. All the signs of occupation told me that this was not the spare bedroom at all.

'Come on, Lara. My arms are breaking under the weight of this teapot.'

I clutched my head in despair. I was going to have to get myself sorted out. Total blackouts were not very useful to a girl who went out drinking with incredibly unattractive men on a regular basis. Taking a deep breath, I wrenched open the door.

'Oh,' said Joe, disappointedly, when he saw me in my jeans and polo-necked jumper, not knowing I had nothing underneath that top. 'Thought I might catch you in your knickers.'

I blushed to the roots of my hair. How had he become so familiar in his tone with me overnight?

'You don't want to see them,' I said probingly. 'They're all grey.'

At least I had still been wearing them when I woke up.

'Are they?' he asked innocently. 'I always had you down for the kind of girl who wears red.'

My tensed up forehead muscles slackened as though they had just been given an injection of botulism or whatever it is that the rich and famous get these days to stop themselves from frowning. He obviously hadn't seen me in my pants. I must have been so drunk that I actually folded my clothes up myself after taking them off.

'Did you sleep well?' I asked. Trying to find out where he had slept without using the words. I edged Joe and his breakfast tray out of the bedroom, scanning the corridor desperately for doorways that might lead to another room as we almost danced into the kitchen.

'Oh, fine,' he said. 'I always sleep on the sofa when I have a guest. It's not too uncomfortable.'

'Oh, thank you, God. Thank you. Thank you.'

'What?' Joe looked disturbed at my grateful outburst.

I waved towards the open window which was letting in chilly blasts of dank February air. 'I mean thank you God for this beautiful day,' I covered.

'Didn't know you were religious,' said Joe.

'Until I saw the light, neither did I. Er, Joe . . .' I was growing bolder now. 'What exactly happened last night?'

'Oh, you got really drunk and then you fell asleep on the table at that bar. I was going to bundle you into a taxi with an address label around your neck but since I'd had one or two myself I couldn't remember whether you lived at number fourteen or number forty so I thought I'd better bring you back here instead.'

I could have kissed him. 'I'll never drink again.'

But I still needed to leave for home as soon as politely possible.

As I was putting on my jacket, Joe told me that our evening together had made him see the light too. He had decided that there was no point mooning about his ex-girlfriend any more. I had proved to him that there were plenty more fish in the sea. I was kind of flattered, but not so much so that I wanted him to make another date, so when he asked if we could do it all again some other time, I said that I had decided to take an evening course in Russian which would start the very next Friday.

'Useful for work,' said Joe, admiringly. 'How about Thursday instead?' 'What? Thursday? I'm afraid that's when I play squash. In fact most week nights are out until the tournament is over and I'll be spending weekends for the foreseeable future visiting my sick grandmother.'

Joe sighed sympathetically. 'I see. I understand. I'm still filled with guilt about the fact that I didn't really visit my grandmother often enough before she died.'

I was filled with guilt too. My last remaining grand-mother had died three years earlier.

'Oh, well,' Joe concluded. 'I guess we'll just have to take it as it comes, eh? Let me know whenever you've got a free moment since you're the one with the busy schedule. Ha ha. I never would have thought that squash was your game though. You should talk to Jerry.' Jerry was our boss. 'He plays squash very well apparently. Perhaps he would give you a match.'

I laughed nervously. 'Perhaps he would. If he wasn't always so busy running Hartley and Hartley. Gosh, is that the time already? I've got to be at squash practice in half an hour. See you on Monday morning, Joe.'

I fled to the door, eager – no make that desperate – to be outside. I wrenched at it so hard that I pulled my arms out of their sockets but made no difference whatsoever to the hinges. Seeing me struggle, Joe walked smugly down the stairs behind me and said, 'You've got to push that button there,' pointing to a little red buzzer on the wall that deactivated the lock.

'Thanks. Bye.' I pressed the button and the door flew open like a greyhound trap. I stepped out on to the pavement. The fresh air seared my lungs. The bright sunshine burned my eyes. I couldn't see where I was going for a second and, while I was waving insanely at a receding Joe, I bumped straight into Hugh Armstrong-Hamilton.

'Lara!!!' the bastard trilled as though the last time he had seen me we had been swopping pleasantries at a jolly tea-party. 'What are you doing here?' We both looked back at the door through which I had emerged. Joe was still standing there. His smug smile had dissolved into a frown.

'Hey. Isn't that the guy from outside the County Arms?'

'Yes,' I said defensively. 'Yes. It is him and what has it got to do with you?'

Hugh raised his hands in surrender. 'Sorry I asked.'

Joe was still hanging about in his doorway, obviously wondering whether I was about to need to be rescued.

'See you on Monday, Joe,' I called again, giving him a wave that suggested finality, before I stalked off down the street away from Hugh.

'Hang on,' he called after me.

I wasn't going to hang on for him. I continued to walk, faster and faster. I didn't even want Hugh Armstrong-Hamilton to live under the same solar system as me, let alone follow me home on a Saturday morning when I felt like one of those fish that lives at the bottom of the sea until it loses all its colour. OK. So the fact that I wasn't wearing mascara was a major point in my decision to flee.

We turned a corner. Me leading, Hugh snapping at my heels like a puppy. When I was sure that Joe would no longer be able to see, I stopped dead and told Hugh, 'Stop following me or . . . or I'll . . .' (I couldn't think of an or.)

'Or you'll have your boyfriend sort me out?'

'He's not my boyfriend,' I corrected quickly.

'Oh.'

'Yes. That's right. It is possible for men and women to be friends, you know.'

Hugh raised an eyebrow. 'Well,' I said indignantly. 'I don't know why I'm bothering to justify this to you, anyway. You never did care who I spent my nights with as long as I didn't pester you.'

'That's not true,' he said smoothly. But I wasn't going to let myself be taken in by his smoothness that morning. 'Anyway,' I said to change the subject, 'hadn't you better rush back to Caroline with those croissants you're carrying? They'll be getting cold.'

'I'm having breakfast alone actually.'

That threw me. 'You are?'

'Yes. Unless you'd like to join me. I'm sure I've got enough for two.'

'I wouldn't eat breakfast with you if I hadn't eaten anything for a year.'

'You're still bitter about splitting up then?'

'Shouldn't I be?'

Hugh shrugged, then he admitted, 'You've probably got every right to be, I suppose. I didn't handle things terribly well, did I?' I shook my head. 'Listen, perhaps I could make it up to you. Perhaps we could go for dinner sometime?'

'I'm quite busy these days,' I lied. 'You know, squash tournaments and things.'

'Ah, yes. The squash. But how about tonight?' Hugh persisted.

As the answer formed on my lips I could hear the voice of Julie in my head. Tonight? I couldn't possibly say yes at such short notice. He would think that I had nothing better to do. That I was just gagging for a date. But Julie would be too busy eating coal to admonish me this time. So I nodded foolishly. Then I underlined the nod with a noncommital sounding, 'OK.'

'Great,' Hugh smiled. 'I'll see you at about half past seven.' Then he kissed me lightly on the top of the head and turned back in the direction he had come from.

It didn't strike me until Hugh had disappeared again that I didn't actually have a clue where I had ended up that morning. I looked at the sign on the corner of the street. Loveday Road. Much as I hated to admit it, it seemed like a good omen.

CHAPTER TWENTY-FOUR

I prepared myself for that evening by putting on my chastity underwear. It was a bra and knickers set I had bought in 1990 which had since gone from pure white to palest grey and which was held together by red stitching and safety pins. It was my way of ensuring that sex would be out of the question that night, or even a snog that breached my shirt buttons. No matter how good he looked, no matter how hard he tried, that night Hugh Armstrong-Hamilton and I would be no more than friends.

We went to La Traviata, of course. But these days I could handle spaghetti. Now that the gilt had been stripped from my image of Hugh by his repeated betrayals, he didn't have the ability to stun me into self-consciousness any more. Though I stayed off the wine just in case, because I couldn't be quite certain.

'So,' I said, getting straight to the point. 'What brings you back into my life? Don't tell me you've been chucked.'

'Caroline and I have split up,' he said, equally flatly.

'That much is true. But I would have called you anyway, Lara. I did promise to be in touch after a month or so, remember? We've had some good times together and I always want us to remain friends.'

I snorted into my glass of Perrier.

'Good times eh? Good times such as on the chair in my sitting room?'

Hugh coloured from the tips of his ears down.

'I can't believe you would tell your workmates something like that. Why should I be your friend now?'

'I only mentioned it to them because that night was so good,' Hugh blustered.

'Not good enough to make you stick around though, was it?'

'Come on,' said Hugh. 'Can't we be adult about this? I just needed a little more time to sort myself out. You can't go on bearing a grudge against me for ever.'

'Wrong, Hugh. If you were to push me far enough I could probably bear a grudge into the next millennium. But I'm not bearing a grudge,' I reminded him sharply. 'It is simply that I object to being used as your second choice when it comes to shagging.'

'That's not true.'

'It's too true. I'm second choice after Caroline. It's obvious. And I'm worth more than that, Hugh. Much more.'

'I know,' he whispered. 'I know.'

'Then why don't you act like you know? Why did you disappear every time Caroline gave you the nod?'

Hugh stared at his plate for a moment, looking thoroughly told off.

'I can't help it. I really can't. It's because of things that have happened in the past I suppose.'

'Don't tell me. You were betrayed once too.'

'Don't make a joke of it, Lara.'

I raised my eyebrows cynically but then Hugh started to tell me exactly what he meant by things in the past. He told me more about Caroline. He told me why he had felt in thrall to her for years and years. First of all, he had been going out with her sister, Fiona. But when Fiona introduced Hugh to Caroline, she all but lost him. Caroline and Hugh had a secret affair until Fiona announced that she wanted to get married.

He couldn't marry her of course. Not because he felt so very deeply for Caroline but because the mere fact of his infidelity proved that he didn't love Fiona. They argued. Fiona drank a bottle of whisky. And driving Hugh home that night, she had the accident which cost him his licence and Fiona her life.

Suddenly it became clear why Caroline had changed the subject every time Fiona's name came up in Wales.

I gasped. 'That's terrible. But why did you lose your licence, if she was driving?'

'Before I knew that Fiona was going to die,' Hugh said slowly. 'I decided to take the rap. Besides, I blamed myself. She had been drinking because of me. Losing my licence felt like penance in a way.'

I sighed. What a noble, noble man.

'Ever since,' he continued. 'I've been unable to tear myself away from Caroline. The accident has been like a guilty glue that has kept us together. Only Caroline and I knew why Fiona lost control of that car. Until now.'

'You mean you've just told me a secret?' I said excitedly.

'Yes. Because you have helped me to break the spell.'

I was astounded. He wasn't an insensitive swine after all. Just confused and misunderstood. No wonder he had been so reluctant to enter into a new relationship with the horror of Fiona's death hanging over him. No wonder Caroline was so reluctant to let him go. I mean, if Caroline's sister died because of her affair with Hugh, she wouldn't want that affair to have been meaningless. She would have had to convince herself that it had been true love.

'I'm sorry,' I said banally. 'If I had known about that I might have been a bit more, you know, a bit more forgiving. What a terrible thing to happen.'

'There's no way you could have guessed. And whatever my excuses, I acted unforgivably. I made you feel a fool. That's why I've bought you this.' He reached into his pocket and brought out a small velvet box. He handed it across the table to me.

'What's is it?' I asked.

'Why don't you open it and see?'

I opened it up gingerly. Surely, it couldn't be a ring? That was too insane. He chucks me. I don't see him for a month. And then he confesses all about his past and buys me a ring. But no, it wasn't a ring. It was a delicate silver bracelet.

'It's not much,' he said. 'But I want it to be a symbol of our enduring friendship.'

I held it up in the candlelight to watch its filigree pattern glitter. It wasn't quite what I would have chosen myself but for a man he had shown remarkable taste.

'It's beautiful!!' I sighed. 'Really beautiful. But you didn't have to do this.'

'It's the very least I could do after all the pain and embarrassment I must have caused you since we first met.' He put on those puppy-dog eyes. 'Can we be friends again now?'

'Friends,' I nodded. How could I refuse? 'Of course we can be friends. Oh, Hugh, I feel so close to you now. I feel as though you really trust me.'

I leaned across the table to land a little kiss on his cheek. What I didn't notice was the way my common sense flew out of the window simultaneously. I had smelled his gorgeous aftershave and I was all but lost. Again.

After dinner, Hugh came back to my place. And I went through the ridiculous rigmarole of changing into some decent underwear in the bathroom while he sipped Southern Comfort in the sitting room. Thankfully, Simon and Valeria were out at a salsa evening in the town hall and a note on the kitchen table explained that they didn't expect to be back before dawn.

I sank gratefully into Hugh's arms, again. Besides, I had convinced myself, even if I went the whole way with my body, which was crying out for attention after a long Hugh-drought, it didn't mean I had to go the whole way with my mind. Hugh slipped his hand up the back of my jumper and fiddled with the catch on my bra.

'That's what I like about you, Lara,' he told me. 'The fact that you're so open-minded about things. You're so generous of spirit. You're always so forgiving.'

I wrapped my arms around his neck and gazed at the beautiful bracelet glittering on my wrist as he began to kiss me. Just your body, I reminded myself. Just your body, Lara Fenton, and definitely not your mind.

The next morning, I bumped into Simon in the kitchen. He was frying eggs, stinking the place out again as he managed to burn more than he successfully cooked. When I floated in, looking beautifully dishevelled I thought as I passed the mirror in the hallway, he looked first at the worn brown-leather jacket hanging from the back of the chair and then at me, his eyebrows raised disdainfully.

'That doesn't belong to you-know-who, does it?' he asked.

I pinched a piece of Simon's toast and said 'Uh-huh.'

'So he's back?'

'Took me out to dinner last night as a matter of fact.'

'Well, Lara,' he said with a sigh. 'Don't say I didn't warn you when it all goes wrong again.'

'Nothing will go wrong,' I said confidently. 'It's different this time.'

'Famous last words.'

'Yeah. But I won't be eating them.'

The moment Hugh had gone, I was straight on the phone to Julie. She took a similar line to Simon and warned me that I was in danger of getting burnt again. But I told her too that this time I had everything under control. This time I was going in with my body but not my heart. Besides, didn't the fact that he kept coming back to me mean something? It was fate, I told her. We were meant to be together. Obviously.

'Well, I hope for your sake that it is going to be third time lucky,' Julie sighed. 'You know where I am if it's not.'

'It will be lucky,' I insisted. 'I'm only ever going to call you with good news from now on.'

Julie snorted.

'I wish you could be more open-minded about this, Julie,' I twittered on regardless. 'That was what Hugh says he likes about me, the fact that I'm more open-minded than most girls and so forgiving of past mistakes.'

'Open-legged and gullible, more like,' Julie told me frankly. 'For goodness' sake be careful, Lara. I don't want to have to start arranging Andrew's social diary so that you and Hugh are never simultaneously in the same room again.'

'Thanks for being so supportive, best friend.'

'Sometimes it's a best friend's job to tell you something you don't really want to know.'

'Oh. Go and knit bootees,' I snarled.

I retired to my room to look at my bracelet. Needless

to say I was disappointed by the response of the two people I considered to be my closest friends with regard to Hugh's return. But we would prove them wrong. I knew we would. Together.

When the phone next rang, it was Hugh. Simon handed me the receiver with a blank expression that rather dampened my elation at receiving the call.

'I'm so glad we got together again last night,' Hugh was saying.

I wanted to simper and giggle and be generally girly, but Simon was watching me with the look of my old French teacher checking a verb test so I couldn't. We arranged to go out that evening and I told Simon magnanimously that he could have the flat to himself.

CHAPTER TWENTY-FIVE

Getting back together with Hugh for the third time did wonders for my performance at work. With the thought of sharing the evenings with the love of my life, the long days didn't seem half so long any more and I was especially tolerant towards my new temp.

Linzi, the Aussie girl, had saved up enough money to go home and had gone, leaving a broken-hearted builder in Beckenham. The new temp was called Eunice, though I often called her 'Useless' when she wasn't too near my desk. She could barely log on to her computer, let alone produce any useful graphics. Before Hugh came back into my life, I had been toying with the idea of planting one of the boss's packets of Polos in her desk and getting her sacked for pinching them. But in my post-Hugh love haze, I would simply re-do all the work I had sent via Eunice and was giving everyone, including her, the impression that she was a super-temp.

Only Joe seemed to be pretty hard to convince.

Since having me wake up in his bedroom that morning,

Joe's interest in me seemed to have cooled. Thankfully. Julie said it was because he had finally got to sniff the aroma of my beautiful hair on his pillow and that had been enough for him. (She was joking. I hoped.) Now, when Joe came to perch shiny-buttocked on my desk, there were no puppy-dog eyes in my direction. Instead he was gazing over towards the desk where Eunice was making more work for me to do.

'Do you think that Eunice is really up to the job?' he asked me suddenly.

'What? I mean, yes. Of course I think she's up to the job.'

'Really? Well I've noticed you correcting some of her mistakes without letting her know what she did wrong.'

'Oh,' I waved my hand. 'Just a matter of saving some time, Joe. Far easier for me to adjust my grammar on screen than send it back and forth to Eunice as though it's a tennis ball.'

'Mmm. But you seem to be correcting more than just the odd thing these days. If she's not working efficiently enough, we could easily ask the agency to send us someone else.'

Joe was staring steadfastly in her direction but his gaze didn't seem to be particularly full of malice. Or even mild annoyance.

'Joe, don't be too hard on her,' I told him. 'It can be difficult, starting a temp job at a place like this where everyone else knows each other so well.'

'Huh. She's been here for a couple of months now. And

she doesn't seem to be making the effort to get to know us at all.'

'A-ha,' I had a Russell Grant-like glimpse of the future. 'Perhaps she's a bit shy?'

'Shy?'

'Yes. I'm sure you were shy when you first came here too.'

Joe straightened up his Mickey Mouse printed tie. (That boy was going nowhere near the Board Room – unless of course, he got a job at Disney.) 'Yes. But I made an effort when I first started. She never joins in with the after-work drinks.'

'Do you ever ask her?'

'Yes. I mean, no. I mean, everyone in this office knows what nights we go to the wine bar. It's just a matter of tagging along. If she wants to be miserable and awkward, then that's up to her.'

'Joe,' I said suddenly. 'If you like her, why don't you ask her out. You asked me and I didn't turn you down.' Joe swivelled towards me and blushed. 'And believe me, I'm picky,' I continued. 'If I didn't have so many commitments what with squash and my grandfather . . .'

'I thought it was your grandmother who was in hospital . . .'

'Oh yes,' I covered. 'But it's grandfather who needs the help at home. Anyway, if I wasn't so busy, I'm sure I would jump at the chance of spending another evening with you.'

'You would?'

'Of course.'

'Then why does she seem so "off" with me.'

I leaned across the monitor to impart some words of wisdom. 'Because sometimes people do act "off" when they actually really like someone. It's a well-known phenomenon. I think people do it because they don't want to get hurt before they know what the other person's intentions towards them are. The only thing is, if you let this being "off" thing go on for too long, you might start to think that maybe you don't like that other person after all. Get in there and rescue her before it's too late.'

Joe looked doubtful.

'Think about when you were at primary school, Joe,' I continued. 'If you had wanted a girl to be yours then, you'd probably have put a daddy-long-legs down the back of her neck. That was always happening to me.'

'I only ever did that to people I really didn't like,' said Joe, annoyingly.

'Joe, take my word for it. She likes you. And all this animosity? It's just passion in embryo. I know.'

Joe left to ponder my wise words and that afternoon, he was perching his grey stay-pressed slacks next to Eunice. Julie rang me while Joe was popping the pub-quiz question. A week into her maternity leave and she was already climbing the walls, aching for adult contact (apparently Andrew coming home in the evenings hardly counted. I had strong suspicions that ten years hence he would be one of those men who pay £200 an hour to dress up like a baby in a custom-built nursery in an ordinary-looking house in Croydon).

'I've just done a good deed,' I told her proudly.

'Oh, yeah.'

'Yes. Joe and the temp in the office. They're totally indifferent towards each other but I'm sure it's because they're really in love.'

Julie laughed. 'Nice theory. You don't know any other couples like that who need pushing together do you, Lara?'

I missed the point completely. 'I'm sure my mother does.'

CHAPTER TWENTY-SIX

Talking of indifferent, Simon seemed to have given up criticising my choice of man. I guess he was just glad that Hugh took me out of the house and out of the way of his beloved Valeria who had now taken to leaving her knickers hanging from the towel rail after having a bath. For my part, I didn't hassle him about the cleaning, or rather the lack of it, and when he was in anguish about how he should celebrate his birthday, I very kindly agreed to a flat party, even though after Julie's engagement party I had decided never to allow such shenanigans again.

I bought a padlock for my door this time, though. Just in case.

As we prepared the nibbles and waited for our guests to arrive, Simon and I talked about our loved ones' shared dislike of sweetcorn like two mothers discussing their babies' first teeth.

'It's funny, isn't it?' I said. 'But from what we've been saying today, it sounds like Valeria and Hugh have got quite a lot in common.'

'Yeah, I bet they'd really get on,' said Simon and I had a brief vision of the four of us as forty-somethings, sitting around a home counties' dinner table talking about school fees.

Valeria arrived first, bringing with her three bottles of strong red wine and a gaggle of Italian friends from her English as a foreign language evening class. Then came the people from work. Julie waddled in briefly and made short work of the Twiglets and half a bottle of salad cream before going home again to rest her aching back. Hugh arrived last, kissing me rather peremptorily on the top of the head while he scanned the room to see who had arrived before him.

'Who's that?' he asked. 'She looks familiar.'

It was Valeria, standing by the window-sill with a couple of her friends. She was laughing loudly about something and smoothing down the skirt of her little black dress. The dress that she had borrowed from me. The one that had seen its first outing on that dreadful night in Wales.

'She's Simon's girlfriend,' I said quickly. The interest in Hugh's eyes was unmistakable. 'Her name's Valeria. And she works in DTP at Partridge Skelton apparently.'

'I knew I'd seen her somewhere before. Nice dress. You must introduce me,' said Hugh.

No fear, thought I, but Simon unfortunately was only too pleased to do the honours.

I watched them shaking hands from the corner of my eye as I chatted to Eunice the temp from work. Then

Hugh said something funny and Valeria put her hand up to her long white throat while she let out a raucous laugh. Simon put his arm around her proprietorially as if he too had noticed the spark that suddenly flew between the two most important people in our lives.

'Where's your new boyfriend, then?' Eunice the temp asked when I met her by the peanut dip. 'Or should I say your recycled boyfriend? Joe tells me you keep splitting up and getting back together again.'

'He's over there,' I pointed Hugh out on the other side of the room. Now he was filling Valeria's glass, his eyes locked upon hers as he poured out the wine. He was totally oblivious of me. If looks could kill I would definitely have shot him a thunderbolt then and there. And her.

'You'll have to introduce me to him when he's not so busy,' Eunice said. I could have sworn that remark sounded pointed but I chose to brush it over and asked her instead about her budding relationship with Joe. It was brilliant, she told me. They had so many shared interests (she had fished since the age of five). She also told me that she never would have thought to look for love right under her nose if I hadn't put the idea into Joe's head.

'Some men are like diamonds,' I said, quoting my mother. 'You just have to see them in the right settings sometimes before you realise how valuable they are.'

'Yeah,' murmured Eunice. 'I think you're right. Ere, your flatmate's quite nice isn't he?'

I nodded just as Simon caught my eye from the kitchen door and reminded me that I was in charge of the sausage rolls.

'Where's Valeria?' Simon asked much later on.

I was pulling more sausage rolls out of the oven at the time. 'I don't know. I've been in the kitchen all night, haven't I?' I snapped. I had been very busy. Far too busy even to talk to Hugh. 'She won't have gone too far.'

'She's not in the flat,' he told me. 'And neither is Hugh.'

'So?' I said, as I blew on the finger I had just burnt on the edge of the baking tray.

Simon looked at me as if I was the most stupid person he had ever met.

'Hugh's probably in the bathroom,' I said by way of an excuse.

But at that moment, the sound of Valeria's tinkling laughter drifted into the flat from the communal gardens down below. Simon and I rushed to the window and peered down into the blackness. It took a moment or two for our eyes to adjust before we could make the figures out. But when we did, it was unmistakably Valeria. She was leaning back against a tree with her arms stretched above her head so that, had it not been for her long white neck, she might have blended into the bark.

'What is she doing?' asked Simon.

I shrugged my shoulders. But I had already guessed there was a man down there with her. He was leaning in towards her, like a vampire, going in for the kill. I mean, the kiss.

'Who is she with?' asked Simon.

We strained to see better. Then wished that we hadn't. Of course. It was Hugh. It just had to be Hugh.

Simon and I looked at one another aghast. But what could we have done? Shouted down, 'Step away from the girl, Mr Armstrong-Hamilton. Leave the girl alone,' with a loud-hailer like they did in hostage films?

'Christ alive, that man is such a slime,' Simon hissed as he rolled up his sleeves and prepared for battle.

'What? He's a slime?' I exclaimed. 'But what about her? She's such a tart.'

'He's trying to seduce her.'

'She's hardly trying to beat him off.'

The scene downstairs was probably continuing to unfold while Simon and I began to argue about which of the players was most to blame. He became so rabid about Hugh and I so vicious about his beloved Valeria that by the time they appeared at the kitchen doorway, smiling like two innocent children, I had almost decided to forgive Hugh just to spite my flatmate.

'Valeria's been teaching me Spanish,' Hugh told us innocently.

'I'll bet she has, you bastard,' Simon spat.

Simon flew at Hugh, fists flailing rather ineffectually. Hugh ducked the punches easily and within seconds he was holding Simon up by the scruff of the neck while his feet kicked the air like those of a hanged man.

Valeria was squeaking her horror in one-hundred-mile-an-hour Spanish. I felt sorely tempted to give her a thump to shut her up but had a feeling that even in her petite hands I would go the same way as Simon, who was now sitting on a stool, rubbing at his sore neck.

'What on earth was that about, man?' Hugh asked disingenuously as he dusted himself off.

'Don't pretend you don't know, Armstrong-Hamilton,' hissed Simon.

'I do not know. Explain what you mean.'

'You and Valeria. Learning Spanish. Learning Spanish, my arse.'

'I not do anything,' Valeria was shrieking indignantly. 'I just tell him how to say "hello" to people who come from Madrid.'

'We saw you from the window,' I told her. 'We saw you kissing.'

The game was up. Valeria looked at Hugh. Hugh looked at Valeria. Simon and I looked at both of them for hope of an explanation which would make the fact that they had been swopping saliva as innocent as him lighting her fag.

'OK,' Valeria said suddenly, shrugging as she did so. 'So I kissed 'im. So big what? I'm not going to say sorry. We go back to my house now, Hugh, you think?'

And they went. Just like that.

CHAPTER TWENTY-SEVEN

Simon and I sat silently in the kitchen while the party broke up around us and everybody else went home. We didn't say anything. I stuffed sausage rolls into my mouth one after another, not making much distinction between those which were burnt or underdone. Simon drew a pattern on the table with salt. From time to time, he made the shape of a heart, then he smashed it to little bits.

'Well, that's the end of that then,' he said, after a long while when the house was empty of everyone else and a CD hiccuped in the player.

'Yeah. Again,' said I.

'I thought she was going to be the love of my life,' Simon sighed.

'Maybe she was. He was definitely mine.'

'Hugh never loved you,' Simon hissed.

'What makes you think she held you in such high esteem?'

'We were doing just fine until Hugh came along.'

'Hugh did nothing. She was a tart long before she met him.'

'You never liked her.'

'You never liked Hugh.'

'Hugh was a shit.'

'Valeria was a slag.'

'You're glad that she's gone off with him, aren't you?'

'Glad? Why on earth should I be glad that she's nicked my man?'

'He nicked her from me.'

'He was seduced.'

'He was looking for something better than you from the moment he walked through that door.'

'He was not,' I gasped dramatically. 'He most definitely was not. You know what your problem is, Simon? Your problem is you wouldn't know true love if it bit you and you ended up with a slapper.'

'That's wonderful, coming from you. You're a girl who really knows how to find a good man.'

We slammed our empty glasses down simultaneously and made for our rooms.

Slam.

Slam.

We closed our doors.

I buried my face beneath my pillow and cried. Simon turned his Dire Straits 'Romeo and Juliet' CD single up to full volume. I guess that was his version of having a good old blub. After he had played it thirteen times, I turned on my East 17's Greatest Hits to cover up the sound.

CHAPTER TWENTY-EIGHT

W e probably would have stayed in our respective rooms for weeks had it not been for the telephone ringing at five o'clock the next morning. Simon and I dashed from our bedroom doors like greyhounds from a trap and scrambled to be the one to pick up the call. We were hoping for Hugh or Valeria, of course, but it wasn't either of them. Instead it was Andrew and he sounded in deep trouble.

'It's Julie,' he panted. 'She's just wet herself all over the sofa. She says it's something to do with the baby coming. I don't know what to do. Lara, you've got to help me. You're a girl.'

'Why should that make me any more qualified to help?' I said petulantly. 'It's not as if I'm ever going to get pregnant with the current state of my love life.'

Simon snatched the phone from me. 'Give me that. OK, Andrew. It's Simon here. We're on our way. Calm down. Breathe deeply.'

'Aren't you supposed to say that to the mother?' I asked nit-pickingly.

337

'I think Andrew's the one more in danger of having kittens at the moment.'

We didn't have to get dressed again, since both Simon and I had been sulking in our party clothes, so we raced straight down to his car and headed for Julie's house. By the time we arrived, she was already sitting at the bottom of the stairs, breathing nice and easily, with a suitcase clasped firmly between her knees.

'Andrew's in the bedroom,' she told us between breaths. 'He thought he was going to faint.'

'Typical man,' I snapped as I helped Julie into the back of the car and clambered in after her. 'He'll have to join us later at the hospital I suppose.'

'How long is it between contractions?' Simon asked.

'How do you know about contractions?' I was surprised.

'Not every man you know is typical,' he replied.

Julie warned us to shut up, since she did not want her first born to arrive head-first into a world full of such bad karma. She'd gone all new-agey in her last two months. Besides, she needed me to talk to her to take her mind off the pain, she said. She was in agony. The contractions were coming so quickly that she could barely count the time between them.

'Haven't we got any gas?' she asked.

'I don't think so,' I said but I looked on the back shelf of the car anyway. I didn't know Simon that well. He might have been carrying anything. 'We've got a fire extinguisher,' I told her.

SECOND PRIZE

'That'll do. Aerosols give off fumes, don't they? That should make me high.'

'Don't be ridiculous.' Simon leaned into the back seat and snatched the extinguisher from my hand before I could find out. 'Just hold her hand, Lara. Rub her stomach or something? Have you got no feminine instincts about this stuff at all?'

'Why should it just be women who have instincts about childbirth?' I exclaimed. 'I was brought up just the same as you. I've got a job in the recruitment industry, for heaven's sake. Nobody delivers anything in our office except photocopies and paper-clips. What do you think I'm supposed to do, Mr New-man?'

Simon suddenly screeched the car to a halt on the lay-by of the dual carriageway.

'What's he doing?' Julie shrieked. 'We've got to get to the hospital. I can already feel it coming out.'

'Come on then, Lara,' Simon was shouting at me from the hard shoulder. 'If you're so bloody nineties, why don't you drive the car and I'll do the caring in the back.'

'Fine,' I said belligerently as I scrambled out of the back seat. 'Let's do that.'

'No,' Julie wailed. 'Don't let her drive. We'll be wrapped around a lamppost before she gets it into second gear.' But it was too late to complain. Simon and I had already swapped positions. Simon took Julie's hand and told her to start her breathing exercises again. She could give his hand a squeeze whenever she started to feel pain.

'Ouch, not that hard. Jesus, I think your fingernails just broke right through my skin.'

'Doing all right in the back there?' I asked smugly. I had yet to turn the engine on. When I did, I bunny-hopped the car out into the slow lane. Julie was swearing like a fishwife. So much for waves of bad karma now. I tried to flick on the indicator as I swung out into a faster lane but all of a sudden the windscreen wipers came on and a Ford Mondeo came tearing past us just five inches away, the driver's hand hard against the horn.

'Didn't you indicate?' Simon cried above the maternal wailing.

'Of course I bloody indicated but the windscreen wipers came on instead.'

'The indicator's on the other side of the wheel, you stupid cow.'

'Why didn't you tell me your car is back to front, you bastard?'

'Why didn't you familiarise yourself with the controls before you set off? You haven't even got your seat in the right position, for heaven's sake. Your foot can hardly be touching the brake pedal.'

'At least I know my braking distances,' I snarled. 'When you were driving we came within an inch of our lives every time we had to stop at the traffic lights.'

'How would you—'

'Shut up!!!!' Julie screamed from the back. 'You've missed the bloody turning to the hospital and it's coming out. It's coming out right now. OhmiGod. I can't believe

SECOND PRIZE

I'm going to have my baby on the back seat of a Ford
Fiesta.'

Looking in the rear-view mirror, I saw Simon's face
blanch. He couldn't believe it either.

'Lara,' Julie pleaded when I started to slow down and
panic. 'Just drive will you. Drive, drive, drive. Simon,
you're going to have to be a man about this now.'

'He is being a man about it,' I quipped. 'Give him some
room to faint.'

But then he regained his composure pretty damn quick.
He tried to help Julie shuffle into a more comfortable
position so that she had her legs bent up on the seat and
he was kind of kneeling between them with his head
squashed up against the roof of the car.

'Right, push,' he told her. 'Push, push, push.'

'Believe me, Simon, I am not trying to hold this
one in.'

I was so gobsmacked by the activity in the back seat
that I missed the next opportunity to get off the dual
carriageway too so that in the end I had to drive the
whole length of it, circumnavigate the roundabout at the
top to a cacophony of horns and drive all the way back
down the other side.

'OhmiGod,' Simon breathed. 'Lara, I can see its head.
What should I do?'

'Just use your instincts, Simon. Just use your instincts,'
I called as if I knew what I was on about but there was no
way I was going to stop the car and let him swap places
with me again.

341

'Urghhh!!! My seats!!!'

It happened just as we pulled into the hospital car park.

Andrew was already at the hospital, having driven faster and much more effectively than me, so the minute he saw Simon's car turn into the car park, he had stretchers and nurses hurtling towards us full tilt. Simon and I were quickly side-lined as the professionals swooped on the car and scooped mother and baby out. Then they were rushed straight inside and we didn't even know what sex the little one was until half an hour later since Simon had been too busy panicking with the umbilical cord to check.

Andrew, the proud father, let us know all the details about his new son while Simon was still trying to mop down the back seat of his car with some of that blue paper stuff they put on the beds in casualty to soak up the blood.

'He looks like me, you know,' Andrew added wistfully.

'From where I was standing,' Simon whispered to me, 'I thought he looked more like an alien.'

We couldn't see mother and baby straight away, so Simon and I drove back to the flat and found ourselves once more at the kitchen table surrounded by the debris of our disastrous party.

'You were really brave,' I told him. 'Not many men would have been able to deliver a baby in the back of such a tiny car.'

'Oh. It was just something I had to do,' he shrugged as

though he did it every day. 'Besides, we couldn't have done it without you in the driving seat.'

'Did I drive OK?'

'For a girl.'

It was broad daylight by the time we went to bed. I lay on top of my duvet, feeling the room warm up as the sun flooded in through the thin curtains, and thought about the little life that had begun in a Ford Fiesta that night. I almost didn't think about Hugh at all.

CHAPTER TWENTY-NINE

A week later, Julie and Andrew's baby boy was home from hospital at last. They had a bit of an argument about the name they would choose for their first born but eventually Julie's choice won through. She wanted him to be called Lawrence, which was the nearest she could get to a masculinisation of Lara, she told me. I was thrilled, though I wasn't so sure about the name Lawrence myself. Andrew got to choose the second name, which was to be Hugh.

It was no surprise to me therefore when Andrew told me that Hugh was to be the other godparent to his son. I smiled weakly into my coffee as Julie and Andrew went over the arrangements for the christening do again and again. It was to take place in the same church as that fateful wedding, with a party afterwards. Julie wanted this party to be a picnic, which would be unusual, original and cheap. I told her I thought it was a great idea – for people who lived in just about any country other than the UK.

I hadn't seen Hugh since he and Valeria left the party together on the night that Lawrence was born so I knew that this christening was going to be agony. I wondered whether I should tell Julie that I'd just become an agnostic and couldn't possibly enter a house of God. No, she would be so disappointed. Besides, it couldn't possibly be as bad as the wedding. There would be no long dresses to step on this time and I would be under no obligation to dance with Hugh. I hoped.

'Now remember,' Julie was telling me. 'If you're talking to Andrew's Auntie Gloria, she thinks that the baby was slightly premature. Under no circumstances must she know that I was pregnant when I went up the aisle, or she will cut Andrew out of her will and I will cut you out of mine. I know that Lawrence was terribly big when he was born but she thinks that he was born at five pounds eleven ounces. We're going to tell her that he's put on a lot of weight in his first two months.'

Lawrence gurgled from his cot on the other side of the room. He had been born weighing almost three stones according to Julie's early reports. She said that he was the size of a baby elephant and she felt as though he had gestated for about as long.

'I'll tell you what, Lara,' Julie continued. 'Don't ever have a christening. It's nothing but trouble from the moment he gets you up the duff until the day itself. You wouldn't believe the politics involved. Choosing godparents was a nightmare. I'm sure we've lost out on a country cottage by not asking one of the cousins on Andrew's side.'

'If you need a spare godparent place, I don't mind stepping down,' I announced, suddenly seeing an opportunity to get out of meeting Hugh again. 'I'll understand that it's just about money and I promise I'll still look after the baby if anything happens to you.'

'No way,' Julie exploded. 'You're my best friend, Lara. I don't care if you won't be able to give Lawrence a decent wine cellar for his twenty-first. I don't trust anyone else to do the job properly.'

'That's very sweet.' I picked a rusk out of the box on the table and began to nibble my way around the edges. Why had I given up eating these, I wondered? They tasted rather nice.

'Lara, put the rusk down. They're for the baby. I've got some chocolate chip cookies in the cupboard if you're hungry.'

'No, I'm not really hungry. This is just comfort eating.'

'Why are you comfort eating?'

'Oh, Julie, guess. I'm just worried about cocking things up again, that's all. What if I'm as much of a clutz at the christening as I was at the wedding? What if I drop the baby in the font? What if . . .'

'Are you worried about seeing Hugh again?'

'No,' I denied it vehemently.

'Well, you can stop worrying. I've told Andrew that no partners are allowed because this christening is going to be a small affair. So Valeria will not be coming to the church or to the reception. Does that make you feel better?'

I nodded. It didn't really. 'Is he still going out with her?'

'Probably. I don't know for sure. Since Andrew moved departments, he doesn't talk to Hugh so often any more. In fact, Hugh might not be able to be a godfather at all. Andrew's left it so late to ask him. He might be playing golf or something instead.'

If only, I thought.

'If Hugh can't make it, we'll be asking Andrew's cousin Jeremy. A much better choice in my opinion. I mean Hugh's loaded, but he hardly flashes it about, does he?'

'What about Simon?' I ventured. 'After all, he was there when Lawrence was born.'

Julie looked at me pityingly. 'I know. But we drew up a list of godparent candidates long before that whole débâcle. If we hadn't needed to borrow his car, then Simon wouldn't have been involved at all.'

'But the fact is that you did end up borrowing his car,' I persisted.

'I know.' Julie fished down the side of the sofa for something to show me. 'He bought Lawrence this.' It was a little model of Simon's Ford Fiesta, right down to the stripe along the side. 'On the note he sent with it he said it was to remind Lawrence of his roots. Let's just hope he never tries to go back to them, eh?'

I was about to tell my best friend that she had become an abominable snob when Lawrence tactfully decided that he'd gone for quite long enough without being the centre of attention and let out a tremendous, eardrum-splitting howl. Julie rushed over to the cot and dutifully lifted him out. 'My God, I swear he gets heavier by the hour,' she complained. 'There's no way Auntie Gloria is going to believe that this lump was premature.'

At least I didn't have to wear a bridesmaid's dress for this occasion. On the Saturday afternoon before the christening, Andrew stayed at home with the baby so that Julie and I could hunt for suitable godmother outfits. It was the first time we'd ever been shopping for dresses in the same size since Julie was having trouble shifting the weight she'd put on for Lawrence. I suggested jokily that she look for something in navy blue, to 'de-emphasise her bum' but she didn't seem to find it funny and asked me if I knew how difficult it was to fit enough aerobics classes in around the four-hour feeds.

I felt old on this shopping trip. For the first time, Julie didn't suggest that we go to Miss Selfridge and try on something insane like those stupid silver hipsters. For all her wildness in our Battersea days, she wanted Lawrence's christening to be a traditional kind of affair and that meant that silver plastic trousers for the god-mother were out, thank God.

But finding something sensible to wear was not as easy as we hoped and by three o'clock we had to retire to a café to rethink our plans. We ordered cappuccinos but this time I also got a croissant. Julie raised an eyebrow but I told her that the size of my hips hardly mattered any more since I was destined to be celibate for the rest of my sorry life.

'You've got to stop thinking like that,' Julie admonished me. 'I mean, I know why you're doing it, because I went through exactly the same thing myself. Thinking that Hugh was the best thing since sliced white and that Andrew could never live up to my expectations. I felt like that right up until our engagement, you know. But the fact is that it probably isn't true. If things with Hugh had gone smoothly for a few months you would have started to see his faults. Apart from the bleeding obvious ones such as, one: he will never get over Caroline and, two: he's been taking your name in vain around the office again.'

I bit into the almond croissant miserably. It seemed like a million years since that first-date-wear shopping trip when Julie had been the one stuffing her face and I had been the one looking on green-eyed with jealousy.

'You've got to move on. We've all got to move on. Honestly, one day you'll wake up and wonder what all the fuss was about. Now what have you decided to buy? I like that green two-piece in Esprit. It'd look lovely with your hair.'

'No,' I said flatly. 'I'm going to go for that dress in navy blue.'

'Darling,' said Julie. 'I'm having that one.'

CHAPTER THIRTY

I knew something was up even before I opened the door when I returned from the shopping trip with the green two-piece. Simon's car was parked outside the flat and though the lights weren't on, I could hear mournful music floating down the stairs. He was listening to Dépêche Mode. It was a tape I quite liked but one which he had told me he would only listen to again if he felt like killing himself. He hadn't exactly bounced back from the Valeria incident but there had been no tears. I had thought he was doing a damn sight better than me after my Hugh Armstrong-Hamilton disaster mark three.

'Simon?' My voice shivered with nervous anticipation of what I might find in the living room. Please, I begged God, please don't let him be hanging from the light fitting and not just because I had only just bought the shade from Designers' Guild.

He wasn't hanging from the light fitting of course and his sympathy index plummeted twenty points when I spotted his feet on the coffee table upon which were ranged more than enough green bottles to sing about.

'Feet,' I said first. Then, seeing his red-rimmed eyes in the weak flickering light of the last of the candles left over from the party, I added out of duty, 'What happened to you?'

He didn't answer but flung a piece of paper in my direction. I retrieved it from the ashtray and began to scan the first few lines. 'Regret . . . unable to renew . . . end of this month.'

'I've been given the sack,' Simon murmured as though he was trying to speak without opening his mouth. 'They've given me the sack. I don't even know what I've done.'

'These things happen,' I said. It was ridiculously flippant. 'You'll get another job.'

'What if I don't?' He looked at me pleadingly, stricken with worry. 'What if I don't? Who'll look after Gran then?'

I folded the letter back up while I played for time. Companies all over London were letting people go in this way. Most of them would be hired straight back on short-term contracts. They'd let the people without dependants go first. Except that Simon did have a dependant whom they probably didn't even consider.

'I don't understand it. I mean, Andrew's my supervisor. He should have told me if I was doing the job wrong before things got so bad that they had to sack me. I thought he was my friend.'

'I'm sure his hands were tied when it came to the

crunch.' I remembered angrily Julie's explanation of why Hugh should be godfather. She must have known even as she spoke that Simon was about to get the chop. And as for Andrew, he was far too weak to let Simon know what was happening in advance when he might still have been able to save his neck. A man who fainted when his wife went into labour was hardly the type to stand up to his bosses in defence of a friend.

'When do you finish?' I asked, trying to steer the conversation into cheerier waters.

'End of the month.'

'That's what? That's nearly three weeks away,' I said cheerfully.

'Two and a half.'

'It's plenty of time to get a new job. Plenty of time to plan. Besides, I'm sure you're owed some holiday money. That'll tide you over. It could turn out to be the luckiest break you ever had.'

'Christ, if one more person says that to me, I swear I'll . . .' He picked up an empty bottle and hurled it against the fireplace so that it shattered into hundreds of glittering green shards. Then he got up, walked out on me and locked himself in his bedroom. I started to pick up the biggest pieces of the glass. He had knocked my favourite ceramic dog off the mantelpiece at the same time, but thankfully it had bounced on the sheepskin rug and remained pretty much intact but for a chip on the ear.

'Never mind, Berkeley,' I told the china terrier. 'I'll paint over that chip tomorrow.' I knew how much Simon's job meant to him. And much as I hated Hartley and Hartley, I wouldn't have welcomed the prospect of a few months on the dole either. Though at least now I had nothing but my Marks and Spencer's Chargecard to worry about.

When Simon had turned up his Prefab Sprout CD loud enough so that I was sure he wouldn't hear me, I picked up the phone to Julie, determined to find out why Simon had been 'let go' and, equally importantly, the chances of him getting a short-term contract. Julie sounded frazzled. She explained that the baby wasn't going to sleep on time. I told her that I thought that babies only ever slept when you wanted to play with them anyway, the rest of the time they were sleepless howling monsters that dribbled from both ends.

'We shall have to get a nanny,' she sighed. 'I can't wait to go back to work. Anyway, what do you want?'

'Simon's lost his job.'

'Has he?' she asked chippily.

'You mean Andrew didn't tell you?'

'He doesn't tell me anything now that he's married to me,' she sighed.

'Andrew is supposed to be Simon's supervisor,' I continued. 'He was supposed to write the report that would get Simon through his probation period. What do you think happened? Simon says he had no clue that things were going wrong until he got the letter asking him to leave this morning.'

'There might have been all sorts of reasons.'

'Such as?'

'I don't know. You'll have to ask my husband.'

'Can I?'

'He isn't here.'

I was sure that I heard an Andrew-like throat clearing in the background.

'Anyway, what are you so worried about, Lara? Simon will get another job. He's got the right qualifications. He's got plenty of experience. Apparently he's a dream to work with.'

'Exactly. So why did they let him go?'

'You're making a mystery out of nothing. I'm sure they must have had some management consultant in suggesting cuts, that's all.'

'Can you ask Andrew to keep an ear to the ground anyway? And to let me know if anything comes up.'

'Anyone would think you cared what happened to Simon. Only a couple of months ago you wanted to turf him out on to the streets.'

'I just want to make sure he can pay the rent,' I retaliated.

'Of course you do, sweetheart. Of course. Listen, I'll mention it to Andrew but I must dash because the baby's screaming away here.'

'I can't hear him.'

'A mother's ear is more finely attuned to these things.'

I made a cup of coffee for myself and tea for Simon. I knocked on his door but there was no answer, so I called, 'There's a cuppa for you. It's outside the door,' and left the mug there before returning to deal with the glass which was now spiking the carpet. I saw Simon's hand quickly whip the cup inside his room so at least I knew he wasn't dead.

I wondered if Andrew really had been in the dark about all this. It was quite possible that he had written a glowing review of Simon's progress but that the powers that be had simply said there's not enough cash. Julie had sounded unconcerned, whereas in the past she would have got into her car and been round like an angel of mercy dispensing the names of her recruitment consultancy friends. Luckily, I still had most of them scribbled in the back of my diary, a legacy from my last stint on the 'rock and roll'. They were largely useless but it might boost Simon's morale to have someone coo with excitement over his job-market potential just because he knew how to log into a computer.

When the glass was cleared up, I sat down and started to watch a film about a man who loses his job and becomes a house-husband while his wife goes out to work. Simon crept out from his room to join me so I turned back to the news.

'I asked Hugh about that money the other day,' he told me.

'The money?' I had almost let myself forget about it but I supposed that Simon would need me to pay him back quickly so that he could make his rent now. 'You did?'

'He says that he never borrowed any money off you at all. He says that you certainly haven't mentioned it to him.

He said, if there's money missing from your account, it will be because of the person who found your card.'

'He said that?'

'Yeah.'

'He told me on the day that he borrowed the card that he had taken that money out but it's probably my fault. I haven't mentioned it to him since.'

'Oh, Lara. You stupid girl. No wonder he took advantage of you the whole time. You should have stood up to him more.'

As Simon had done. First because of Valeria and now because of me. It suddenly struck me that Andrew wasn't the only man at Partridge Skelton who would have had a say in whether or not Simon's contract was renewed.

The next day was a Sunday so at least Simon didn't have to face his workmates before he had got used to the idea that he had just been sacked. I thought I would try to cheer him up by cooking a fabulously fatty breakfast just like the ones Valeria used to make. Sausages, bacon, eggs and fried bread. I set off half the smoke alarms in the building before I had finished.

'Ta-daa,' I swung open the door of Simon's room and lurched in with the tray, complete with a flower plucked from one of my precious plants. But there was no one in Simon's room to appreciate my efforts. His bed was empty and neatly made. He must have got up really early because I hadn't heard him go out.

So I ate his breakfast myself, faintly worried that Simon

was not in the flat to be checked up on. While I was eating the telephone rang. An efficient sounding woman asked for Simon, but when I said that he wasn't around her tone turned to exasperation.

'When will he be back?'

'I really don't know,' I said. 'He left the flat before I got up.'

'I'm calling from his grandmother's nursing home. It's important that he comes in to see her at once. She's been asking to see him all night. Says she wants him to bring the photo album in. She won't stop going on about it and it's driving my nurses wild.'

'I don't know what I can do about that,' I muttered. I felt as though I was getting a ticking off.

'Well, can't you bring it in? You must know where he keeps it if you live together.'

'We don't live together like that,' I began, but the nurse cut me short.

'Quickly as you can, dear.' She put the telephone down.

I sat and stared at my empty plate for a while. What could I do about it? I didn't even know which nursing home Simon's grandmother was staying in, let alone where he kept his photo album, or even which photos she wanted to see. (I suspected that he had taken some compromising snaps of Valeria in their time.) Then the phone rang again and made my mind up for me.

'She wants some Yardley talcum powder as well,' the nurse announced without even asking who she was speaking to. 'Quick as you can. I really don't have time to attend to the emotional needs of my patients as well as their physical ones.'

'Where are you?' I managed to ask before she hung up on me again.

'Bluebird House, dear,' she said as if the fact that I didn't know confirmed how neglectful I had been of the poor woman. Moments later I had my shoes on and I was clutching a photo album in my hands. In it were pictures of Simon at various stages in his development. I discarded the one of him as an undergraduate flashing his bum which I had found tucked into the back of the book.

I located Bluebird House in my *A to Z*. It was a lot further away than I had imagined and I was just looking forward to an agonising Tube journey when I spotted Simon's car keys on the top of the fridge. If I was doing him a favour, I thought, then surely he wouldn't mind if I borrowed his car to do it. After all, this time at least I would know which side of the wheel the indicator was on.

Bluebird House was the kind of place that could make you ill just by passing through the double doors. As I stepped into the reception area, carrying the photo album and the biggest tub of talc I had been able to find on a Sunday morning, I suddenly wondered whether this was such a good idea. I mean, would it be of any comfort to Mrs Mellons at all to have a complete stranger turn up in her grandson's car? But I had come this far and I had scoured south London for an open chemist's shop to sell me the talc, so I figured I might as well at least drop the stuff off. The nurse showed me down a dark corridor to Simon's grandmother's room. The air smelled faintly of disinfectant-mopped sick and urine. If this was the best place Simon's money could buy, I shuddered to think how they'd cope on National Health.

I was dreading the moment when the door to Mrs Mellons' room swung open. I imagined her shackled to her bed by numerous drips and catheters. I imagined her distraught beyond belief when she dragged herself momentarily from her coma and saw that I was not her grandson.

But she wasn't even in the bed. She was sitting in a chair by the window. Not even dressed in nightclothes but wearing a well cut lilac-coloured suit. I cleared my throat and she looked at me expectantly.

'I live with Simon,' I began. 'He isn't at home this morning so I hope you don't mind that I decided to bring this stuff over myself.' I deposited the things on the bedside table as though they were scalding hot and burning through my hands. 'It sounded quite urgent,' I added, to excuse my intrusion further.

'What, dear? Oh don't tell me that dreadful woman phoned you.' I nodded. 'She takes everything so literally since my neighbour made an official complaint that her wishes weren't being passed on. She's on her probation period that woman, you see. I only mentioned that I needed some new talc.'

'I thought it was a matter of life or death,' I said and immediately wished that I hadn't.

'Well. Thank you anyway. It's very kind of you to bother. You must be Valeria.'

'Er. No,' I said, almost apologetically. 'I'm Lara.'

'Ah, Lara the housemate. I've heard a lot about you. Didn't you iron one of his shirts?'

'Accidentally. It was at the bottom of a pile of my own.'

Mrs Mellons laughed. 'Good. I thought for one terrible moment that you were encouraging him to be lazy.'

'Oh, he isn't lazy,' I said hurriedly. 'In fact he's quite good around the house.'

'That I find hard to believe. You know, when he was at school—' But I was never to find out what he'd done, because just at that moment Simon burst into the room.

'Gran,' he cried in a voice full of anguish. 'Are you OK? I got the note and came over as quickly as I could. But I didn't have the car.'

'I'm perfectly fine,' she said serenely. 'It was just a misunderstanding on the matron's part but your friend here has been looking after me very well.'

Simon looked at me blindly and despite his grand-mother's reassurances, he still raced to her side and spent some time just holding her hands. He looked as though he had been crying and I wondered whether I should leave the room. I cleared my throat but they didn't seem to hear me so I slipped out into the corridor and waited. An old man wandered past, dragging his drip on a trolley behind him. 'Renee,' he called when he saw me. I felt guilty when I told him that he had the wrong girl.

Simon stayed with his grandmother for another half

hour. I watched the minute hand creep around the dial of a dirty white clock and picked at my fingernails. I thought of how I had scoffed when Julie told me what a good man Simon was, ploughing all his worldly goods into making his grandmother's last days comfortable. Then I thought of my own mother, rallying round with the Tupperware and how much I still relied on her, much as I hated to admit it.

'You didn't have to do that,' Simon told me later on, when he was driving us back to the flat.

'I know,' I blustered. 'But the nurse kept calling up and it sounded so urgent I didn't know what to do.'

'You were driving my car without insurance,' he added.

'I thought the Tube might take too long.'

He managed a smile. 'Don't suppose it really matters anyway.'

'No. I didn't run into the police.'

'Oh yeah,' said Simon. 'But they're after you. There was a message on the answerphone. They've got film of someone taking money out of your account and they need you to make an ID if you can. Soon as you can get down there.'

I nodded. This news should have made me glad but I had a sense of impending doom because I knew whose face I would find.

'I'll wait until after the christening, eh?' I told Simon, explaining that I didn't want the face of a criminal to be in my mind while I took sacred vows to look after my godchild. Simon just snorted. Perhaps he knew as well as I did that I didn't want to upset my best friend by causing one of her carefully chosen godparents to be indisposed.

CHAPTER THIRTY-ONE

The christening was to take place that afternoon.

I arrived at Julie and Andrew's house early to help make the sandwiches for the celebration picnic which was to take place in spite of warnings of rain. Andrew had suggested egg mayonnaise sandwiches but Julie didn't want 'dangerous' eggs within three miles of her precious Lawrence so we were doing smoked salmon and ham. Julie was becoming, before our eyes, a very cautious mum.

Andrew looked at his watch nervously while Julie and I cut and buttered. The godparents, me, Andrew's brother and Hugh, were meant to be at the house by midday to go through plans for the day. Andrew's brother and I had been early but Hugh had yet to arrive.

'I'll give him a call,' Andrew said when Julie pestered him about the matter for the twentieth time. 'You know what he's like. Always a bit late.'

A bit late? It was getting on for half past one. The christening was to take place in less than an hour. When

Andrew came back into the room he reported that Hugh had not picked up the phone. It meant that he was on his way. Obviously.

But a quarter to two approached and we needed to leave for the church. Still no Hugh. Andrew suggested that he might have gone straight to the church to wait for us there.

'Well, what are you going to do if he isn't there?' asked Julie irritably. 'We've only got ten minutes before the service goes ahead. What about your cousin?'

'He's already said that he's not going to come to the christening because we didn't ask him to be godfather in the first place.'

'Oh,' Julie stamped her foot. 'I should have known this would happen. I should have told you to ask your cousin. Hugh Armstrong-Hamilton has always been about as reliable as an alarm clock with no batteries.'

'He was a good best man at our wedding.'

'What? How can you say that? What about that ridiculous scene he made with Caroline and that other man? He nearly had the whole of the wedding party thrown out of the hotel?'

I didn't dare butt in and explain that that wasn't exactly what had happened.

'Now we're one godparent short,' Julie ranted. 'We'll have to call the service off. And my aunt has come all the way from Dingle. I bet he doesn't even have the decency to send Lawrence a present. Well, what are you standing there like that for? Go and sort it out, Andrew, for heaven's sake. Start calling people to tell them the christening's off.'

While Julie was blubbing into the sliced white, there was a knock at the kitchen window. Simon had let himself into the back garden.

'Are you Church of England?' I asked him in a whisper as I let him in.

'No, I'm an atheist.'

'That'll do.'

Unlike the wedding, the christening ceremony went without a hitch. I didn't rip Julie's dress and when it was my turn to hold the baby, I managed to hold him without once thinking he was going to end up on the floor. Simon very gamely read out his vows and lit his candle for Jesus as though he actually believed in what he was saying. Lawrence kept quiet throughout, even sleeping through the bit where the vicar dripped the water on his forehead. In fact, the only person to cry was Lawrence's mum.

It was while we were standing outside the church, taking it in turns to hold Lawrence for the pictures, that Hugh Armstrong-Hamilton turned up in my life for the very last time. He ran around the corner into the churchyard, tie flapping, long legs all over the place, and froze at the bottom of the pathway when he saw that Lawrence's dipping was already done.

I saw Julie's eyes narrow with hate and exasperation. I hoped she wasn't simply annoyed that she'd been diddled out of a filthy rich godparent for her son by a delay on the London Underground.

'I thought you said it was happening at three o'clock,' Hugh said desperately as he shoved a hastily wrapped present into Julie's Lawrence-laden arms and kissed her perfunctorily on the cheek.

'No, two o'clock. Two o'clock,' said Andrew. 'I reminded you every single day last week.'

I could tell that Andrew was trying to lay the blame firmly with Hugh. He had had enough trouble that morning because of Hugh's absence and he didn't want Julie to think that it was because he had told Hugh the wrong time.

'I'm sure you didn't say two o'clock,' said Hugh, laughing nervously.

'I'm sure that my husband did.'

It was Julie. She handed Lawrence to me and squared up to Hugh with her hands on her hips. 'But it probably didn't sink in because it's not directly in your interests to be here, is it? Dear Simon here had to step in for you at the last minute and, in retrospect, I have to say that I'm very glad he did. At least we can rely on Simon. You barely made it to our wedding and now you've let down our son on the most special day of his life.'

'Now, hang on a minute,' Hugh blurted.

'No. You hang on. You don't care about anyone but yourself, Hugh Armstrong-Hamilton. You're interested in nothing that doesn't have something in it for you. Well, let me tell you something, there's nothing for you at our son's christening picnic, so you may as well go home now.'

Hugh struggled to find a reply. Maybe Julie was being a little bit over the top, but certainly no one was rushing to defend him from her attack. I looked along the line of gobsmacked christening guests at Andrew and at Simon. Simon certainly had reason to hate Hugh, but Andrew? I imagined that Hugh could make things quite impossible for him at work.

Suddenly Andrew spoke. 'Yes. And you can forget about me coming in with you on your little scheme,' he stuttered. 'Simon's my friend.'

Hugh's jaw dropped. So did Simon's.

'What scheme?' asked Simon innocently.

'You'd better not say any more,' said Hugh.

'I'm not having arguments in front of my baby.'

I was seconded immediately to escort Julie and Lawrence to the car while Andrew, Hugh and Simon circled each other like gun-toting cowboys on the church steps and the other guests feigned disinterest, but craned their necks to catch a view on their way back to the cars.

'What's going on?' I asked Julie. Andrew never did anything without telling her first, no matter what she claimed. 'What is this scheme they're talking about?'

'It's Hugh. He wanted to have Simon out of the way after the Valeria incident. It was he who wanted to have Simon's contract terminated but Andrew has been fighting to renew it.'

'Hugh wanted Simon sacked? That's terrible.'

'That's Hugh.'

'And you wanted him to be godfather to Lawrence?' I said accusingly.

'Yes, and you wanted him to be your husband. But I don't think either of us was really thinking straight. Seeing Simon in the church, taking everything so seriously even though he knew he had been asked to step in at the last minute, I realised that money and great christening presents were no substitute for the care and attention that Simon could give. Besides, I hardly think that this is going to turn out to be a great christening present.'

She had given me Hugh's present to hold along with the baby. 'Let's have a look, shall we?' I produced the parcel from my pocket. She opened it and looked at the plastic rattle inside with disdain.

'Huh. Four ninety-nine if it was a penny more. And that man owns half of Pembrokeshire.'

'It's the thought that counts,' I said, remembering that I hadn't been able to spend much more.

'But not much thought went into this.' She peered at the rattle closely. 'See, it's already got toothmarks on it.'

'He didn't get Lawrence a second-hand rattle, surely?' I said incredulously. 'The baby who had it first could have had all kinds of germs.'

'If only it had been chewed by a baby. I knew I'd seen this somewhere before. It belonged to Hugh's black Labrador Phoebus, or Fleabus as he was more commonly known.' She flung the rattle out of the window where it landed with an angry noise on the kerb.

'I didn't know he had a dog.'

'Probably doesn't like to talk about it. Fleabus died last year. Probably of something like distemper! OhmiGod!' Suddenly, she gave out a loud sob and snorted into her hankie. 'To think, if Hugh had been godfather, I would have had to let that rattle go into my precious lamb's mouth. He might have died. Oh, Lara. What would I have done?'

At that moment, Lawrence was trying to cram his father's mobile phone into his mouth instead. I guessed that he was the kind of kid who could handle a few germs.

'He could have killed my precious baby!!! Perhaps he wanted to—'

Thankfully, Andrew came back to the car before Julie filed the court case. Simon was behind him, looking as white as only a person who knows how narrowly they have kept their job can.

'I told him where to go,' said Andrew manfully as he got into the driving seat. 'Simon's keeping his job now.'

'Oh, darling,' cooed Julie. 'You were so brave.'

Simon gave me a strained smile.

'And we defended your honour too,' Andrew added to me.

'Quick,' said Julie, sparing me the details. 'We must get to the picnic. I expect half the guests are going in the wrong direction already. Pass me the mobile, Lara, so that I can call Minky's car and check that she hasn't

369

gone wrong. She's got half the food in the boot of her
Mazda.'

I extracted the phone from between Lawrence's gums
and he fastened them instead on one of my buttons.

CHAPTER THIRTY-TWO

M inky hadn't gone her directions wrong. Neither had anybody else. And when we got to Julie's carefully chosen spot by a babbling brook that would be safe enough for any toddlers present, Julie's mother had already started to lay the picnic tables with goodies.

I, the world's least successful cook, had actually made a cake. I'd used a mould in the shape of a teddy bear and iced it to have chocolate fur and a blue fondant ribbon. Unfortunately, it had suffered a little in transit and now looked pretty much like my own bear, who still had pride of place on my bed, well loved and limbless after twenty-odd years. Still, Julie's mother had placed my cake pretty centrally and when I carried my new godson over to look at it, he stretched out a hand and promptly covered himself and me with goo. I handed him back to Julie, who was keen to keep him close by anyway, after the shock of that rattle.

There were a few speeches. Thankfully not as long or as embarrassing as the ones at the wedding since I had managed not to rip or drop anything all day. Afterwards there was a reasonably restrained rush for the food and the party split into little cliques, gathering beneath the largest trees they could find for the shade.

I'd heard the rattle story once too often by now, so I found a weeping willow on my own and lay beneath it, listening to the chatter of the brook across stones. I looked up at the sky through my canopy of leaves and thought about the year that had passed since the night of the engagement party.

One year. Autumn to autumn. I had known Hugh for a year and I asked myself what I had learned in that time. How not to ride. How not to eat spaghetti. How not to get my fingers burned. Only just.

When the party was over I would have to go to the police and identify the man taking money from the cashpoint with my card. I knew who it would be and it made me only a little sad. The Hugh Armstrong-Hamilton who had let little Lawrence down was not the man I had fallen in love with. But then again, he had probably never been the man I had fallen in love with, just a man-shaped piece that had almost fitted the jigsaw of my life.

A shadow fell across my face.

'Mind if I join you?'

It was Simon, juggling a plate of dainty sandwiches with the crusts cut off. I noticed that he was also about to risk a piece of my teddy-bear cake. That was loyalty.

I moved closer to the trunk so that he could sit beneath the umbrella of the leaves.

He smiled at me shyly. 'I bought you a present this morning. When I went for a walk.'

'Oh, really. What is it?'

'It's a ring, of sorts.'

'A ring?' I almost choked on the vegetable samosa I had been saving until last.

'Yeah, it's one of those ceramic things you put around the light bulbs. When they heat up they give off a nice smell. Thought it might cover up the stink of my trainers if we used it in the hall.'

I recovered the bit of samosa that had got caught in my windpipe and managed to say thanks. 'That was a really nice thought.'

'There's something else as well.'

'What?' I asked. 'No, don't tell me. It's a toilet brush.'

'No. I didn't know where to get one of those from. But I've decided to have you insured on my car.'

'You have?'

'No,' he said sarcastically. 'But it'll only be third party so you'll still have to avoid getting into an accident.'

'Me get into an accident?' I said. 'I'm the best driver you know.'

'Don't make me present the evidence against that before I do the deed.'

I took the hint.

'Wow,' I said, after a moment's consideration. 'Wow. I can't believe you're really going to do that.' It was the most faith someone had shown in me since Mum bought me my first pair of ballet shoes. (I never got round to needing a second pair.) Simon was actually saying that he trusted me with his car. From a man, that was like saying that he trusted me with his signed Man United shirt or the future care and well-being of his children.

'What are you laughing at?' he asked.

I lay down on the picnic rug and watched the clouds drifting overhead, still nowhere near big enough to spoil our fun. But then a shadow did pass over me again. It was Simon, leaning across me, looking down into my face.

'You've got to promise to be careful,' he told me seriously.

'I promise I'll never even take it into fourth,' I replied.

'I'm not talking about the car any more,' he said solemnly.

'You're not?'

'No. But I think you know what I mean.'

Typical me. Always slow on the uptake. A year since the engagement party when Julie had told me that Simon would be perfect for me, I finally realised that she might be right.

'Are you going to kiss me?' I asked with a squeak.

'If you think you can shut up for long enough.'

His soft pink lips brushed gently against mine.

EPILOGUE

After the nightmare of the cashpoint-card fiasco and finally having to face up to the reality that my one-time Prince Charming was in fact King Rat, I didn't hear about Hugh Armstrong-Hamilton again for quite a long time.

In fact, the next time anyone breathed his name anywhere near me was, believe it or not, on my hen-night. My mother's fondest wish had come true. At last there was someone else to worry about my pension plan for me and with whom I might even get a mortgage. The only bitter-sweet aspect to the whole wedding thing was that Simon's grandmother wouldn't be there to see him make an honest woman of me.

Julie was in charge of the hen-night of course, since she was going to be my maid of honour (I insisted on bridesmaids' dresses in peach). I couldn't have my final night of freedom at the flat for obvious reasons, so we went to a club in town that had a ladies' night with bad male strippers every other Thursday. We got into a sort of screaming and whistling contest with the table next to ours while a guy dressed up as Batman did his stuff. The other table's bride was in the loo with her bridesmaids, apparently having started the festivities altogether too early that night.

When my fellow bride-to-be finally emerged from the girls' room with her friends in tow, I almost choked on my maraschino cherry. Though she looked a wee bit paler than when I had last seen her beneath Tim at Julie's wedding, I knew at once that it was Caroline Lauder, flanked by Antonia and Cecilia. Caroline didn't even look in my direction at first but Cecilia recognised me straight away, though we hadn't seen each other since the night our cathartic bonfire almost burned down her house.

'What are you doing here?' Cecilia asked me.

I pointed at my veil which was garnished with a learner plate. 'I'm getting married next weekend.'

'You're joking?' she said. 'Caroline is too!'

'I guessed that.' Caroline had a learner plate and three water-filled condoms taped to the back of her dress.

'Everybody's doing it. Antonia and I had a commitment ceremony in the summer.' Cecilia showed me a glittering eternity ring. I told her I was glad for her and listened to the details of her hen-night patiently, though all the time I was desperate to find out who Caroline's groom was going to be. Finally, Cecilia finished describing great-aunt so-and-so's outrageous hat and I was able to ask.

'It's Tim, of course.' As if it could have been anyone else.

SECOND PRIZE

My heart, which had been waiting in my mouth, got back into its proper position.

'It's wonderful, isn't it? Thank God Hugh Armstrong-Hamilton finally got off the scene. And she's made up with her sister too since Hugh stopped interfering.'

'Caroline's sister?'

'Yes, Fiona. She's flown back from Australia just to be a bridesmaid.'

Caroline and her almost identical-looking sibling gave me a little wave.

'Fiona?' I asked again. 'Hugh told me she was—'

'What?' asked Cecilia brightly.

'Oh, nothing,' I said. What was the point of bringing all that up?

'Anyway, who's your lucky man?'

'I don't think you know him. His name's Simon.'

Cecilia gave a mock sigh of relief. 'Phew! For a minute there, when you looked so odd about Caroline's sister being here, I thought you were going to say that you were marrying the dreaded Hugh A-H yourself.'

'Me?' I laughed. 'He should be so lucky.' But I felt a pang of something as I said it. Was it loss? Disappointment? Maybe it was plain old embarrassment.

So there had never been a car crash. Just as Hugh had never been in love. Not with me. Not with Fiona. And probably never even with Caroline Lauder. Hugh Armstrong-Hamilton had loved no one but himself. To everyone else he only dished out lies so that he could act like a pig and still get the sympathy vote. I remembered

Hugh's face as he told me the tale about Fiona just to make sure he could get me into bed when he had pushed me almost too far and for a moment I thought that I was going to get angry. For a moment I thought I might just open up that can of worms again after all, tell Fiona what he had said about her and make sure that Hugh Armstrong-Hamilton never ate breakfast in a girl's house again. But then I saw Caroline laughing with her sister and a tug on the back of my veil from my bridesmaid reminded me that I'd moved on too.

'What's the matter, Lara?' Julie asked. 'You've stopped drinking. Do you want that Caroline Lauder's mates to think we're a big bunch of pussies?'

Well, that was fighting talk. So I filled my glass from the half-empty bottle of champagne in front of me and raised it in a toast to my one-time rival.

'Hey, Caroline. Here's to winning second prize,' I said.